BELL RINGER

An Adam Perdue Mystery

S.J. Spain

ISBN-979-8-9913354-3-0

Cover design by: Ivan, Bookcoversart.com
Library of Congress Control Number: 2024917681
Printed in the United States of America; Published in Wilmington, NC

This book is dedicated to all who are experiencing or have experienced homelessness and those who provide them aid and comfort.

Special thanks to my beta readers and editors extraordinaire: Beth Cameron and John Hill.

Ring the bells that still can ring
Forget your perfect offering
There is a crack, a crack in everything
That's how the light gets in

LEONARD COHEN

HANDS OFF

I don't recommend sleeping on the street in Orman. The summers are scorching, the winters are frigid, and it's humid all year round. The metal bench I was curled up on was as hard and cold as a mortuary slab. A blanket, long underwear, and wool gloves made it almost bearable.

I was looking for a woman no one really wanted found. Michelle Rathborn was one of three surviving children of Charles Rathborn, founder of the Quickie Buy chain of convenience stores. Quickie Buy stores are located in the more marginal neighborhoods of Orman and a couple of other nearby towns.

The stores' losses from shoplifting and hold-ups are more than made up for by the huge mark-ups on their merchandise – and the lack of any competition in the areas where they did business. Most of their customers refer to the local franchise as the "Stab & Grab."

Michelle was the sole beneficiary of her father's majority stake in the operation. Her brothers weren't happy that they were required to try and find her if they wanted to challenge the will expeditiously. They had cheered up a little when the deceased's brother and executor, whom they called "Uncle Unctuous," had made it clear that proof of death would be even better than finding her.

With the information her loving siblings provided, it hadn't taken me long to follow the tracks of the prodigal daughter's downward spiral from two tours as a decorated medic in Afghanistan to just one more entry on Orman's annual count of the homeless. I had traced her to the night shelter at the Veterans Assistance Center over by the bus station, but she had been tossed out of there a week before for drinking.

One of the other residents had told me that Michelle liked to sleep in a dead-end alley in Village South. The Village is a sixteen-square-block area that morphed from squalor to gentrification and back again several times over the last few decades. It finally settled in as an upscale artists' enclave, with a subculture of illicit drugs and sex that its residents protected as fiercely as they did the art deco facades on some of the brownstones. For the third night in a row, I pretended to sleep while watching the mouth of the alley.

An owl appeared in a patch of sky between two buildings, wings outstretched and rigid, diving in an arc that brought it over a dumpster. It dropped and then rose with its wings beating, a squirming rat clutched in its talons. Who needs television? I had the Raptor Channel streaming live right in front of me.

Someone must have been messing with the remote, because a car turned the corner, high beams bouncing and tires squealing. The startled owl dropped its prey and disappeared into the night. The car, a black limousine, pulled up along the sidewalk and stopped.

The back door opened, and a passenger emerged and walked toward the alley. The driver stayed inside, hidden behind the tinted glass. I couldn't get a good look at the passenger, either, who was wearing a long raincoat with a raised collar. It could have been Rathborn. Of course, it could have been almost anyone. It didn't figure that a homeless addict would arrive by limo to sleep in her favorite alley, but it was an excuse to get up and move around.

In case it was just a smallish guy who needed to take a leak, I paused for a minute before walking toward the alley entrance, blanket wrapped tightly around me. Anyone who's ever been homeless knows the trick to using a blanket as a coat is to hold one corner from the long side tightly in each hand and then cross your arms over your chest. When you uncross them, you look a bit like Dracula opening his cape. That's not the worst look to have when you're living on the street.

I shuffled along in the controlled stagger of someone who is used to being drunk, ignoring the limo. Enough of the streetlights in the alley were still working for me to see that it was empty. It was lined with trash cans set outside sturdy metal doors. Whoever was in the car must have gone into one of the townhouses. Not Michelle. Not my business. I turned to go, and a movement on the ground caught my eye.

It was the rat, squirming on its back like a flipped over turtle trying to regain its feet. As I watched, the rat stopped struggling and lay still, chest rising and falling rapidly. One eye was gone, and the other was staring at

3

me. Not glancing in my general direction, or looking at something beyond me, but staring me straight in the eye. Blood pulsed from a hole in its neck, beading up into a blob and dissipating into its fur.

I steeled myself to walk past. After all, it was just a rat. If not for the limo's sudden arrival, it would already be owl chow. As I moved away, the rat's one eye followed me like one of those creepy paintings in an old horror movie. I suddenly had a vision of myself wrapping the rat in my blanket and walking into Mercy Hospital with it. That would be a hoot. Much hilarity would ensue as hospital security tried to figure out a way to make me leave without actually touching me or my rodent patient.

The demand for emergency mental health beds in Orman so outstrips the supply that I wouldn't even be in the running for one. A derelict seeking medical attention for a wounded rat fell into the psychiatric category of "catch and release." The mental health issues involved are too small to put him in the live well. He has to be unhooked and returned to the stream so his mania can mature and spawn before finally making its way to the therapeutic dinner table.

Maybe the rat would just die. It was bleeding a lot. How long could it last? Maybe it was dead already? I squatted down. It wasn't dead, and its eye was still fixed on me. It was wheezing as it breathed: "Ehee, ehee, ehee." I reached out and put one hand over the rat's chest, firmly pinning its body to the ground, and with the other I twisted its head sharply. The squeaking stopped.

I carried the rat to the dumpster and placed it inside. It wasn't a very dignified send-off, but a full dumpster has got to be about as close as it gets to heaven for a rat. I considered tossing the bloody gloves in, too, but it was cold and I still had several hours to go on the stakeout.

I walked to the end of the alley and back before stretching out on the bottom step of the brownstone nearest the dumpster. I could see the entire alley and was sheltered from the wind. It was more comfortable than the bench, and I dozed off for a while.

A door slammed shut in the alley behind me. I got to my feet, leaned against the dumpster, and muttered to myself. I heard footsteps coming closer, the hard slap of real leather soles against cobble stones. Not Michelle. Probably the limo passenger.

Professional curiosity required that I try and get a look to be certain. I pushed myself away from the dumpster and turned. It was a man, slightly built, and as he passed me, his lips twitched in what could have been a smile. He looked familiar somehow, like someone I knew who had changed his hair style, or shaved off a beard, or usually wore glasses. I couldn't place him, but I knew the guy from somewhere.

He was out of the alley before I could call out to him or catch up and get another glimpse of his face. An engine roared. The limo came flying forward, jumped the curb, and crushed the man against a building. I stepped back behind the dumpster faster than my brain could articulate the thought, "What the fuck?"

The limo backed off, and the man crumpled to the ground. The driver got out, a pistol in his left hand and a hatchet in his right. He stared down the alley, and I willed myself to become one with the dumpster. It must have worked, because he didn't come and shoot me or hack me to death. There was a pop followed by two thumps.

I wasn't exactly frozen with fear, though I was definitely cold and plenty afraid. It was more that I was stuck in fight-or-flight mode, with neither option holding any appeal. My gun was in a car that was parked two blocks away. The only way out of the alley was about twenty feet from the guy who was currently giving new meaning to the phrase "full-service limo driver."

Dropping into a crouch, I poked my head out from behind the dumpster. The driver was bent over the body. I could hear the purr of the limo engine and something else. Whistling. The sick son-of-a-bitch was whistling.

He wiped the hatchet blade on the dead man's coat and wrapped something in a towel. He stood up, looked at the body for a moment, and nodded. He popped the trunk and deposited the towel before getting back in the driver's seat. The limo backed off the curb and roared away. I stared at the back bumper through a cloud of exhaust. The license plate was covered with mud.

I pulled out my phone, hit 911, ignored the operator's questions, gave her the location, and said only "Hit and run. Gunshot." I closed the call and walked over to the body. I really wanted another look at his face, to see if I could place him. Half of his head and face was a bloody mess. I stared at the other half, squinted, tilted my head one way and then the other, trying to isolate whatever was familiar, but I couldn't quite get it. I knew this guy. Not well, maybe. But I knew him. I moved closer and bent down. Still nothing.

The sound of sirens drawing closer caused me to straighten up and take stock of my situation. I was standing in a pool of blood. My foot was right next to one of the coat cuffs – where a hand should have been. I stepped back and looked at the man's other arm. That hand was missing, too. The pop had been a gunshot to the face, from inside his mouth by the looks of it, and the thumps had been the hatchet hacking off his hands.

The first officers arrived on the scene before I'd gotten more than a few feet from the body. Reasonably enough, they pulled their guns and shouted for me to raise my hands and get down on the ground. They looked scared.

Being a patrol cop is 95% boredom and 5% terror. Bored cops can be open to conversation and sometimes even argument. Not frightened cops, though. It's best to do exactly as you're told and keep your mouth shut until absolutely certain that they aren't afraid anymore. I raised my hands in the air and knelt on the ground.

They cuffed me, bagged my hands and feet, and put me in the back of a squad car. The bags would preserve the evidence on my bloody gloves and shoes until I got to the station. More importantly to the no-longer scared and therefore now-bored cops, they prevented a mess in the back of the car that would have to be dealt with at the end of their shift.

From the outside, the Orman Police Headquarters is a stately building that fits in perfectly with the courthouse and City Hall across the street. It features marble steps leading up to a columned archway, and the sign over the entrance is polished copper. Inside, it looks pretty much like every other police station I've ever seen, with scuffed metal furniture, scratched tile floors, and sagging walls coated in peeling layers of once-white paint.

A not so polished copper sat across from me in the interrogation room. Detective Woodward "Woody" Wales was familiar to anyone working either side of the law in Orman. Crooks hated his guts, and other cops hated him just a little less. Folks like me tried to stay clear of him.

Word is that his mother's the only one in the world who ever has a kind word for him, and even then, it's usually followed by a muttered, "Asshole!" and a slap to the back of his head.

I was still cuffed, but the bags had been removed, along with my gloves and shoes. The linoleum under my stockinged feet was warm. There must have been a heating pipe running underneath the floor. It felt nice.

"So, we've had a busy night, have we, Perdue?" He lowered himself into a chair on the other side of the table. The chair had no arms, which was good, because Woody is a very large man.

"Just the usual."

9

He gave me a look that I imagine he usually reserves for a smear of dog poop found on the sole of one of his favorite shoes. Woody's chair wasn't bolted to the floor, and it had a lot of suspicious scuffs and scratches on it. I found myself hoping that someone was on the other side of the wall-length mirror, hopefully Lieutenant Squire. She and I are friends. I think.

"It's rat's blood, you know, on the gloves." I got only a stare in reply. At first glance, I may have seemed like a pretty good suspect, standing over the body in a pool of the victim's blood. It was readily apparent on second glance, third at the most, though, that I didn't do it – at least, not alone.

The man had been nearly cut in two by a vehicle, shot, and partially dismembered. My undamaged car was parked two blocks away. I didn't have a gun or anything with which to perform amputations, and when told to put my hands up, I had only the regular complement of two with which to comply.

"Let's cut to the chase, Perdue. You were found on the scene, your hands covered in blood, with your bloody shoeprints all around the body. I have a lot of questions, and you better have a lot of answers. Got it, Shit-for-brains?"

I nodded.

"OK, then. Where are the victim's hands?"

"I don't know."

Woody brought a grapefruit-sized fist down on the table. "*I don't know* is not an acceptable answer! Try again."

I shrugged. "The guy who killed him must have taken them, I suppose. He wrapped something in a towel and tossed it in the trunk of the limo."

"You saw this guy who you say killed him?"

I nodded.

He brought both fists down this time. "No nodding, no shrugging, no batting your pretty eyes at me. Use your words. When I ask a question, you answer it, nice and loud and clear. Understand?"

I caught a nod halfway and answered a little too loudly, "Yes, I understand!"

Woody wasn't sure if the extra volume was the result of defiance or fear, but he let it go. "What did this mystery perp look like?"

"I didn't get a good look at him. He was wearing a coat and a hat, and I was a couple hundred feet away. I'd guess he was a little under six feet, medium build maybe – but, again, with the coat it was kind of hard to tell."

"White, black, or other?"

"Dark."

"Dark, huh? Black, Hispanic, or Asian?"

"His coat?"

"The man, Jerk-off!"

"I don't – uh, I couldn't tell. I told you I never saw his face. His coat was dark, though. Navy, dark gray, black. Something like that."

"Well, I'd better get a BOLO out right away! 'Be on the lookout for an average height man of average build and unknown race. May be wearing a dark coat.' We'll have him in cuffs in no time! You're sure it was a man, though, right?"

"Well, not certain, I guess. He moved like a man. But I'm not even sure what that means. It was just my impression that it was a man."

Woody raised his arms, fists clenched. They hung in the air for a moment, and then he lowered them slowly and placed them behind his head, where most people's neck would be, and rubbed the back of his head and shoulders.

"We're going to try one more time. You're going to give me answers that mean something – answers that get you or somebody else in front of a judge and jury asking for mercy – or you're going to be held for as long as the law allows before we charge you. No bail, no phone call, nothing but the company of some drunks and druggies for the next 36 hours. Now tell me what the hell happened out there!"

I walked him through it: the stakeout, the owl and the rat show, the whole thing. He stopped me a couple of times to ask more questions for which I had no answers, but mostly just let me tell my story – as he should have done in the first place.

He had to know that I'm a private detective in good standing – or at least as good standing as any dick could be with the "real" police. He also had to know that no gun had been found on the scene, no implement that could have amputated the victim's hands, and no car that could have cut him in half. The odds were pretty slim that I had conspired with someone else and then hung around to talk to the police. He was just yanking my chain, because that's what assholes do. I pitied his mother.

After a few more minutes of repeated questions, including his favorite "Where are his hands?" the door opened and Squire came in.

"Do you have what you need for the moment, Woody?"

"As much as I'm going to get, I guess. Not exactly the observant type, this one." He shrugged and flipped his notebook closed. "This case is going to be a major pain in the ass. Respected citizen cut nearly in half, shot, and mutilated, and we've got nothing? I'm glad you're the one who gets to handle the media pricks, Lieutenant – and the dick pricks, too." He threw a last glare in my direction and headed for the door.

"The cuffs, Woody." I held my hands out. Woody glanced at Squire, who nodded, and then removed them.

After a shower, change of clothes and a quick check-in with Uncle Unctuous, I met Squire for coffee and cherry pie at Tuck's Diner. Tuck's Diner is a converted rail car. It's been a long time since Orman had passenger rail service, but when you sit in Tuck's you can almost hear the rhythmic chugging of a coal-fired engine and feel the gentle sway of a dining car.

That's because there's an appliance manufacturer next door with a metal-stamping machine that runs all day and most of the night, and the whole car rocks every time a customer enters or exits using the original metal steps.

Squire slid into the booth across from me. She moved with the grace of an athlete, which she had been in college: basketball and volleyball. She wore a well-tailored suit and a pleated Oxford shirt that shouted "white collar professional." The sidearm holstered under her left shoulder spoke more softly but delivered a stronger message.

"This is a fine mess you've gotten yourself into, isn't it Adam?"

"Well, this mess just kinda found me." I took another bite of pie, chewed it slowly, and swallowed with satisfaction. I figure Tuck's cherry pie is one item that is on the menu in both rat and people heaven. Not a crumb of it ever makes it into a dumpster. "Thanks for getting me out of there. If Woody had asked me where the guy's hands are one more time..."

"Woody's an ass, but he's a pretty good cop. I doubt he ever thought you had anything to do with it. Which is more than I can say for me, when I first saw you. I thought you had finally lost it and gone all Hannibal Lecter on us. You were a sight. If not for the quick and dirty lab report that the blood on your gloves wasn't human, I'd have been leaning on you harder than he did."

"Yeah, I didn't consider how the homeless look would work against me if there was trouble. It's great for stake outs, though. Nobody even sees homeless people."

"Except for cops."

"And social workers, sometimes."

Squire knew this wasn't my favorite subject. I had spent my first couple of years in Orman on the street. Not technically homeless much of the time, but pretty hard to distinguish.

"Speaking of stake outs.... What can you tell me about your client?"

"Everything I know. He was happy to be helpful to the police, once I had given him a few lurid details about the murder." I gave Squire the rundown, and she seemed to be in agreement that my case had nothing to do with the murder. Just me being in exactly the wrong place at exactly the wrong time. Everybody has talents, and that's one of mine.

"You really strangled a rat?" she asked, before shoveling in a huge forkful of pie.

"Broke his neck. He was dying, and in pain. Hell, it just seemed like the right thing to do at the time. I didn't know some crazy son of a bitch with a hand fetish was about to drop a corpse in my lap."

"I've seen lots of owls around downtown. Eagles and hawks, too. We raze the forests and crush the cliffs into sand to make lumber and concrete for our buildings. Then the birds of prey wind up building their nests on the ledges of our high rises. There's something poetic about that."

Danielle Squire's that rare cop who has a thoughtful side and isn't embarrassed to show it. Her reputation as someone who thinks hard about things got her to her current rank of lieutenant fast. Normally, it would also put a pretty low ceiling on her career, as anything higher usually requires the kind of political instincts that aren't compatible with being thoughtful. Somehow, though, Squire manages to please her superiors and earn the respect of her subordinates – without pissing off either.

"Well, Woody was right about one thing," she sighed. "This is going to be a media cluster fuck. No one's got the story yet, but once the interns check out the morning blotter, I'll have print, TV, and the whole social media brigade on my ass. Even I would want to know the story about this one."

"Woody said the vic was somebody. Who was it?"

"According to the license and credit cards in his wallet, a guy named Ellis Bell. He's some kind of hotshot investment advisor."

"Maybe that's why he looked familiar. His face show up in the paper a lot, or maybe on TV?"

Squire shrugged. "He was a one-man shop with a few very big clients, as I hear it. More about discretion than self-promotion. Honestly, I don't know much about him, though." She took an 8x10 glossy photo out of her folder and slid it across the table to me. "That the guy you saw last night?"

The photo was a professional head shot, crisply focused against a soft gray background. Bell was a decent looking guy, with thick dark hair sculpted into a wave that started at the part and crested just above his ear. His nose was large for his face and a little crooked. It certainly looked like the guy I saw, at least the way he looked before he had half his face blown away. But something was off. I shook my head and slid the photo back.

"Yeah, that looks like him, but I couldn't swear to it."

Squire tucked the photo away. "His wife, who was soon to be his ex-wife according to his lawyer, is going to try and ID him at the morgue, but as you know…."

"Yeah, not a lot to look at there. Maybe he's got a tattoo or birthmark that she can confirm."

We ate and drank in companionable silence for a few minutes. I couldn't shake the feeling that I knew the victim, but I don't know any investment advisors. "You gonna look at the wife for hiring it out, Squire? Or are you thinking he pissed off a client?"

"No telling at this point. He sure pissed somebody off."

"Taking his hands is weird, and so is sticking the gun in his mouth and blowing half his face away instead of a quick shot to the temple. Why take the time to do that? He had to be trying to make it hard to ID the vic."

"Could be. But according to your statement, it only took a few seconds. Bang, chop, chop! And if they wanted to stall us IDing him, it was pretty careless to leave his wallet." Squire stood up and dropped a five on the table. "I've got to get back to headquarters. Good luck finding the Stab & Grab heiress."

She walked in to my office like she was walking right off a yacht.

On a plank.

She elbowed the door open, avoiding the doorknob. It's antique brass, with a splotchy patina of *verdi gris*. I think it gives the place some class.

The tall redhead stepped gingerly toward my desk, her high heels maneuvering around the more obvious stains on the carpet. I keep promising myself to replace it with laminate after my next big case. But I don't really have big cases.

Her head swiveled between the two available chairs in front of my desk, clearly unhappy with the selection. I stood up and waved at the offending furniture with what I thought could reasonably pass as graciousness.

"Please, have a seat Ms. –?"

"Forris. Gayle Forris. You are Mr. Perdue?" She remained standing. She had a lovely English accent, the kind you hear on the BBC or on a GPS instructing you to "turn left on Main Street and then right on Front."

"I am, though you can call me Adam." I sat on the edge of the desk, splitting the distance between remaining on my feet and sitting back down. "And what can I do for you, Ms. Forris?"

"I am hoping that you can locate my, uh, partner, Trent Argent." She didn't add, "And call me Gayle."

I found myself wanting to call her Gayle.

"What sort of partner is Mr. Argent? Business? Romantic? Your partner in crime, perhaps?"

"We live together, and we are romantically involved."

I sighed. It didn't look like I'd be getting to call her Gayle anytime soon. "Domestic cases are not my area of expertise." I indicated the card holder on the desk and she took one.

"Adam Perdue. LSI, Inc.," she read aloud. "Specialists in finding misplaced persons." She threw me a 100-watt smile that made me want to find a puddle just so I could throw my jacket over it in an act of unprovoked chivalry. She self-consciously lowered the wattage. "Misplaced persons?"

"Missing people no one really misses, mostly insurance and probate beneficiaries who can't be located, spouses who haven't signed their divorce papers, that sort of thing. Clients pay me to find them, so they can get signatures and close the file. It's my niche. I can recommend an agency that is very good with domestic cases, if you'd like."

I didn't want her to leave, but it probably would be better for everyone if she did before Julia returned from lunch. Julia is my assistant, and we were once "uh, partners." Our personal relationship is complicated, and we carry what is probably an unhealthy load of jealously and protectiveness toward one another.

With impeccable timing, Julia threw open the outer office door and breezed in. "I'm back!" she shouted, lowering her voice at the end, when she saw that I was with a client.

"Can you bring us a couple of cards for agencies that do domestic cases?"

"Pervy stuff or garden variety?"

I inclined my head toward Ms. Forris, who rolled her eyes.

"This is not a domestic case." She demonstrated her resolve not to be talked out the door by swallowing her distaste and lowering herself into one of the visitor chairs. Her bottom seemed to hover just over the cracked leather cushion rather than settle into it, but I got the message.

Julia retreated and gave me a look that let me know that she had noticed me eyeing our client's backside. Of course, I noticed her admiring it, too. Like I said, complicated.

"No offense, Ms. Forris, but missing boyfriends usually turn up. How long has he been gone?"

"Since Sunday. Three days. And his car is still parked in front of our flat. The police took a report yesterday but made it quite clear that they don't intend to do anything about it."

I nodded. "They have higher priorities. It's like if you call the fire department to get your cat out of a tree. They'll tell you that they've never found a cat skeleton in a tree and that when it gets hungry, it'll find its way home. It's a fair assumption that the same holds true for boyfriends."

"I got that impression. There are some special circumstances in Trent's case. That's why they recommended I come to you."

"And what are the special circumstances?"

"Trent works at the Veterans Assistance Center, night shift at the shelter. A couple of weeks ago, one of the regulars disappeared. He didn't think much of it at first. But this particular client receives a monthly disability check. When that arrived and a few more days passed without him making an appearance, Trent started asking around about him."

"Do you know the client's name?" I asked.

"I'm afraid I don't remember. Trent told me, but..."

She flushed from her forehead to her neck. I caught myself wondering how much lower the blush might go.

"... I didn't think it was important at the time, so it didn't register."

"Of course. Go on." I thought it was cute that she was embarrassed not to remember a homeless guy's name. Of course, I probably would have thought it was cute if she hocked up a loogie and spit it on the floor.

"When he came home from work Sunday morning, he said he had a lead. A few other guys have gone AWOL lately, and folks on the street are talking about some new religious ministry that's running an invitation-only shelter. They're calling it the 'Homeless Hilton.' It's supposed to be somewhere outside of downtown, but they have street vans that cruise the whole city."

"Did he mention the real name of the shelter?"

"Maybe. I don't remember that, either. None of this seemed very significant at the time. I know you probably hear this all the time, but Trent's just not the kind of person to take off without a word. I know that something has happened to him."

"Actually, given my particular niche, I almost never hear that. The folks I look for are *exactly* the kind of people who take off without a word. I get why the police sent you to me, though. I have a lot of contacts in the homeless community. I've probably met Trent before, if he works at the vets' shelter. He's the night manager, you said?"

"Yes. Mostly, he does a lot of paperwork. That and checking in folks that the police and EMT's drop off in the middle of the night."

"Then, I'm certain we've met, though it may have been while I was staying there as a guest."

"Oh, are you a veteran?"

"No, but playing things that I'm not is part of the job."

"I guess it would be."

"Do you have a picture of Trent?"

She pulled out her phone, scrolled through it, and handed it to me. I recognized the face, with a small sting of shame. He had checked me in more than once back in the bad old days, when I was the kind of drunken fool that the police dropped off when it got so cold out that it wasn't safe on the street.

On nights like that, the VAC takes all comers and puts them on cots in the lobby. A lot of the vets there – staff and clients, both – look down on the cot crew. Many aren't veterans and most are drunk or high on something. The shelter at the VAC is "dry." Nobody under the influence is allowed in, and using while on the premises results in a swift kick to the curb.

This Trent guy treated folks all right. My memory of those days is pretty fuzzy in general, but I remember every act of kindness I received or observed. There weren't that many.

"Okay. I have another case right now that's a priority, but I'll do what I can. It's $200 a day, plus expenses. If that's a problem for you, I have a sliding scale based on income."

"No, it's not a problem. I shouldn't say so, I suppose, but it's less than I expected."

"Normally, it would be $400 a day, but I've got this other case that dovetails nicely with yours. So, you get a bargain rate. It could change at any time, though. I'll let you know."

I fiddled with her phone. "I'm sending yours and Trent's contact information to my phone, and Julia's to yours." The printer in the corner of the office hummed to life. "I'm also printing copies of Trent's picture."

I handed her phone back, along with one of the photos. "Write Trent's date of birth, Social Security number, the names of family, friends, co-workers – anything that you think might be helpful." She looked at the picture for a moment before turning it over and placing it on the desk. She leaned forward to write on it, and I couldn't help but notice her blouse pull up out of her skirt and expose the small of her back. It was freckled.

My reaction wasn't quite the same as it would have been a few minutes before. Now, her boyfriend wasn't an abstraction. He was a real person, and one who had been decent to me when he didn't have to be. I'm not saying I looked at her like a sister. But it wasn't the same "God, I'd like to throw her over the arm of the sofa and..." look that it might otherwise have been.

She handed me back the photo.

"Do you and Trent use any particular ride share company?"

"No. We have our own vehicles, and I have my employer's car service. If Trent needed a ride, he'd probably use a regular taxi. He used to drive a cab himself when he was at university."

I took Trent's picture into the outer office and gave it to Julia. In a low voice, I asked her to make the usual rounds of emergency rooms and the morgue. In a normal voice, I added, "Take this around to the taxi companies at shift change and see if anyone remembers giving him a ride between Sunday and today."

Like me, Julia Waters has a past. Hers included taking a lot of taxis. She's also an attractive woman to whom many of the drivers would be only too happy to talk.

I returned to my office, where my client had her checkbook out and pen poised. "How much do you need up front?"

"Make it for three days, $600."

Julia piped up from the doorway, "There's a $30 fee for returned checks." Our client looked offended.

"I'm out of here," Julia shouted cheerily. "I'll let you know what I know when I know it."

Gayle Forris stood in the middle of the floor, unsure what to do next. It was a pretty normal reaction. "Go home, Ms. Forris."

"I just feel like I should be doing something more to find Trent."

"You've done what you can for now. When he looks for you, he'll be looking at home, right? Be there for him. Hell, he might be there right now, trying to come up with an excuse for ditching on you. If you go out to work, or the grocery store, or whatever, leave a note, so he knows where to find you.

"Julia and I are on the case. I'll let you know when we find something. We'll call you at least once a day, even if we don't have anything to report. What's the best number to reach you?"

She pulled a card from her purse: *The Orman Times Gazette*, the last print newspaper still alive in the city. "The best number to use is my cell. It's on the card. You should already have it from when you texted yourself from my phone."

"What do you do at the Gazette?"

"I'm a journalist. I cover crime and politics."

"Potato, potahto..."

She gave me a weak, "never heard that one before" smile and opened the door. DK, the office cat, darted inside and settled onto the seat she had vacated. She flashed the 100-watter at me again. "It doesn't cost me any extra, does it, if you have to strangle another rat?" She turned and left without waiting for an answer.

My reputation in Orman was growing. Like a boil.

"I didn't strangle it, I broke its neck," I muttered. DK licked himself, unimpressed.

It's pretty rare that I get paid for two cases at once. Orman isn't that big, just over a quarter million people, including the near suburbs. With my very specific niche, it was much more common to have no cases at once. It's not great for the bank account, but it does wonders for my cribbage game.

The Trent Argent case was a little outside my usual work zone. He actually had someone who wanted him found. He had gotten lost in my backyard, though, doing kind of the same thing I do. Exceptions must be made.

My first stop was the VAC shelter, where the paths of several of my targets intersected. The lobby was empty, as clients are required to be out during the day. They would start lining up around 4:00 PM for a bed and a locker in the dorms, or "the barracks" as they called them. For anyone who arrives after 6:00, it's the lobby cots.

The day desk was covered by a very serious looking woman I didn't recognize, probably a relatively new hire. Her gray-striped black hair was pulled tight into a pony tail, and she literally looked down her nose at me when I approached her elevated desk.

I adopted my very best "Aww, shucks" manner and stopped at the line of tape on the floor two feet in front of the desk. She nodded approval, and cocked her head to the side, inviting me to speak.

"Ma'am, I was wondering if you could help me with something." One of the few places you can get away with "ma'am-ing" a woman of your own general age and class is in the military. The VAC works hard to recreate the military environment for its clients, reminding them of when they had once been a part of something important.

"That would depend. Are you checking in?" My heart warmed for her a little. I was dressed in business casual and had shaved that morning. My hair was a little long, but clean and neat. I didn't look like a homeless person, and it was obvious that she knew that lots of homeless people don't, either.

"No, ma'am. I just wanted to ask a couple of questions about –"

She smiled coldly and picked up the phone. "I'll just get someone from the communications office for you. Are you a reporter?" I shook my head and tried to look a little offended. "You're *not* a police officer. They always display their badge like it's a free pass to the world. And they don't stop at the tape." One hand held the phone and the other was poised above a keypad.

"Not a reporter, and not a cop. I am looking for somebody. Actually, I'm looking for two – no, make that three – people. And I'm hoping you can help."

"I'm sorry. We don't give out any information about the guests, even whether someone is here or not. I can take the name of the person you are looking for and your name and contact information. *If* we have someone by that name, I'll pass it on."

"I understand. But the main person I'm looking for is a staff member, Trent Argent."

"Mr. Argent works the night desk."

"Not the last few nights."

"I will get someone from human resources to take care of you." Her hovering finger finally got to punch in some numbers. "Are you a friend, or family member?"

I shook my head. "I'm here on behalf of his partner, Gayle Forris."

She looked like she wanted to say something, but then someone must have picked up in human resources. "Teresa? I have someone here asking about Trent. No. He says that he's 'here on behalf of his partner.' Trent's, not his own." She nodded several times, then said, "All right," and put the phone down. Her hand came out with a card. "No one can see you right now. You can have Ms. Forris call Ms. Jones and make an appointment for herself or you."

I had to step over the tape to take the card. "Thank you, Sergeant – uh?" She had non-commissioned officer written all over her.

"Very good. Do you guess people's weights at the county fair, too? It's Sanderson. My friends and the guests here call me 'Sandy.' You don't need to call me anything at all, because our business is finished."

I stepped back. "Ms. Sanderson, I really do need some help here – and I doubt that Ms. Jones can provide it.

I'm sure you know that Trent has disappeared. His partner has hired me to try and find him. She believes that he was looking for one of the guests here who has vanished, too. As it happens, I am also looking for another person, who was a guest here up until a couple of weeks ago – now, also missing."

She looked at me steadily, but said nothing. It was standard interrogation practice. Get someone talking, refuse to fill the pauses, and they'll just keep blurting things out. Maybe she had been an MP. Or the parent of a teenager. Requires the same skill set, really. Of course, it's SOP for PIs too. In this case, though, I thought a little more blurting might be in order.

"Look, the police don't care what happened to your guests, and they think that Trent is shacked up with a mistress somewhere. If you don't care about any of them, either, then I'll just leave. Give me a call when someone you *do* care about goes missing." I stepped forward again and gave her Ms. Jones' card back, along with one of my own. I flashed her a big, false smile and turned to leave.

"Mr. Perdue."

I stopped and turned slowly around, sure that I was finally going to get some information.

"Have a blessed day." She tossed my card onto her desk, cracked a smile – I was reminded of an iceberg shearing in half – then looked down at some papers. Dismissed.

Outside, I looked around the square. There was a donut shop up the street. Odds were good that some of the shelter clients would be there, nursing a cup of coffee. But I wasn't looking for anyone who had a couple of bucks in their pocket.

Orman is laid out on a grid, like many American cities founded in the mid-1800s. Numbered streets go east and west, named roads go north and south, and avenues go diagonally. In the downtown area, there are alleys between the streets and roads that allow access to loading docks, service entrances, and off-street parking. These alleys are the daytime hangout for many of Orman's homeless.

Jacob's Alley runs between First and Second Streets, behind the vets' shelter, the courthouse, a dry cleaners, two coffee shops, a ten-story condo complex, a pizza place, law offices, and a bail bondsman. Downtown Orman is a hodge-podge of businesses and residences. The Chamber of Commerce likes to use the word "eclectic."

The locals' pride in their city center is based on how far it's come. Ten years ago, the coffee shops were tattoo parlors, the pizza joint was a strip club, and the site of the condos was an empty lot that was home to so many junkies that you couldn't have found a haystack hidden among the discarded needles. The dry cleaners, law offices, and bail bondsman had been there as long as the courthouse, since about 1920.

I strolled down the alley, pretending to smoke a cigarette. Each puff that I drew into my mouth and exhaled without taking any smoke into my lungs was a small victory over my lifelong addiction to nicotine. If you're looking to catch flies, then it's worth arguing the relative merits of honey over vinegar. If you want to hook a hobo, you stick to cigarettes.

Someone to whom you've just given a smoke is a lot more likely to talk to you than someone you approach with questions. Say what you want about people who end up on the streets, but they have their own sense of honor and debt. A cigarette freely given deserves at least a little courtesy.

"Hey, man. You got a spare smoke?" A scruffy man of indeterminate age was seated on the curb, hands stuffed in his pockets and one leg snaking through the strap of the backpack beside him to defend against a snatch and run.

"Sure." I pulled a cigarette out of the pack and tossed it to him. He caught it awkwardly in his left hand and put it to his lips. I kept up my pace so it appeared that I was going to keep walking.

"How about a light?" I slowed and reached into my pocket for a lighter. It was playing out just as I wanted. It was all his idea to engage with me. The only problem was that his right hand hadn't left his jacket pocket. I like to see a stranger's hands before I get too close. Caution and suspicion are essential to life on the street. As John Lennon put it, "Paranoia is just a heightened sense of awareness."

I tossed the lighter at him a little hard, and directly at his right arm. As his hand came out of his pocket, I glimpsed a flash of metal. My heart skipped a beat.

The lighter clanked off his prosthetic hand and landed between his feet. He picked the lighter up with his left hand, took a long draw as he lit his cigarette, getting a big butane hit along with the tobacco smoke, and tossed it back. "Thanks."

"Hey, sorry about that. Bad throw." I tucked the lighter into the half-full box. He gave me an "all's well that ends well" shrug and lowered his eyes to the ground. It was now or never.

"Look, can I ask something?"

He didn't look up. "Is it about my arm?"

"What? No, not about that."

He raised his head. "Good. Some people get their freak on about prostheses. For some reason they seem to get more turned on by the crude metal one."

He held up the limb, opening and closing the two "fingers" and gauging my reaction.

"You'd think it would be the fleshy-looking one, but it's definitely the pirate special that does it. What's your question, then?" He rested his arm across his lap, apparently satisfied that I wasn't a prosthesis pervert.

I squatted down on the opposite curb. "Are you staying in the veterans' shelter?"

"Some nights. Depends on the weather. No offense to my fellow warriors, but I generally prefer my own company."

"A couple of folks I know there seem to have gone missing."

"Is that right?"

"A gal named Michelle who was a guest, and Trent who worked the night desk."

"Sergeant Argent's gone AWOL? Hadn't heard that."

"What about Michelle Rathborn? Army medic. Served in Afghanistan."

He stubbed out his cigarette, and I tossed him the pack. "You're not a cop. A cop wouldn't have bothered to play me into bumming a smoke. Are you intel?"

I laughed. "No, but thanks for the compliment. I'm just a lowly private detective."

"It wasn't a compliment." He opened the cigarette box and took inventory. "Eight cigarettes. That's eight questions you can ask, plus two for the lighter. Up for a game of ten questions?"

"Okay." I handed him my card.

"LSI, Inc. Not very informative. I like that. Ask away, Adam Perdue."

"Do you know who Michelle Rathborn is?"

"Meth head alkie whose disappointed daddy owns some convenience store chain. That's one."

"When was the last time you saw her?"

"Maybe two, three weeks back. It was raining like hell, that's why I went into the shelter. You can check the weather records. Only night in the last month that it came down hard all night long. That's two."

"When did you last see Trent Argent?"

"The same night, probably. No, I take that back. I saw him out here last week, either Friday or Saturday night. Well, actually, early Saturday or Sunday morning, more like. Right around dawn. He brought a coffee urn and some donuts out from the shelter. He'll do that sometimes. It drives Cookie nuts. Three."

"Were either of them acting oddly recently, or doing anything differently than usual?"

"That's two questions. Four if I wanted to be a hard-ass." He took several puffs off his cigarette, focusing on it intently, as if he was a neglectful social butterfly who had just returned to his date at a party and wanted to give her his fullest attention.

"Michelle pretty much always acts odd, and it's been a while, so I've got nothing there. I guess Sergeant Argent was a little different. He usually just drops off the coffee and donuts and leaves. But last week he hung around and talked to a few guys. That's four and five."

"What did he talk to them about?"

"I don't know. He didn't talk to me. Six."

"You're sure you have no idea what he was talking about? Nobody said anything after he was gone? I think he was looking for one of the guests, but I don't have a name. He went missing on Sunday, so it's kind of important."

"He might have been looking for one of the clients. I didn't hear a name. Seven."

"Do you remember who he talked to?"

"I remember a couple of guys, maybe. It wasn't like I was paying hard attention, you know? I was sucking down some coffee and donuts out on the edge of the crowd. Eight."

"Are you telling me the truth?"

"Yeah, so far. But if I wasn't, I'd say the same thing. Nine."

"If I offer you $50 to find out a name, do you think you could do it?"

"Probably could. But I'd want it to be an exclusive deal, for a day anyway. I don't want to go poking around and then find out you already got the name from someone else. That's ten."

"I'll give you an exclusive for twelve hours, and make it $100 bucks if you get the name. Deal?"

"Deal." He put out his left hand, turned thumb downward so that it was easy for me to shake with my right.

"I'll look for you right here in 12 hours, then. What's your name?"

"You used up all your questions. If you need to find me, ask for Captain Hook. That's what everybody around here calls me."

AND SQUIRE MAKES THREE

My office is on the fourth floor of the Sutter Building. It's the oldest office building downtown, and it shows. LSI moving in didn't bring down the tone of the building, which says a lot. The only business with any kind of prestige at all is the Second Bank of Orman, which occupies the main floor. The higher up you go, the sketchier the tenants become. There's a temp agency, Working4U, a couple of jewelers, a chiropractor, half a dozen independent insurance agents, and several contractors whose names appear in the paper a little too often. A bail bondsman and two attorneys round out the directory.

The LSI office suite includes an extra room with an attached bathroom, complete with a shower. I have one of those half-size dorm refrigerators, a microwave, and a hotplate. Technically, no one is allowed to live in the building due to zoning, but I'm not the only one who calls it home. I do my eating, sleeping, and relaxing in the office and mainly work out of my car. But clients like to visit offices, and Julia definitely does not like working in "Old Yeller," as she refers to the ancient Oldsmobile that I drive.

When I pointed out that it was more cream-colored than yellow, she clarified that her reference was not to the paint job but rather to the old Disney movie. "That poor thing needs to be put down."

LSI has a resident cat, DK. His proper name is Dumpster Kitty, but Julia thinks that's demeaning, so we settled on the initials. No food of any kind is safe from DK. The appearance of anything edible drives him into a frenzy. You can take the kitten out of the dumpster, but you can't take the dumpster out of the kitty. DK is a lazy, aloof, and entitled creature who barely tolerates our presence in his home. In other words, he's a cat.

I pulled the elevator's metal door closed and hit "4." Nothing. I opened the door and shut it, then tried again. I jiggled the door handle while punching the button, and it finally lurched upward. The elevator, like most temps at Working4U, appears functional and is always available, but it only works when the spirit moves it – and then only in its own quirky way.

Squire was perched on the edge of Julia's desk, giving her plenty of height to fully enjoy the view as Julia bent over an open file drawer. I'd have called her on being a perv if it wasn't for the fact that Julia never files anything, and wouldn't retrieve it if she did. Sometimes it's a fine line between harassment and flirting. This wasn't one of those times.

"Oh, Adam. There you are!" Julia straightened up, her face red.

"Were you looking for me in the file cabinet?"

"What? No, I..." She gave me a look that could pierce Kevlar. "Lieutenant Squire is here to see you."

We exchanged nods, and I led Squire into my office. DK jumped off one of the guest chairs and lunged through the doorway, nearly tripping us both.

"What can I do for you, Squire? Anything happening with the Bell case?"

"Maybe. It would help a lot if you had anything on the limo driver. Could you tell if he was black or white, or maybe Middle Eastern?"

I stopped my head in mid-shake. "Middle Eastern? That's a funny thing to ask."

"Not really. Orman has several thousand citizens of Middle Eastern origin, some going back generations. And then there are the refugees the State Department resettled here after the Iraq war, and a batch of Afghans when that mess wound down.''

That was true enough, but it didn't explain why Squire would be looking at them for the Bell murder. I was about to irritate her by pointing out that Afghans aren't Middle Eastern, when my coin dropped.

"The hands."

"The hands," Squire confirmed. "It seems that our Mr. Bell's customer accounts are missing quite a bit of money. And the largest discrepancy was in the account of the Zakat Trust, LLC – a charitable foundation managed by the Levant family."

The Levants have lived in Orman for almost a century and own a piece of just about everything. The patriarch, Noor, emigrated from Lebanon in the 1930s and turned a single hole-in-the-wall takeout store into a chain of fast-food restaurants that went nationwide. There is a

Baba Ghanoush in more than 300 malls across the country.

Noor's son Abraham had a knack for picking stocks and multiplied the family's fortune. And *his* son David now runs the empire. None of them had ever shown any inclination for leaving Orman for the big city. Omaha has its Warren Buffet, and Orman has David Levant.

"But the Levants aren't old school, Squire. I don't see them cutting off the hands of a thief."

"They aren't the only ones with funds in the foundation. There was a big influx of cash during and after the Iraq and Afghanistan wars. Not everyone who resettled here was a penniless refugee. Homeland Security has been keeping an eye on the foundation. They make a lot of grants to charitable organizations in the West Bank and Lebanon."

"I bet they make more right here in Orman." There isn't a nonprofit in the county that doesn't receive some kind of funding from the Zakat Foundation. "Anyway, I really didn't see the guy's face at all. I couldn't tell you if he was an Arab or a Swede. So, the feds are working the case, too?"

"Thankfully, they don't seem very interested. The guy from Homeland thought it was funny that Bell had ripped the foundation off. I get the feeling they don't really care if we solve the case, or find the money."

It belatedly occurred to me to wonder why Squire was telling me all this. Her idea of information-sharing is complete access to everything I know in exchange for a rumor from one of her less reliable snitches. Could be she just wanted to hit on Julia, or could be she had something else in mind. The only sure thing was that she hadn't expected me to suddenly remember that I had seen a face after all.

"What do the Levants have to say about all this?"

"David Levant politely terminated our interview once he figured out that I was trying to make a connection between the missing hands and the Islamic punishment for stealing. Which was interesting, since I didn't mention the hands and it's been kept out of the media so far."

I had done a job for Levant a couple of years before. A resettled refugee, Amin Abad, had gone on a drinking binge, working his way down from the hotel bars, through the clubs and neighborhood dives, until he wound up on the street sucking on half pints and begging for change. His wife and kids were in a jam, because the relief payments from the resettlement program were electronically deposited in an account in his name, and he had the debit card for their food assistance, too.

Levant had paid me to find him and get the cards and PINs from him. It had been easy to find him, and he handed over the cards and codes without a complaint. He was wracked with guilt over his failure to get a job and provide for his family. He wasn't the first man in Orman to try and drown those particular sorrows. Employers seem to come and go pretty fast. The City Council has incentive programs that are really just bribes

43

to prospective businesses. They work, until some other city raises the ante. Then the jobs catch the next bus out of town.

I felt sorry for Amin, so I set him up with a week's rent at a flop house and a job cleaning out foreclosed houses. I took him to an AA meeting, and when he stayed sober for a week, I became his sponsor. Sometimes it sticks the first time. Not often, and not for me. But for Amin it did. He turned himself around and made things right with his family. They live in a nice little condo on the fringe of downtown, and he still goes to two meetings every week. Last I heard, he had become a sponsor. Pay it forward.

And what's that got to do with the price of hummus in Baghdad? Well, one day Squire and I went to grab lunch at a Baba Ghanoush. When we got to the register, the kid behind the counter rang up Squire but wouldn't take my money. I thought he must be mixed up. Cops get their meals comped, not private eyes.

The kid showed us a laminated sheet that was on a stand next to the register. There were pictures of about a dozen people with the words, "No charge" printed underneath. Mine was among them. It looked like it might have been an old mugshot. Squire thought it was hilarious and had me tell her the back story.

"So, you want me to talk to Levant for you? Why would he do that? I'm not even working the case."

"That's what I'm here to talk to you about. The fiscal year just rolled over, and we've got a few bucks for

44

consultants. I think we have enough left over after paying the psychics, snitches, and techno trolls to buy some old-fashioned shoe-leather help in a homicide case. Two hundred dollars a day, the standard city rate, three-day minimum. Expenses are on you. You find out anything you can about the Bell murder, starting with a conversation with Levant. What do you say?"

My immediate instinct was to say no. Three paid cases at once was unprecedented, and there's a reason for that. Julia and I can only cover so much ground, with some help from our modest network of folks living on the margins who had lost pretty much everything but their wits.

Besides, I'm not sure I wanted to use up whatever credit I had with David Levant on a case that didn't even involve me. Except, of course, that it did. It had happened on my watch, even if there hadn't been anything I could do to stop it. And there was that feeling I just couldn't shake that I knew the victim somehow.

"On one condition."

"Which is?"

"If I lose my free pass at Baba Ghanoush over this, you buy me lunch once a week for the rest of my life."

"Deal." Squire laughed and held her hand out. "With your nose for trouble, it's not like it's gonna be a long-term commitment."

We shook on it, and I saw her to the door.

"Nice to see you, Julia. Try and keep your boss away from any more murders for a while, okay?"

"That's my job. You be careful out there, too."

Once Squire was safely on her way down to the lobby, I turned to Julia and looked at her, eyebrows raised. She raised hers back.

"Do you and Squire have something going?"

"No, and it wouldn't be your business if we did."

"If your business gets in the way of our business, then it *is* my business. But that's not why I'm asking. She's good people. You both could do a lot worse. You both *have* done a lot worse."

"She's all right," she replied in the tone of voice that made it clear that she was much better than just all right. "But we kind of come from different worlds. Hell, for all I know, she may have busted me back in the day. I didn't pay much attention to who was slapping on the cuffs."

"Everybody has a past. Squire, too. Anyway, you do have one thing in common."

"What's that?"

"Yours truly."

"You've got a point there. Nothing can bring two people together better than mutual loathing. At least we know our tastes in people are compatible."

"You cut me to the bone. Why don't you draw up a standard retainer agreement for the $600 Squire promised and get her signature on it. I'm sure she'd be willing to meet you somewhere halfway between here and the station, like Tuck's maybe. She's a sucker for their coffee and pie. Meantime, I'm going to reach out to David Levant."

The 2nd Street garage is conveniently located a couple blocks from my office, right next to the on-ramp for Interstate 13 North. Take that for seven miles and you get to the Interstate 28 interchange going east and west. There wasn't a better location for getting out of Orman in a hurry. In fifteen minutes, you could be out of the county, and within 45 minutes you could cross the state line in three different directions. Not that I ever think about needing to get out of town fast. Not me.

I eased Old Yeller out of the garage, which always made me feel like I was breaking an elderly and infirm relative out of the nursing home. Same challenge in getting her started and turned in the right direction, same suspicious look on the gate guard's face as I wheeled her out.

My best guess is that Yeller has over 300,000 miles on her. When I bought her, she was thirty years old and the 5-digit odometer read 78,787. There were two scratches on the dashboard plastic to the left of the odometer. The car dealer took just enough exception to my theory that they represented the number of times it had rolled over – without actually denying it outright – that I figured I was on the money. It had rolled over once since I bought it, and I had dutifully added another scratch.

David Levant runs the Zakat Foundation out of the Baba Ghanoush headquarters. It's at the Atrium, one of those artificial villages that incorporate office, retail, residential, and recreational facilities. The people who live there liked to brag that they never need to leave the place. I'd be okay if I never needed to go into it. It's a little too Stepford Wives for my taste.

Levant let me sit in the waiting room for about ten minutes, long enough to remind me that he is an important man but brief enough to impress the receptionist. I bet she's seen the mayor wait for longer. Of course, the mayor is a dick and deserves to wait.

"Adam, Adam. Come in. Long time, no see." He spared me a glance and a smile, waving me to sit on the couch, then studied the papers on his desk for another minute. I looked around his office. Gayle Forris would have been happy to sit anywhere, including the floor covered in oriental carpets.

Bookshelves held leather-bound tomes with bright embossing in various languages, some in Latin script, others in Arabic or Persian, and still others in Cyrillic. Paintings graced the walls, and small works of art were scattered on all the surfaces. It was an unusual mix: modern and ancient, European, Asian, African, and Middle Eastern.

He gave the papers a final shake of his head and then came and joined me. "Tea?" he asked. I nodded, and he dropped sugar cubes in our glasses, poured steaming green tea over them, added a small spoon and a slice of lime into each, and slid one toward me.

Levant is a third generation American who has that special kind of pride in his heritage that comes to those whose parents and grandparents had worked so hard to assimilate that their descendants are free to celebrate their background as enthusiastically as any Irish-American who wears a "Kiss Me, I'm Irish" t-shirt on St. Patty's Day.

"You said on the phone that it was a confidential matter, but there is little in Orman that stays confidential for long. I assume that you are here about the Bell murder? I understand you witnessed it."

I nodded. "I have a personal interest in the case. I don't like having people murdered and dismembered on my watch. But I also need to tell you that I have been retained by the COP to investigate." The City of Orman Police has a great acronym.

"Of course. Do you think that Mr. Bell's hands were cut off as some sort of message, as Lieutenant Squire implied?" His voice lost just a touch of its warmth.

"I honestly don't have a theory on that, Mr. Levant. The more traditional take on it would be an attempt to obscure the victim's identity, but leaving his wallet kind of contradicts that. What do you think?"

"In my office and in my home, you must call me 'David.' If you wish to be more formal in public, I leave it up to you." He continued only after I smiled in acknowledgment. "It does seem unlikely that someone would have the foresight and calmness required to cut off a victim's hands but not think of his driver's license. Did he really whistle while he worked?"

Levant clearly had someone in the COP feeding him information. "Yeah. It added to the creepy factor, which was already at a pretty high level. He went about it all very calmly and professionally, like he was following a checklist."

"What was he whistling? Was it a tune, or just freestyle?"

Neither Woody nor Squire had thought to ask me that. Hell, I hadn't thought to ask me that. I replayed the scene in my head. "Freestyle, I think. Not a tune I recognized, anyway. I don't remember too clearly."

David nodded and waited for me to continue. He was well aware that he had thrown me off my game a bit.

"Well, another mystery is why did our freestyle whistler have orders to cut off the hands but not to take the wallet? I'm sure you can understand why Squire has to check every possibility."

"Of course. But she – and you – should understand that taking the hands as some sort of Sharia punishment for theft makes no more sense than obscuring his fingerprints and leaving his wallet. The purpose of cutting off a hand for theft under Sharia is as a deterrent, for the thief himself and for everyone who sees the price that he has paid.

"There is no purpose to cutting off the hand of a dead body, as there is no deterrent. Any such message is sent with the murder and not enhanced by the removal of the hands. Also, desecrating a body in this way is forbidden under Islamic law."

"Okay. I'll buy that. Who do you think might have wanted Bell dead, with or without his hands?"

"Me, obviously. And anyone else who gives to the Zakat Foundation. But most were unaware of his theft until the police brought it to our attention. We received regular statements that showed our investments with Mr. Bell were doing very well. I had received a tip that there might be something funny going on with Bell, but I had not informed anyone else involved with the foundation. I assume there are others whose money he embezzled?"

"So I've been told, but they all suffered relatively small losses. You mentioned the other contributors to the foundation. Do you think any of them could have found out that he was embezzling the money and then taken matters into their own hands?" I winced at the expression, and Levant smiled at my discomfort.

"I suppose it's possible. But if so, they would have been in on it with him. If any of us were certain about his theft, we would have gone to the authorities, not kill him. With him in custody, restitution is possible. Dead, there is no way to get our money back. Only Bell and any accomplices he may have had now know where it is.

"I don't wish to cast suspicion on anyone in particular, but if I were investigating his murder, I would look at his close friends and family. Isn't the idea to follow the money? And if you have difficulty following it, try and discover who else is trying to follow it."

Levant was right, of course. Nine times out of ten, find the money and you find the murderer. "So where would you look, if you were looking for someone who was looking for the money?"

"I would start with the widow, of course. But I would probably find that she is neither sufficiently clever nor industrious enough to be an important part of such a plan. I don't think her ambitions are even as large as the generous insurance settlement that is coming her way. I would not rule out her being used in some way, but she is not a planner."

He ran his hand through his hair, closed his eyes for a moment, and then exhaled deeply. "The next place I would look is the other investors. A wise collaborator would want to be hurt by the scheme, but not hard enough to draw attention. The Zakat Foundation has been hit hard enough to draw a great deal of attention, which may be exactly what was intended. While no educated Muslim would have cut off the hands of Mr. Bell, someone less knowledgeable, like your Lieutenant Squire or yourself, might do so to draw even greater attention to the foundation's investors as suspects."

I nodded and tried my best to give the impression that he was confirming something that I had already considered. Private detectives don't always have to be a step ahead of everyone else, but they should never look like they're a step or two behind. When people pay you to find out things, they like to believe that you're better at it than they are. I find it's wise to support their delusion. A quick change of subject is a convincing way to disguise a revelation as familiar territory.

"How well did you know Bell, David?" I made a mental note to get the full list of Bell's clients from Squire.

"Well enough, I suppose. We met quarterly to discuss foundation business. I would see him in between at social and charitable events. We shared an interest in antiquities. To be more precise, I should say that we had different interests in the shared topic of antiquities. Mine is an aesthetic and historical interest. His was in their value as investments."

"You mean like stocks and bonds?"

"More like precious metals. While not highly liquid, they are easy to transport and generally increase in value. That saying about why real estate is a good investment also holds true for ancient artifacts: they aren't making any more of them. There has, however, been an increase in supply over the last decade due to the chaos and governmental collapses taking place around the world."

"I recall reading something about looting at the Iraqi and Afghan national museums and various antiquities appearing on the market in Europe and the US."

"Yes. Much of the looting in Iraq – and the smuggling – was done by NATO troops. The Afghan museums were looted by warlords and the Taliban who sold them to servicemen and diplomats. Disgraceful all around. Those artifacts are a window into the world's past, and sadly many of the gold and silver pieces have been melted down and sold for their precious metal value alone. Such a loss."

"That's about all you can do with something stolen from a museum, right? Everything is catalogued and photographed. You've got to melt it down to make it saleable."

There is another way, but I wanted to see if he would go there.

He did.

"Or you can find a private collector who isn't too fussy about his purchases."

I looked around the office. Just on the nearest set of shelves, there were carved stone friezes, miniature paintings on silk, and what appeared to be a piece of Roman glass. He caught me looking and laughed. He pushed an album across the coffee table to me.

"The items on that shelf are on page 17, I believe."

I opened the book. Each page was filled with photographs captioned with descriptions of the item's provenance and the date and source of Levant's purchase. The first half dozen pages were just carpets.

"I compiled that for insurance purposes. But I find that it is helpful for answering guests' questions as well. I do not buy stolen antiquities. They can't be insured, and it's selfish and anti-social to hide away such treasures. But it's not as bad as melting them down.

"An artifact or a work of art squirreled away by someone with more money than conscience may eventually be returned to the world. A metal ingot simply passes from hand to hand and bank to bank, enriching the holder and no one else."

David Levant is not someone who wastes time or meanders in his conversation, so I couldn't help but wonder why he was sharing his thoughts about ancient treasures. My area of expertise is unwanted people, not highly sought after objects.

"You wonder why we're having this conversation about antiquities, don't you?"

Note to self: don't play poker with David Levant.

"I assume it has something to do with Bell."

"Indeed. As I stated earlier, Mr. Bell has an interest in the investment side of antiquities. He offered me a number of items, among them an ancient sword, one of great historic importance to Muslims. I doubt very much that he had the actual item, which was lost to the world a thousand years ago. But the photo he showed me was of an appropriately fashioned weapon.

"One can tell little from a picture, of course, but even a centuries-old replica of this sword would be extremely valuable, of great interest to scholars, and possibly very dangerous. There are many in the Shia Muslim community who believe that it will be wielded in the end times by a messianic figure who will conquer the world in the name of Islam."

"You mean, like a Muslim version of the Anti-Christ?"

"More like a Muslim version of Jesus returning after the Rapture. In any event, Mr. Bell indicated that it had come from the vault of either the Baghdad or Kabul museums, though he would not say any more than that. I agreed to pay him $50,000 in cash for the sword if it passed my inspection and contacted a friend at the FBI who deals with art theft."

"So, what happened?"

"You saw what happened. Mr. Bell was crushed, shot, and mutilated – all, unfortunately, before he had delivered the sword to me. And before I had delivered him to the FBI, which I assumed would be able to track down the source of the stolen article. I would still like to find out who has it and how it came into their possession." He looked at me.

I didn't feel as good about the ten-minute wait now. Ten minutes for a meeting I wanted was impressive. Not so much when it was a meeting *he* had wanted.

"I am already working for the COP, so it would be a conflict of interest for me to work for you on the same case."

"But I am not interested in who murdered Bell. Well, I am, of course. But that is not what I want to hire you to do. I would like you to find the person or persons unknown who are attempting to sell Iraqi and Afghan antiquities – in Orman, of all places. And it wouldn't hurt if you found a lead or two on the money stolen from the Foundation.

"That seems more like a confluence of interest than a conflict. I will pay twice your normal rate, or twice whatever the COP is giving you, whichever is higher. More importantly, you will be doing the right thing." He leaned forward and held my eyes. "*And* doing me a favor, which is always the right thing."

Four clients? This was getting ridiculous. I tried to do the math in my head and gave it up. It's not that I'm all about the money, but this was adding up to a whole lot of what I'm not all about.

"You realize that I'm going to report our conversation to Squire. She'll be looking into Bell's antiquities business, too."

"Of course, I'm counting on it."

"What the hell, then. In for a penny, in for a pound. I'm getting $200 a day —"

He shut me off with a wave of his hand. "Send me whatever paperwork is needed. You need a retainer to begin, correct?" He pulled his wallet out and counted out ten $100 bills. "Will that be sufficient?"

I took the money, and Levant stood. He walked me to the door of his office. As I reached for the handle he spoke again.

"I was having Bell followed. The day before his murder, he paid a rather long visit to a place called New

Life Ministries, some sort of homeless shelter, I believe. I mention it because Bell was not the philanthropic type, and because such places are an area of expertise for you. That is why I want to hire you. That, and the fact that I had to fire Register from the job."

Clyde Register was the big dipper in the Orman private investigators' firmament. He had all the car repo, insurance scam, and skip trace business in the county. Every once in a while, an independent set up shop for a few months, or a couple of years at most. If they were any good, Clyde bought them out and paid them better than they had been able to pay themselves. If they weren't any good, they didn't last long anyway. Clyde didn't want my business, though, so we got along okay – doing cross-referrals and only stabbing each other in the back when absolutely necessary.

"Why'd you fire Clyde?"

"Because his tail lost Bell the night he died. He sat outside Bell's house the whole night and somehow missed him getting into the limo, or sneaking out the window, or whatever he did to get himself down to Village South that night."

"Interesting about Bell being at a homeless shelter. The night he was killed, I kept thinking he looked familiar but couldn't place him." I didn't want to tell Levant that I had never heard of New Life Ministries. When you hire a guy for his expertise on Skid Row, you expect him to be familiar with all the establishments.

The truth is, places open and shut all the time. Mostly they're one-person operations, true believers who hear a calling and sink their life savings into trying to save some very difficult to salvage souls. But Bell had visited New Life Ministries, so I was going to have to get to know them.

"Maybe he volunteers there or something," I suggested to David.

"My money is on 'or something.' He isn't the volunteering type."

People think that private detectives get paid to find things. The way I see it, I get paid to look for things. If I find them, that's a bonus. But as long as I'm looking, I'm keeping up my end of the deal. So not finding what I'm looking for doesn't bother me. It's just part of the job. But when I have a client and I can't find anything to look for, I start to feel a bit like a fraud. So, having *four* clients and no clear path to look for anything or anybody made me very antsy.

There was a time when I thought I had hit rock bottom and lost everything, including my integrity. As it turned out, I found a way to thrash around on the bottom with sufficient enthusiasm and endurance to squirm my way even lower. But that's another story.

Integrity is a funny thing. It has to be given up to be lost. It's not like a reputation. No one can take it away with lies, or even with the truth. It can't be lost to bad luck, or fate, or even the will of God – if you believe in such things. But once it's been surrendered by the person who had it, it can only be restored by the faith of others.

Not that long ago, when I was going through the pockets of my soul looking for spiritual spare change, or a claim check for my conscience, or something similar – I forget exactly what – I discovered my long-lost integrity. It turns out that enough people have developed sufficient faith in me that it had been restored. I vowed then to never lose it again.

That's why I hit the streets, determined to find something to look for. I didn't care if I was looking for Michelle Rathborn, Trent Argent, Ellis Bell's murderer, or an unknown purveyor of stolen antiquities. I might not find any of them, but I damn sure was going to look for at least one of them.

I walked the alleys around the veterans' shelter but couldn't find my source. A cigarette and a handful of change got me his favorite morning hangout, which I should have guessed: the donut shop. I found him at the counter, prosthetic arm tucked in his pocket and eating an egg sandwich. He nodded at the stool next to his, and I sat.

"I got you a name."

"Then I've got you a c-note." I started to reach for my wallet, and he glared at me.

"Not here. Not now."

I pulled out a ten and waved it at the waitress. "I'll have a chocolate glazed and a medium coffee, black with one sugar." Hook pointed at his half-eaten sandwich and twirled his finger. "And another egg sandwich." I nodded to the waitress.

"Sergeant Argent was asking around after Herb, one of the regulars."

"You got a last name?"

"Ryan. Army. Served in Afghanistan. Helmand, I think."

"So, Herb Ryan, Army."

"No, 'Herb' is his street name. Weed is his drug of choice. His real first name is Sean."

"Okay. Any idea of his rank?"

"You never served." It was a statement, not a question.

"Uh, no."

"Herb's a grunt. I'm a grunt. Everybody on the street or in a shelter's a grunt. Officers have their own mess." He laughed. "Man, that has some serious multiple meanings."

I raised an eyebrow.

"Mess as in 'mess hall.' Their own private place to eat. Mess as in 'messed up in the head.' Mess as in 'This is another fine mess you've gotten us into, Stanley.' Serious shit multiple meanings."

"So, any idea why Argent was looking for Sean Ryan?"

"Just 'cause he was missing. Like I said, he was a regular, and then he was gone. Poof! Like he was beamed up to the Starship Enterprise. Or maybe caught a Greyhound outta town. Same difference. No, a puff a smoke! That's it! Herb disappeared in a puff of smoke."

"Hey, I appreciate the information." I slid the plate with my donut in his direction. Just a corner of the bill I had slipped under it showed. He pulled out his artificial arm and laid it on the counter with a thump, while palming the bill casually with his good hand. Misdirection, just like a magician.

"So, what's your name, if I need to find you again?"

"Just ask for 'Captain Hook.' Like everybody else."

"I'd like to know your real name."

"I'll give you a choice, Perdue. I'll tell you my name, if that's what you really want to know. Or, I'll tell you where people are sayin' that Herb went. Where they told Argent that Herb went. Which do you want to know?"

I wanted to know Hook's real name, of course. But I *needed* the information about Ryan. "Where did Sean Ryan go?"

He looked both disappointed and relieved. "Herb went looking for a new life. Or it went looking for him. One of the guys saw him get into that New Life Ministries van. Last anyone's seen of him." New Life Ministries again.

A lot of people don't believe in coincidences. It's human nature to want to cover the stark nakedness of random happenstance with the clothing of order and purpose. But they are real. As frustrating as it can be, sometimes shit just happens. Lightning does strike the same place twice, or even three times.

I didn't figure there was any connection between Bell giving support to New Life Ministries and Herb seeking it from them. But it was a three-fer: looking into the place would help me earn my pay from at least three of my four clients. For all I knew, it might prove helpful in finding Michelle Rathborn. Staking out her favorite alley certainly hadn't been.

Old Yeller was waiting for me at the curb. My car may be chipped, dented and worn on the outside, but it has a couple of newer touches on the inside. Charlie at Fender Bender Garage had fitted the oversized glove compartment with a laptop on a retractable arm that allows it to be used from any seat in the car. In the center console, where the cup holders used to be, he had mounted one of those internet hot spot thingies that use cell signals to give you WIFI. I more often bemoan the loss of the cup holders than appreciate the addition of the internet, but this wasn't one of those times.

By putting "New Life Ministries" and "Orman" into the search bar and scanning the results, I was able to give myself a quick education on the shelter. It had opened up in Orman just about a year ago and had a lot of positive local press. In fact, its founder and director, Pastor Janice Shelley, was receiving a "Local Heroes" award from the mayor that very afternoon.

I glanced at my watch, which indicated that it was 2:30 PM, a half hour after the presentation on the steps of City Hall. That meant I had half an hour to get there. The stem had broken off the watch, so I hadn't been able to adjust for the most recent time change. Easier to be an hour ahead half the year than to find someone who could repair a watch stem, even in a relatively retro place like Orman.

There was a decent sized crowd at City Hall. I recognized the directors from a couple of the shelters, the mayor, chief of police, and a local TV reporter. Gayle Forris was there, voice recorder in hand, trying to elbow her way toward the mayor.

"Nice to see you, Miss Forris." She started a little when I spoke from just behind her.

"Mr. Perdue. What are you doing here?"

"Call me Adam. Same as you, working."

Any further conversation was cut short as the city manager tapped the microphone, making the speakers crackle, and introduced the mayor. The mayor spoke about how important the issue of homelessness was to him and praised the work of all the service providers who had representatives in the audience.

He recited some year-over-year statistics on homelessness in Orman, which were on a decided downward trend. There was loud applause from the audience. He then went on to credit the decrease in homelessness largely to Pastor Jan and New Life Ministries. Applause from the other shelter representatives was more muted, but still polite.

"And all this has been accomplished without a dime of taxpayer money! All New Life Ministries services are provided free of charge and supported by private donations. In fact, I'm an enthusiastic donor myself. After you hear Pastor Jan speak, I know that you will become one, too. Without further ado, Pastor Janice Shelley of New Life Ministries!"

Not using city money would make them popular with the other shelters. Taking up some of the caseload while not dipping into the limited funds available will make you some friends in the provider community.

As Pastor Jan stepped to the microphone with a young man in a suit, Gayle whispered in my ear. "Why exactly are you here? Do you think New Life Ministries is involved in Trent's disappearance?"

"No," I whispered back. "Not at this point. There just seem to be a lot of coincidences involving that place, and I thought I'd get the measure of its director."

"Thank you, Mr. Mayor for that glowing introduction. If New Life Ministries has seen some success in the last year, it has less to do with me and more to do with the incredible courage and commitment of the clients who come to us seeking a way back into being productive members of society. They deserve the credit – they and Jesus Christ, through whose grace and love they have been redeemed. With us today is just one of the many guests at New Life Ministries who has rejoined the community as a solid citizen."

She nudged the man forward. I recognized him from the AA meetings I had attended years ago. He was one of those people who couldn't stay on the wagon, but climbed back on after every fall. He had accumulated enough of the short-term white and red chips to fill a checkerboard.

"Hello, my name is Horace Alpert. Thank you for having me here today."

She gently pulled Horace back from the mic.

"Eight months ago, Horace came to us a broken man." She looked to him for confirmation, and he nodded. "Today, I am proud to say that he is managing his own landscaping business, providing employment for three people and helping to make Orman more beautiful." She paused as the audience applauded.

"His story is just one of many at New Life Ministries. And did the mayor mention it was at NO cost to the taxpayers of Orman?"

The rest of her speech was just as well-constructed: deflection of credit, acknowledgement of efforts of the wider community, thanks and praise to Jesus – all leavened with an occasional humorous aside. Most importantly to everyone in attendance, it was short.

"Let me know if your interview turns up anything interesting," I whispered to Gayle. She nodded before wading through the departing crowd to get close to the guest of honor. I made my way toward Horace, who seemed to be looking for a way out.

"Hey, Al. Congratulations!" Al was the name he had used at AA.

"Uh, Adam. Yeah. Thanks."

"Long way from the basement of the Y."

"Not so far. I'm still going to Wednesday meetings there. Haven't seen you in a while."

I shrugged. "Good for you. Are you still staying at New Life, or do you have your own place?"

"I've got an apartment on Grove Street. I graduated from NLM a month ago." He was gone by the time Ryan would have gotten there.

"Terrible thing about that guy who got murdered. I hear he volunteered at the shelter. Did you ever meet him?"

"Sure. He did the financial literacy classes, helped me set up my company."

"Wow, nice guy to give his time like that."

"I wouldn't call him nice. He always acted like there was someplace he'd rather be. But he knew his stuff. Uh, speaking of someplace I'd rather be, I've got a job I need to check on."

"Sure. Nice to see you again. Maybe I'll stop in at a Wednesday meeting one of these weeks." He smiled and slipped away.

Back in Old Yeller, I looked up New Life Ministries again and found an address on Railroad Street in the Old North Quarter, an area of industrial and warehouse buildings, about half of which were vacant at any given time. It was an unlikely place for a homeless shelter, as it wasn't on the bus line, and it was a good thirty-minute walk from downtown. Definitely worth a visit.

I figured I had some time before Janice Shelley got back there and pushed *8 on my cell phone to get Squire. Old Yeller was less of a Luddite than me. Even though my phone had a voice assistant and other high-tech conveniences, I still liked to use ancient-but-familiar tools like speed dial.

"Hey, it's Perdue checking in." I repeated the important parts of my conversation with David Levant. She wasn't pleased that the cut-off hands weren't much of a clue, but she was even more unhappy that I'd taken Levant on as a client.

"You can't work for us and a suspect – a potential suspect, I should say – at the same time."

"I'm only looking into the antiquities thing for him. He understands that any leads I get on Bell's murder go to you. I think he referred to it as a confluence of interest."

"I'm beginning to wonder if I shouldn't have just hired Claire, after all."

Claire Driscoll went to high school with Squire. After a couple stints as a meteorologist for a local TV station, she had found her true calling as an all-purpose healer of sorts. She offers traditional and new age therapies, communes with the departed, prescribes healing crystals, and realigns chakras – among many other things.

She offers a kind of psychic warranty and repair program called the Karmachanic Program. For $120 a month, you can choose up to 4 hours of services from her entire menu. Or, you can just follow her recommended maintenance schedule and wait for a text reminding you that your aura was due for its six-month burnishing, or whatever. She had her last name legally changed to "Voyant" a few years ago.

"Maybe I should ask Claire about New Life Ministries." With Squire, the best way to get information is to tell her you're going to ask someone else.

"Why would you do that?"

"Its name sounds right up her New Age alley. Any reason I shouldn't ask her?"

"No, but I'd be surprised if she knew anything. You'd be better off asking His Honor. It seems to be his pet project. It's in an office and industrial area, and the zoning doesn't allow for it to house people overnight. The mayor twisted the Planning Board's arms to get them a special permit, then he made the fire department okay their safety inspection even though the place is a fire trap.

"The gal running the place must have some kind of serious juice. The mayor never gave a crap about homeless folks before, but suddenly the city's supposed to fall all over itself to make this place feel welcome."

"Yeah, I just saw him give some kind of award to the lady who runs it."

"Janice Shelley. Goes by Pastor Jan. Nice looking, in a churchy way. Spooky eyes, though. Word is, she and the mayor may have something going." Suddenly, Squire realized she was answering questions instead of asking them. "Hey, why are you asking about that place, anyway?"

"Bell was a benefactor or volunteer of some kind. It also came up in a couple of recent cases." She was mad enough that I was working for Levant at the same time as her. I didn't think it prudent to remind her I had two additional cases going. "It's funny. I hadn't heard of the place before, and it's kind of on my beat."

"Maybe you need to go on a bender and get a refresher course in life on the street. They've been around almost a year but keep a low profile. They have a couple of outreach vans that pick folks up and take them to the Old North place. Supposedly they do detox there, provide medical and dental care, and have a job training program.

"They're picky, though. They don't take walk-ins or drop-offs. The only way to get services there is to be picked up by the van. We had some damn cold nights last winter, and all the other shelters set up cots in their lobbies for the overflow, but the folks at New Life wouldn't take anybody. 'Program rules,' they said."

"And Mayor Marks is a fan?"

"They have a ridiculously high success rate at getting people off the street. The last homeless census was down 20%, and His Honor thinks it's thanks to NLM."

I was surprised that Squire knew so much about New Life Ministries and that she was sharing information so readily. Perhaps she had her own suspicions about the place.

"Say, can you get me a list of Bell's clients?"

Squire agreed. I signed off and gave Julia a quick call. I got her working the computer in search of everything she could find on New Life Ministries.

I headed out to the Old North Quarter with only the most basic plan in mind. I would pose as a freelance writer doing a story on homelessness in Orman and see if I could get permission from Pastor Jan to talk to some of the clients and staff.

In my line of work, it doesn't always make sense to measure twice and cut once. Sometimes it works better to not measure at all and just keep cutting until you get the job done.

I arrived at New Life Ministries and parked across the street. The sign above the front entrance of the main building displayed the shelter's name and, below it, the quotation: "We shall not all sleep, but we shall all be changed." Okay.

The sprawling complex was made up of a two-story concrete block office structure with wings stretching off of it on three sides. Seen from the high ground where I parked, it looked a bit like a cross. The whole thing, including the curved metal roofing, was newly painted a hideous bright green. Not forest or Kelly green, or even neon, but something up at the "baby's first poop" end of the fecal tone scale. Presumably, it had been donated by the manufacturer. They sure weren't going to sell it to anyone.

The property covered a couple of acres and was surrounded by an eight-foot-high chain link fence with three strands of barbed wire on top. It showed signs of recent repair. The barbed wire was in a straight line, not bent inward or outward: equally effective for keeping people out or in. There was a single gate, one of those sliding ones controlled by a guard in a booth. It was the tightest security I had ever seen at a homeless shelter. I gave Julia a call to see what she'd pulled up on New Life Ministries.

Just because I don't like to plan doesn't mean I want to be completely unprepared. With good preparation, winging it works. Some of the time, anyway.

"Not a lot to tell. Incorporated with the state and applied for their tax-free status with the IRS a year ago. They list their charitable purpose as: 'To provide shelter, food, medical services and pastoral care to the homeless in order to provide a New Life to all who seek one.' The sole officer of the corporation is a Reverend Janice Shelley. That's probably an alias. I can't find any reference to her, except in relation to New Life Ministries.

"She's not ordained in any of the mainstream religions, as far as I can tell. There is a reference on the NLM website to the New Life Redemption and Salvation Church of Dothan, Alabama. I can't find anything by that exact name in Dothan, or anywhere in Alabama. There are about a hundred Janice Shelleys in the United States. She doesn't appear to be any of them. The social security number she gave in her IRS application is for someone named, and I'm not kidding, 'Purdy Outhouse' in Poughkeepsie, New York."

"Seriously, Purdy Outhouse?"

"Yep. He's 87 years old and in a nursing home. She just borrowed his social. As a non-profit, they won't be paying any taxes, and they'll be filing under the charity's tax ID number anyway. There's no reason anyone would check it. It's just a space you have to fill out on the form."

"What about their funding? I've been told that they don't get city money. Can you see where they get their cash from?"

"Nope. Not until they file their 990 with the IRS, and they don't have to do that until six months after their fiscal year ends. I didn't find any foundation that lists NLM as a grantee, or pictures in the paper with the Grand Poobah of the Loyal Order of Dancing Ferrets presenting a giant foam board check. Nothing. Just their own website and a few references in the newspaper.

"Look, they could be legit. A lot of charities start out as one-man bands with a few small donations from friends and the public – or one or two big ones from people who like to stay anonymous. Usually, though, the founder had some sort of life before the charity. This one doesn't smell right to me. You be careful in there."

"Will do." I hung up and walked toward the front gate.

A man came running around the side of the building, in bare feet, boxer shorts, and a tee shirt. His legs were churning and his arms were flailing – like a cartoon character running away from a bear. The bear turned out to be two men in security uniforms. We all reached the gate at the same time. Boxer shorts attempted to climb it, and the uniforms pulled him down. A man came out of the security box next to the gate, carrying a taser.

"Mister! They won't let me go! I want to go, and they won't let me go! You gotta help me!" The uniforms each had one of his arms, and they were holding him up so that he could just touch the ground on tiptoe. He flung his head from side to side, unable to move any other part of his body. He had a tattoo of a rat on his neck, which seemed to squirm and crawl with his movements.

The man from the box noticed me for the first time and looked momentarily confused. Then he put the taser back on his belt and jerked his head in the direction of the building. The uniforms started to hustle boxer shorts in that direction.

"You can't keep me prisoner! I want to go! I want to go! I want to go!" He looked at me, desperation in his eyes. His upper lip was quivering, making the long droopy mustache that topped it dance like a caterpillar on a hot frying pan.

"You need to let go of him," I said in my most authoritative voice. It was enough for the uniforms to pause and look at the gate man.

"This isn't any of your concern, sir. This man has some mental health challenges, as you can see. We can't let him just go running around in his underwear. Not in this neighborhood."

"I don't see why not. Anyone can see that he has nothing to steal."

"I just want to leave. Why can't I just leave?"

He was upset, but he didn't seem any more unstable than many folks on the street. The whole Stalag 13 look of the place bugged me. And the well-equipped security was very suspicious for any homeless shelter. I wasn't sure what I was going to accomplish on this trip, but I sure as hell was getting this guy out.

I pulled out my detective ID with the impressive gold badge insignia and flashed it at the gate guy. I saw him look fearful for a second, then it was clear that he recognized it as a private dick badge. "I'm going to need to talk to that man." I pulled out my phone.

They all ignored me and the gate guy told the other two: "Get him back to his room."

"What's your name?" I shouted at boxer shorts.

"Watkins. Sam Watkins. I want to leave! I should be able to leave!"

"Well, I think the police will agree with you." I raised the phone to my ear and caught the gate man's eye. "Your call, boss. Either you let Mr. Watkins go or explain to the police."

He sneered at me. "Go ahead and call the cops. I got my orders. No one leaves without paperwork. And unless he's hiding it somewhere I don't want to look, Watkins here doesn't have any paperwork."

"Okay, have it your way." I spoke into the phone. "Hi, this is Adam Perdue. I'm consulting on the Bell murder. Can you patch me through to Lieutenant Squire?" Whether it was mention of the Bell murder, which was all over the media, using Squire's name, or the realization that it hadn't just been an idle threat, something changed his attitude in a hurry.

"Now, no need to waste the police's time coming out here for nothing. I'm sure we can work something out. Let me make a call." He pulled out a radio and talked into it.

"Hi, Squire. It's Perdue again. I'm out at that New Life Ministries place. We may have a situation." I nodded at the phone. "Well, it may be a case of illegal confinement. Or it might just be a misunderstanding. I'll let you know in a minute."

"It's just a misunderstanding," the guard confirmed. He opened the gate. "Mr. Watkins' personal effects are being gathered right now and will be brought out to him. Pastor Jan will bring them herself. She asks that you wait for her here." He nodded at the uniforms, and they released Watkins. He immediately scurried over and put me between him and the guards.

"I don't need any more clothes. I just need to go."

"OK, Squire, I think we're getting squared away here. I'll call back in ten minutes and confirm. If I don't call, I'd appreciate if you sent someone by to check on the situation." After a short pause, I laughed loudly. "Will do. Talk to you later." I pushed the hang up button on the phone and ended the nonexistent call.

Ned let me into the compound, and we all stood around awkwardly for a few minutes until a woman approached, a cloth shopping bag in each hand.

"I have all your things here, Mr. Watkins. You should have come to me and explained that you wanted to leave. You're free to go at any time, of course, but you don't want to leave dressed like that, do you?"

In her presence, Watkins looked embarrassed for the first time by his lack of clothing. "Thank you, Pastor Jan," he mumbled as he took the bags.

"You can put on some more appropriate clothing in the booth there. You don't mind, do you Ned?" It was clear from the look on his face that Ned did indeed mind, but he forced a smile and shook his head.

"And what brings you out here, Mr. – ?"

"Perdue. Adam Perdue." I handed her a card while flashing my PI badge. "And you are Janice Shelley?"

"Yes, though most people just call me Pastor Jan. Pleased to meet you." She put her hand out and we shook. Her hand was small and soft, but her grip was tight. She held on for just a beat longer than necessary while she looked me up and down like a tailor evaluating a customer for a suit – except that she paid special attention to my face. There are two areas on men where tailors' eyes don't tend to dwell. The face is one of them.

"Likewise, Ms. Shelley. I saw you earlier today at City Hall." I gave her my best friendly-but-harmless smile while I tried to think up an answer to her question about why I was there. My plan to claim to be a reporter had been blown when I interceded on Watkins' behalf. It was time for the last resort: something approaching the truth.

"I am looking into the murder of Ellis Bell. I understand he was a patron of yours?"

She laughed. "I guess you could say that. We have a number of people who support our work in various ways. Ellis was one of them. I am guessing that the investigation is not going very well."

"Why do you say that?"

"Well, I don't imagine that the police hire private detectives unless they are pretty desperate. And I wouldn't think that a detective would spend much time on such a peripheral part of a victim's life unless he had few other places to look."

Watkins exited the booth, fully clothed and carrying his bags. "I want to leave," he said to none of us in particular. Pastor Jan nodded, and the guard opened the gate. Watkins walked out into the street without another word.

"I don't think that I can help you, Mr. Perdue, but if you do have more questions, my office would be a more appropriate place to ask them."

I wasn't sure, but it seemed that there might have been a hint of having something to say that she didn't want to spill in front of her security team. "Thank you. If you have a few minutes to spare, I would appreciate it."

Pastor Jan nodded, turned toward the building and walked toward the front door. I fell in beside her. She was of average height, slender, with dark blond hair and hazel eyes.

"Don't forget to call the police back and let them know everything is fine," the guard called out. There was just enough concern in his voice to make me wonder where Pastor Jan recruited her team.

I pulled out my phone. "I'll text them." Instead, I typed a quick text to Julia, asking if she had any additional information on NLM or Shelley. Hopefully she would text back. Receiving texts during an interview can be very handy. It gives a reason to pause, and I can often work them in somehow, either to pretend to receive important information, or as an excuse to leave.

"Please have a seat." Pastor Jan indicated the chairs in front of her scarred wooden desk. These were the Goldilocks of visitor chairs. If the ones in my office were too skeevy and the ones in Levant's too elegant, these were just right: worn but respectable cloth-cushioned wingback chairs. I settled into one, and she sat in the leather executive chair on the other side of the desk.

Even though she was at least six inches shorter than I am, she was looking down at me. She took a long look at my face again, turning her head at different angles, like she was getting ready to paint my portrait – or maybe wondering how my head would look mounted over a mantlepiece. She smiled, but only with her lips. Squire was right. Her eyes were spooky.

"You are correct, of course," I began. Potentially hostile conversations often go better when started with a concession. "There aren't a lot of leads in this case. That's why I'm just trying to get all the information I can about Mr. Bell."

"Well, I can't tell you much, I'm afraid. He was one of our more generous donors, giving both financially and with his time. He taught financial literacy courses to our guests. I've found that one of the few common denominators among the destitute is that they don't know how to budget their money. Even if you have very little and you're just going to drink it away, you might as well do it frugally.

"Ellis was quite happy to explain things in terms our guests could relate to. He would have some of them do a worksheet comparing the cost, quantity, and proof of cheap wines to find the best value. His suits cost more than many of the people here have ever seen in a month, but he connected to them in a way that I could not. He will be missed."

This was interesting. No one else had ever spoken highly of Bell, and she was the first person to express any regret at his death. She was a minister, of course, and he had been providing services to the homeless people in her flock.

"I don't want to speak ill of the dead, but Mr. Bell appears to have been universally loathed. You are the first person to say anything kind about him."

"Don't get me wrong. Ellis was a first-class conman, and I don't doubt that he stole those Arabs' money. But there was a bit of Robin Hood to him, too. I think he deeply regretted not having a band of merry men. That may have been why he enjoyed coming here."

My phone buzzed in my pocket. "Sorry, Ms. Shelley."
I took it out and looked at the message from Julia: *pastr jan shel not in any db until year ago*. I looked at the screen for an extra moment and decided it was time to change the subject.

"Do you have a client here named Sean Ryan?" I may have imagined it, but for just a fraction of a second, Pastor Jan seemed to lose her composure. But it was back so fast, I couldn't be sure.

"We refer to the people we're working with as 'guests.' We do not confirm or deny the presence of any individual, unless requested to do so by an officer of the court. I am happy to take your name and number and if we have a guest by that name, I will pass it along to them. It will be up to them whether or not to contact you."

Standard operating procedure. She did seem a little too relieved to have been able to launch into a rehearsed answer, though. I figured it was time to break out one of my few true talents. I'm a natural irritant, like sand.

My late wife Sarah used to call me Sandy when I got on her nerves. And she would have hated being referred to as my "late wife," as she was obsessively punctual. But I couldn't call her my "dead wife," even in my head.

When I would point out to her that sand in an oyster often produces a pearl, she would reply that sand in your shoe almost always gives you blisters. In my line of work, blisters can be as valuable as pearls. Whatever it takes to get someone to reveal something that they didn't intend to reveal.

"You mean, like it was up to Watkins whether he could leave or not? If I hadn't happened to show up, he would have been dragged back to wherever you had him by the cheap muscle you have guarding this place."

She definitely lost her composure. When I asked about Ryan, it had just fallen from her face for the briefest of moments and then been inhaled back in. Bringing up Watkins and her thugs caused it to fall to the floor and scurry away. Anger and frustration showed in her expression. With a visible effort, she made her face passive.

"I do not appreciate your attitude, Mr. Perdue."

"Yeah, very few people do."

I find that in verbal fights, just like physical ones, it makes sense to hit people hard when they're back on their heels. This is particularly true when one is over-matched, or when the other party can decide to just leave the ring. I didn't feel over-matched by Pastor Jan, but I knew that at any moment she could stop talking and the fight would be over. So, I threw everything I had at her.

"How did you feel about Trent Argent's attitude? When he came around asking about Ryan?"

She stood up. "You may leave now."

I nodded but remained seated. No "Who the hell is Trent Argent?" No confusion about having all these names thrown at her. Just cold determination not to answer. Might as well throw in the kitchen sink, too.

"Not until I speak with Michelle Rathborn. She's another one of your 'guests,' isn't she?"

"Get out! I have asked you to leave politely. If you do not do so immediately, I will call the police and have you removed."

This time it was more than annoyance. This time I saw fear in her eyes. And anger. What the hell was going on at this place? I had one corpse, three cases, four clients, and three missing people – and they all were somehow related to New Life Ministries.

I like to throw things against the wall and see what sticks. It helps me to weed out the stuff that doesn't matter and focus my investigation on the stuff that does. I had thrown everything I had against the wall that was Pastor Jan and New Life Ministries, and it had *all* stuck! I didn't know what to ask next, so I played for time.

"I got the very distinct impression from Ned that he would not welcome a visit from the police. I don't think you really want to call them."

She looked at me in silence. With her fingernail, she traced one of the long scratches in her desk. When she reached the end, she ran her finger backwards to where she had started. She repeated the motion several times, but her eyes never left my face.

"Mr. Perdue. Our interview is ended. You are not welcome here. I have asked you to leave. If you do not do so, I *will* call the police and have you removed. Ned, like many of those who live and work here, has a past. In his past, the police have not always been his friends.

"In the present, however, the chief of police, as well as the mayor, *are* my friends. This is a place for healing, and for – yes, *new life*. At the risk of sounding more New Age priestess than Protestant pastor, your bad energy is a threat to the fragile recoveries that are taking place here. If you are on this property in five minutes, you will be prosecuted for trespassing."

She swept out of the office, leaving the door open behind her. I was pretty sure she was bluffing about calling the police. But there was also not much point in sitting in her empty office. Still, I stayed for a full minute anyway. Just to make a point. When I left, there was a guard standing in front of every doorway except the ones that led me out. No one said anything to me. Ned opened the gate when I approached and closed it after me.

Once outside, I looked back at the place. New Life Ministries had certainly provided new life to my investigations.

I drove around the neighborhood, hoping to find Watkins. I figured he could use a ride, and I knew that I could use some information. As usual, my inner wiseass had made things more difficult for my outer PI. There had been more information to be gleaned from Pastor Jan, but I just hadn't been able to resist antagonizing her into silence. Of course, her reaction to my asking about Ryan and Rathborn was good information in itself.

I didn't find Watkins, so I drove back to my office asking myself the questions I wanted to ask him. How do folks get into the shelter? What services does it offer? Are people really kept there against their will? Were any or all of Rathborn, Argent, and Ryan inside? What really goes on at New Life Ministries?

Then I started asking myself the questions that Watkins wouldn't be able to answer. What is the connection between two missing homeless people, the night manager at the veterans' shelter, and a dead con man? Who was Pastor Jan before she became Janice Shelley?

Questions tend to lead to more questions, and answers lead to more answers. In every case, there is a turning point when I find myself running out of questions and piling up answers. I wasn't there yet. I needed to find Watkins, but I didn't know where to start looking. There were two large shelters in Orman besides NLM and the VAC, and a handful of smaller ones. I had no idea whether or not Watkins was a veteran, but I headed to the veterans' shelter first.

The never helpful Ms. Sanderson was on duty at the front desk. I stopped at the tape and waited for her to look up from her computer screen. She ignored me for one minute, then two. Finally, she looked up, feigning surprise.

"You're back, Mr. uh, Tyson, was it?"

"Perdue. Adam Perdue."

"Right. Of course. I use mnemonic devices to remember names. The association for you is frozen chicken parts. Just got the name of the wrong chicken king. I'll get it right the next time. What can I do for you today?"

"I'm trying to get a message to one of your guests, a Mr. Watkins. If I leave it with you, can you see that he gets it?" I held out one of my cards. On the back, I had written *Mr. Watkins, please call me ASAP*.

She took the card and threw it on her desk. "As you know, I can't confirm or deny the presence of any guest at the shelter. Does your Mr. Watkins have a first name?"

I searched my memory for a moment, and the image of Yosemite Sam from the Warner Brothers cartoons popped into my head. The droopy mustache.

"Sam. Sam Watkins." What do you know? Mnemonics work.

"Well, I will deliver it if I can."

"Thank you, Ms. Sanderson. That's all I can ask." I turned to leave.

"Mr. Perdue," she commanded in a low voice. Yep, definitely former MP. "Approach the desk." Her tone was that of a particularly pompous judge summoning counsel to the bench. "Trent was looking for someone when he disappeared."

"I know. Herb Ryan."

She lowered her voice to a whisper. "I shouldn't tell you this, but I think I know where he is. We got a request for his records from a social worker in Billings."

"Montana?"

"You know another Billings? Yes, Mr. Perdue, Montana."

"Do you have the social worker's name or where they worked?"

"At a civilian shelter. I don't remember the name. That's all I know about it, and like I said, I shouldn't even be telling you that." She straightened up and returned to command voice. "Have a blessed evening."

I left and started cruising the alleyways. Ms. Sanderson's change of heart bothered me. It was obvious that she had no interest in helping me the last time I was there. Now, she was giving me leads? There was no harm in following it up, though, so I popped in some ear buds and speed-dialed Julia.

"Hey, how's everything on the office front?"

"Boring. Except for Squire. She's been by twice to get updates. She dropped off a list of Bell's clients. Anything I can tell her the next time she comes by?"

"Yeah, tell her to stop romancing my assistant and call me on my cell phone if she wants to know how I'm spending COP's money."

"I suppose I could do that. She's kinda cute, though. In a smarty-cop kind of way."

"Too much information, Julia. Look, I need to check something out. One of the homeless folks I'm looking for has supposedly turned up in Billings, Montana."

"Homeless in Orman to 'Home on the Range.' Is that a step up or an out-of-the-frying-pan-and-into-the-fire sort of thing?"

Julia fancies herself a big city kind of girl. Orman may not be Manhattan, but it isn't Montana, either.

"That's what I want you to find out. His name's Sean Ryan, former Army. Supposedly he's staying at a shelter in Billings. The vets' shelter got a records request from a social worker there."

"OK, boss. Which of our four cases does this relate to?"

"Trent Argent."

"Oh." Her disappointment came through loud and clear in that single syllable. She was enjoying Squire's attention and would have preferred something that she could relay to her.

I don't feed pigeons. They're nothing more than rats with wings. They'd happily eat the old folks who throw them popcorn in the park, if they could. But Julia is nobody's pigeon. She is a sweet woman who has known more sourness than anyone should have to in one lifetime. I had a bag full of random morsels of information. There was no reason I couldn't toss her a couple.

"If you see Squire, let her know that I'm making some progress on the Bell case. It's tied up with New Life Ministries in some way. How smuggled antiquities, embezzlement, and murder relate to a homeless shelter, I don't know. But I'm tracking down a lead, a guy who's been staying there. It's not much for $200 a day, but it's what I've got. And if you get the time, do some basic research on that client list of Bell's."

"You got it. I'll get back to you ASAP on Ryan."

I put the ear buds back in my pocket. They were very handy when working undercover, especially when I'm posing as a street person. Any conversation I have can be put down to a crazy person talking to himself. Fortune makes some folks brokers and others bums. Bluetooth makes them all look equally demented as they walk down the street holding conversations with invisible people.

"Hey, PI man!" Captain Hook was sitting on a loading dock smoking a cigarette.

"Hey, yourself." I walked over. Just inside the warehouse, men sat on boxes eating and drinking.

"Got myself some honest work unloading trucks. Hey, don't look so surprised. Longshoremen use a hook, mine's just built in. How's the search for Herb going?"

"It's going. Your information was very helpful. Now I'm looking for someone else, a guy named Sam Watkins. Squirrely little guy. Last time I saw him, he was wearing a trench coat and carrying all his worldly possessions in a couple of bags."

"Dude, you've just described half the people on the street. Hell, that describes at least three people I've seen this morning."

"Any of them have a droopy mustache and a rat tattoo on the side of his neck?"

"There's a guy, I think he goes by Sam. He has rat tattoos on both sides of his neck, though."

"I only saw one, but there could have been two, I guess. He just left that new place in the Old North Quarter where you said Herb went."

"New Life Ministries? That'd be a first. People who go to the Emerald City don't end up back here in Munchkin Land. Word is, they fix everything that's wrong with a person and send 'em on their way as productive members of society. 'Clip, clip here, clip, clip there! We give the roughest claws that certain air of savoir faire, in the Merry Old Land of Oz!'" he sang.

"High success rate?"

"Either that or they're making 'em into meat pies! Either way, I haven't heard of anyone who's gone there ending up back on the street. Maybe you ought to be looking for this Watkins fellow up on High Street. Probably drives a beamer and has a job with one of the banks or insurance companies now. Wears a suit to work. Has a wife and 2.4 kids out in Highgate."

"They sound like miracle workers."

"Yeah, I suppose. But maybe folks don't need as much fixin' as some people think. Hey, what's Helen Keller's favorite color?"

"Corduroy."

"Ha! You knew that one." A loud beeping announced that a tractor trailer was backing down the alley to the loading dock. Hook hopped up and flicked his cigarette away.

"Gotta get back to work. I'll keep an eye out for Rat Neck. If I'm thinkin' of the right guy, he's a serious pot snob. Only smokes the best hydroponics. If he really did flunk out of New Life, I bet he's looking to score some smoke. Try poking around Brown Town, but he won't be buying any Mexican dirt weed – he'll be looking for some Señorita Sinsemilla."

Brown Town is two square miles of commercial and residential neighborhoods running along both sides of Brown Street. It's where most of Orman's Hispanics live. It's mainly Mexicans and Central Americans on the south side and Cubans, Puerto Ricans and assorted other Caribbean folks on the north. The nickname started out as a derogatory one, but the residents co-opted it and use it proudly.

When suburban day-trippers attend the annual Cinqo de Mayo Fiesta, they stick to Brown Street's restaurants, shops, and open-air markets. They don't venture off the main drag and into the neighborhoods where many of the people live, the ones who serve them in restaurants, cut their lawns, repair their gutters, clean their houses, and care for their children.

They don't need to. They've seen the real thing: vacationing in Cancun, building houses on mission trips to Haiti, and surfing in Costa Rica. The really adventurous ones have been to Cuba and smuggled back a box or two of cigars.

In Brown Town, you can get the same box for half the price of the government store in Havana, if you know where to look. And you can get a whole lot more, too. The police don't like to venture far off Brown Street, either.

Like any city, Orman has tiers of individuals and families who hold an outsized influence on local affairs. They own much of the land, run profitable businesses, serve in government, and chair the cultural, social, and economic committees that set the city's agenda.

Once in a while, one of them suffers financial ruin or becomes entangled in an especially lurid scandal that causes them to lose their place among the Brahmins. Even more rarely, a self-made outsider can crowbar themselves into the top tier through extraordinary personal success or popular acclaim.

People raised in Orman know who the important people are and sense changes in the hierarchy the way an experienced sailor knows whether the sea will be rough or calm. Newbies like me, though, have to try and pick up what's going on through observation, analysis, and eavesdropping. I've developed a pretty good handle on who's who in Orman, for an outsider. Like a video game, though, the only reward for mastery is ending up on a new level with new rules.

Brown Town has its own set of influencers. Jaime "Jimmy" Diaz is one of them. He's what some folks derisively call an "anchor baby." His Mom crossed the border while pregnant with Jimmy. Though she never lost her thick accent, she wouldn't let Jimmy speak any Spanish at home. He was the first non-white Homecoming King at Metro High. He's currently a member of city council. If I was a betting man, I'd give even odds that he'll get elected mayor in the next ten years.

Of course, I *am* a betting man, and I have a $100 bet on it with Squire. In a nice bit of wagering symmetry, I also have a bet in the same amount with Jimmy that

Squire will be Orman's first non-white, non-male chief of police.

Another *hombre de influencia* is Javier Herrero. He lived up to his last name, which means "warrior," fighting with Fidel and Che in the mountains for a few years. But he didn't like the direction the revolution went in and was given the choice of prison or exile. He chose exile and pulled some strings to get into the US.

Part of the deal was that he was to resettle in some out of the way place and keep a low profile. Orman qualified. He started a trucking and warehousing company that supplies all the restaurants, grocery stores, and mini-marts in Orman. He's in his late nineties, and I'm betting he makes it past one hundred.

I've got another c-note on that with Squire.

A third is Juan Cartel, no accent over the "e." His father ran a live theater in Bogota. As a teen, Juan would be dispatched by the actors to pick up their performance-enhancing drugs. He noticed that the actors rarely had any money, but the dealers were rolling in it.

He gave up his stage ambitions and made a career in smuggling drugs and people. He is rarely in Orman – some folks say he's never been here at all – but he rules Little Bogota's underworld via text message and a rotating cast of enthusiastically violent proxies.

The lone woman with a place in Brown Town's Star Chamber is Maria Santos. Her grandfather was a migrant worker who organized his fellows in the fields. Many of them went from being pickers to growers during the area's agricultural boom between the two world wars. Abuelo Santos was the most prosperous of them all.

When farming gave way to industry in the 1950s, he retired and his only child – Maria's father – used the family's modest fortune and considerable land holdings in the county to build factories and warehouses. His wife died giving birth to Maria.

As sole heir to the Santos empire, she attended the best private schools and eventually graduated with honors from Mount Holyoke College. Unfortunately, her father didn't live to see the first member of his family earn a college degree.

When Maria returned to Orman to take up the family business, she discovered that it was mostly gone. Her father had mortgaged everything to the hilt buying rental units during the housing boom. When it went bust, so did he. All that was left were a dozen mostly derelict industrial and commercial properties and the family foundation.

The properties had little value. The foundation's funds were restricted to providing college scholarships, so while they hadn't been leveraged and lost in any of her father's deals, they weren't a ready source of capital or income, either.

Evaluating applications and handing out checks is a part-time gig, at best. Maria gives considerably more time and attention to her other enterprise, growing and distributing most of the marijuana in Orman and the surrounding area. It turns out that those run-down industrial buildings were well suited for the discreet growing and processing of marijuana.

The police are willing to ignore the illegal nature of her business. It's only a matter of time before the state legalizes pot, as so many others have, and it isn't like she's selling fentanyl or meth. The fact that plenty of cops' kids receive scholarships through the Santos Foundation further contributes to their willingness to look the other way.

If Watkins was looking for quality grass, it was likely that he was going to get it from someone in Maria's organization. Since I was looking for Watkins, Maria was a good place to start. A couple of years ago, she had hired me to locate one of the Santos Scholarship kids who never made it to her first day at college.

Sandy McCoy was a standout student at Carver High who suffered from severe test anxiety. She was allowed to take all her exams in a room by herself. When it came time for the SATs, however, the College Board wasn't willing to provide her with a similar accommodation. A friend introduced her to Adderall, which allowed her to focus and relax at the same time. She aced the SATs and was accepted to Stanford.

The summer after high school graduation, she discovered that she liked being relaxed and focused pretty much all the time, and that speed balls – a combination of crystal meth and heroin – did the job way better than ADHD medicine. When her money ran out, she found that she liked relaxing more than being focused and took up heroin full-time. The men who paid to have sex with her didn't seem to mind the lack of focus.

I found her living in a shabby room above one of Alejandro Cartel's clubs. Tricks paid the barman for her services, and he kept her supplied with heroin and fast food. Maria bought Sandy's freedom from Cartel and put her scholarship money toward a stint at rehab instead of Stanford.

Walking down Maria's street, I drew a lot of attention from her neighbors. A white man venturing that deep into Brown Town naturally aroused a bit of curiosity. I was stopped at her gate by a man working in her garden. He reached into his pocket and pulled out a pistol, smiled and put it back. Then he reached into another and pulled out a cell phone. He hit a key and then pointed the screen at me. It was blank for a moment, and then I saw Maria.

"What can I do for you, Mr. Perdue?"

"A few minutes of your time?"

"Why not?" She raised her voice. "Jose, Mr. Perdue can come in." I handed the phone back to the gardener. He snapped it shut and waved me toward the house. One of the young boys who had been watching me ran up to Jose, took the phone from him, and popped the battery out. He pulled an identical phone from one pocket and a hand-held scanner of some kind from the other. He scanned a small barcode on the phone's case, handed it to Jose, then ran back to his post.

"To what do I owe the pleasure, Adam?"

"A case. Several cases, actually. I'm trying to track down a guy who may be able to help me with all of them. From what I hear, he has fondness for your product. I was wondering if you could put out an alert on him with your people."

"Hmmm. That's not good for business, you know. Our customers depend upon our discretion."

"All I'm asking is that you give me a heads-up if you spot him. Make the sale and send him on his way. Just give me a buzz. I'll run into him accidentally."

"I see. And exactly why would I do this?"

"As a favor to me. I would owe you one."

"One can never have too many favors, I suppose. For whom will my people be looking?"

"His name's Sam Watkins. He's white, fortyish, thin. Not altogether there. He has a rat tattoo on the side of his neck. Or maybe two. I only saw one, but someone else told me he had one on each side."

"This man has one – or possibly two – *rat* tattoos on his neck?"

"Hey, there's no accounting for taste."

"I suppose not." She opened a coffee table drawer. It was divided in half. One half had a dozen or more identical low-end cell phones. The other had one smart phone.

"Alex!" she shouted, and a teenager came running in from the kitchen. "This is Alejandro, who prefers 'Alex.' He is my tech wizard." The boy, who couldn't have been more than sixteen, blushed happily at the description.

She jerked a thumb toward the drawer. He nodded, gathered up the big pile of phones, and ran back out.

"Burner phones. I get them from Chicago. They've been purchased at retailers all over the country."

Alex returned with a large plastic bag full of phones, which he emptied into one side of the drawer. He used a scanner in the drawer on one of the phones and handed it to Maria.

"Excuse me a moment while I text my network to be on the lookout for your rat-necked friend." She tapped away at the screen for a minute. Then she threw the phone into the empty half of the drawer, scanned another and put it next to the smart phone.

"One phone, one call is my rule."

"What's the scanning all about? The boy outside did that, too, when he replaced your gardener's phone."

"My gardener? Oh, you mean José! Well, you got the first syllable right. He's my guard. But he bores easily, and I don't want a bored bodyguard. He likes to garden, so I let him garden. He has quite the green thumb."

"The scanner?"

"Oh, that. It's some incredibly complicated inventory system. It tracks which phone is with whom and then sets it up – and the whole network – accordingly. For instance, José is in my speed dial as #4. After he called me, he got a new phone and number, and I did also. But when I hit #4, my new phone will still know to ring José's new phone. But any call records will show two entirely new phones being used."

"I didn't know you were so tech-savvy."

"It's not really an interest of mine. It's a turnkey solution provided by the people in Chicago. It's seamless on our side, as long as we use the scanners. Very expensive. But peace of mind is one of those things that you will never have if you worry about the price. The local police don't have any problem with my business, but the feds still do. I like to imagine all the Campbells running around in circles trying to figure out what's going on."

"Who are the Campbells?" I imagined some Scottish gang – in my mind's eye, they looked like extras from the movie Braveheart – who were trying to move in on Maria's turf.

"You know, like Cambell's alphabet soup. FBI, DEA, ATF, et al. The Feds."

"You have a strange sense of humor, Maria."

"Which you will indulge, as I am doing you a favor – and an expensive one at that. Everyone I texted has to switch phones now. One complete turnover of phones runs about $500."

"You have a lot of security for a business that is almost legal."

"Yes. That 'almost' creates substantial risk. Because the Feds do not approve of our product, we can't accept credit cards for purchases, and banks can't accept our deposits. We have a lot of cash in a lot of places."

"I can appreciate —" I was interrupted when her cell phone buzzed. She looked at the screen and laughed.

"I am told that El Rata Flaca —the skinny rat – made a purchase about half an hour ago at 7th and Marseille. But not from us, and not our product. He bought a bag of heroin from one of Juan's boys. Apparently, his tastes have evolved."

"Thank you, Maria. I owe you one."

She smiled. "And I think I know how I will collect on it. For now, though, go trap your rat."

I found Watkins in an abandoned triple decker that had become a shooting gallery. Thankfully, he was on the ground floor. The stairs to the upper floors did not inspire confidence, having more spaces in them than the grins at the old folks' home on denture-cleaning day. I had come equipped with a giant-sized coffee and a box of donuts from the Quickie Buy. I was okay with interviewing Watkins while he was high – in fact, it was probably preferable – but I needed him semi-coherent, at least.

He was lying on the remains of a couch that no self-respecting bed bug would be caught dead infesting. He wasn't asleep, but he wasn't really awake, either. His eyelids were below half-mast, and a stream of drool was escaping from the side of his mouth. He looked very content.

"Hey, Sammy! What's shakin'?" I sat gingerly on the bare wood of the couch's one remaining arm, down by Watkin's feet. He had on sneakers held together by duct tape. The corners of the room were piled with fast food wrappers and feces. Luckily for me, a trip through my car's windshield had destroyed my sense of smell.

It also had done a Humpty-Dumpty on my face. All the best surgeons and all of their thread couldn't put Adam together again. Little did I know that losing my sense of smell and what I had been told were my good looks would turn out to be such benefits in my second life as a PI.

It's not that I'm "children screaming in terror" ugly now. It's just that they put me back together again the way you might reassemble a broken pitcher, with more attention to its ability to hold water – or, in my case, what passes for brains – than for restoring its original look. There weren't any visible scars, but the bones in my face didn't quite line up anymore, and the symmetry was off. Somehow, the whole effect was to make me very forgettable – a great asset in my chosen profession.

Watkins' eyelids twitched then went still again, succumbing to the languor of the drug riding the vein train nonstop to what was left of his brain.

"Mmph!" he uttered cheerfully.

I took the lid off the coffee and poured a little on the floor so it wouldn't spill too easily. I held the coffee under his nose. He smiled but didn't move. I got a donut out of the box and held it to his lips, leaving a white smear of powdered sugar behind. His tongue flopped out and retracted. He smiled some more. It was no use. He was in a better place at the moment than coffee and donuts could tempt him to leave.

I located his stash in one of the trench coat pockets. Three paper bindles of heroin and a newish looking syringe. A butane lighter, charred spoon and two empty packets lay on the floor beside the couch. I hid his stash under the couch, handling it gingerly. The syringe was capped, but still.

"Why'd you have to go from weed to heroin, man?"

"Once you try smack, you never go back!" Watkins mumbled in a sing-song. It sounded like an answer to my question, but it may have been an unconnected utterance – like someone talking in their sleep.

There was nothing for it but to wait.

Patience is not only a virtue but a necessity for stakeouts. That's why detectives are often described as hard-boiled. A good dick has to be able to watch the pot for as long as it takes, even if it never boils. Of course, eggs don't have the luxury of catching up on their email or texts while bobbing in the roiling water.

I moved into an alcove where I could keep an eye on Watkins and called Julia.

"What do you want first, Saving Private Ryan or Shelley's Frankenstein?" She was pleased with herself.

"Ryan."

"Sean, aka Herb, Ryan is residing in the Gospel Rescue Mission in Billings, Montana. He has a regular gig out of Work Now Day Labor and never misses a counseling session. He is the very model of a modern major janissary."

"Janissary. Nice word."

"I read books."

"And Shelley?"

"Now, that's a horse of a different color. A friend checked her out in the motor vehicle database. They're a little fussier than the folks who register non-profits. You remember Purdy Outhouse, right?"

"Who could forget Purdy Outhouse? The legitimate owner of the social security number on Pastor Jan's IRS exemption application."

"Correct. But the social in the DMV records actually belongs to someone named Janice Shelley. Or, I should say *belonged* to."

"The way you say that makes me think it's not our Pastor Jan."

"Not unless she's been re-animated, Eeyore."

"That's Eyeore. But thanks for noticing me."

Julia and I share a fondness for Mel Brooks movies in general and Young Frankenstein particularly. And who doesn't love Winnie the Pooh's sardonic donkey friend?

"The DMV's Janice Shelley disappeared two years ago. Just last week, a body was found in an Omaha park. It was in pretty bad shape, but the cops there have a kickass missing persons' desk. Their SOP is to require DNA samples from relatives at the time they file the report. The victim in the park was a sibling match to the sister who reported her missing."

"So, our Pastor Jan is using someone else's identity. Someone who turns out to be dead."

"Yeah. Creepy enough, right?"

I loathe dramatic pauses, but Julia is a big fan.

"Wrong," she continued, just before the point when she knew I'd get annoyed if she didn't. "It gets creepier. When the original Janice Shelley went missing, she was homeless. Her last known address was a shelter called the Small Mercies Refuge. Small Mercies closed its doors a month before New Life Ministries opened up here in Orman."

"You think maybe Pastor Jan was a resident at the shelter and stole Janice Shelley's identity?"

"That would fit. But not as well as this: Reverend Ann Ickes, who ran Small Mercies, dropped off the map along with her shelter."

It took a moment to sink in.

"What are we dealing with here, Julia? Some kind of sociopath with a homeless shelter fetish?"

"Hey, I just find the pieces, boss. It's your job to put them together. But I don't think they're going to make a very pretty picture."

"Look, I'm running down a lead now – a guy who's been staying at New Life. After I talk to him, I'll come back to the office and we'll try and make sense of this."

"You want me to call Squire? Or the cops in Omaha? They might want to know that their vic has a doppelganger on the loose."

"Not yet. We don't really have anything but a possible identity theft charge to lay on Pastor Jan. And that's not enough leverage to get anything important out of her. Hold off until I get back."

"OK, boss. Watch your back."

"Always."

I had been so engrossed in my conversation with Julia that I hadn't even been watching my front. As I hung up and headed back to Watkins, I heard footsteps from the entranceway. I glided back into the shadows of the alcove as two men came into the room. One went over and looked at Watkins.

"Yeah, that's the little shit. Knew we'd find him in one of these dives. Give me a hand, and we'll carry him out to the van."

His voice was familiar. In the dim light, I couldn't really make out either of their faces, but I was pretty sure that they were New Life security goons. I patted the pocket that would have held my gun if I had brought it in with me like a sensible person.

I was going to have to bluff my way through. But there was no reason not to have some insurance. I hit *8 on my phone – the shortcut for Squire – and laid it on the floor.

"Hey, boys! Mighty far from home, aren't you?"

They dropped Watkins, and he landed half-off the couch.

"What the fuck?" They turned toward me, drawing the guns that they hadn't been stupid enough to leave behind.

"Oh, threatening me with guns, are you?" I was almost shouting, so Squire would understand my predicament.

I could faintly hear a voice coming from my phone. The only word I caught was "address." Yeah, that would be a good idea.

"Seventh and Marseille," I said loudly. "Is a long way from New Life Ministries."

"It's a long way from anywhere, asshole!" The two men headed toward me.

Watkins was stirring, but clearly still out of it. It probably didn't help that his heroin-soaked blood was running to his head. I raised my hands. At least I'd gotten my current location, and a possible future one, to Squire.

One of the men kept his gun trained on me. The other one walked up and pistol-whipped me. As I fell to the floor, the last thing I remembered for a while was hearing the voice on my phone, "We no deliver that place!" and a click. I had hit *9 by mistake. Lee Fong's Szechuan.

I woke up, sort of. At least I reached some level of consciousness that made me aware that I was lying on my back. I willed my eyes open. One of them obeyed. The other seemed stuck. Wherever I was, it was filled with a pale blue light. It featured a ceiling with a web of cracks and a large water stain that glowed purple. Probably not heaven, then. Rooms in heaven ought to have perfect plaster as pearly white as the fabled gates.

My head hurt, bad. I tried to recall why and remembered getting pistol-whipped in the shooting gallery. With a twinge of embarrassment, I also remembered dialing my favorite takeout joint instead of Squire. I raised my head a little and then dropped it back when the dull throb changed to stabbing pains behind my closed eye. Definitely not heaven. I wondered briefly about Lucifer's position on ugly ceilings.

Using my hands, I explored what I could without further movement of my aching head. I was lying on a firm couch or futon with cloth upholstery. It had a soft, high nap. It was relatively new, or at least unworn. Although depth perception with only one eye is tricky, the stained plaster ceiling seemed pretty high. That made me think it was probably an old house.

If I moved my head slowly enough, I could turn it without bringing on the ice pick orchestra. That allowed me to see some more of the room. The windows were tall and covered in thick drapes. The floor was dark oak, worn but still beautiful. At the very edge of my field of vision, there was a desk with a computer monitor. That was the source of the blue light. There was something familiar about the room, but I couldn't quite place it.

Having reached the limits of sight and touch, I focused on hearing. If there was anything happening in the bass spectrum, I couldn't detect it over the dull thudding of my own pulse. Any highs were getting drowned out by the ringing in my ears. I tried to find something in the mid-range, and finally picked out a rhythmic clacking sound that seemed to be growing louder. Footsteps.

I closed my eye and made my breathing slow and steady. A door opened. The clacking grew even louder, and then stopped. Silence. I was overwhelmed by the smell of honeysuckle. It transported me for a moment to my childhood and the backyard of the house in Maryland where I grew up.

The fence had been covered in the fragrant vines. We used to pinch off the base of the flower and pull the long thread through the center of the blossom to steal the single drop of sweet nectar that lured the parched tongues of children and honey bees on hot summer days.

It was more than just honeysuckle, though. There were other floral accents. Two things hit me at the same instant: I was smelling my late wife's favorite perfume, *Le Chevrefeuille*, and I was *smelling*. The memory of her and the realization that I had regained my lost sense of smell shocked me out of my feigned sleep. I opened my eye, half hoping and half dreading that Sarah would be there.

Maybe I really *was* dead and it was time for my long overdue reckoning.

I wasn't dead, and Sarah wasn't standing there. Maria Santos was. She was holding a tray. That's why the room looked familiar. I had been there earlier today, or maybe yesterday?

"You're awake. That's good."

When I said nothing, she knelt and placed the tray on the floor. It had two bowls and two towels. One bowl was steaming, and the other was filled with ice. The towels were the little fancy kind that you find in guest bathrooms – if you spend time with the sort of people who have guest bathrooms.

Maria dipped a towel into the steaming bowl, wrung it out, and gently wiped my forehead. It hurt like crazy, but it also felt good. I closed my eye and breathed in the perfume, letting the memories of long-ago lazy summers and the scent of Sarah act as a kind of anesthetic.

"Quite a deep gash, but I don't see anything life-threatening." She wiped around my eye and I felt the lid come loose.

I opened both eyes and found myself staring at Maria's cleavage. She was wearing a silk bathrobe, and her efforts had worked it loose to the point that the long "V" of flesh it exposed went almost to her waist. Her breasts were still mostly covered, but the indentation of her nipples could be seen moving beneath the thin material. I caught my breath audibly.

"Sorry." She wiped my face even more gently before putting away the cloth.

"That's got you pretty well cleaned up. Hold this on your head while I get some bandages."

I put my hand on the makeshift ice pack, brushing hers in the process of the transfer. I closed my eyes and tried not to think of her hips moving beneath the robe as she walked away with the same clack-clack with which she had arrived. Who would have thought that Maria Santos was a high heels and silk robe kind of woman? I certainly hadn't, but just as certainly always would from then on.

Holding the ice pack gently against my head with one hand, I pushed myself into a sitting position with the other. My head swum for a moment when I swung my legs onto the floor, but it passed.

The throbbing began to diminish as the ice and my more upright position moved more blood to the rest of my body. I did a quick inventory, moving all my fingers and toes, flexing my knees and elbows. I seemed to be in good shape other than the head.

Nice of Pastor Jan's goons not to kick the shit out of me while I was down. I'd remind myself to feel bad for not returning the favor if the opportunity presented itself.

Maria returned to the room, carrying a phone in one hand and my jacket in the other.

"We got your jacket into the wash quickly enough to get the blood out. Your shirt is probably ruined, though." I looked down at my chest. My shirt was covered with blood. She placed the phone on the coffee table and the jacket on the arm of the sofa. It was warm and smelled like fabric softener.

"Not to be too cliché, but how did I get here?"

"My people brought you, after the men in the van left with the Rat. I couldn't leave you lying there in a crack house."

"I appreciate that."

"You would have been stripped faster than a broken-down car on the interstate in Wildewood. Eventually, someone would have called the police, and that would have been awkward. Frankly, my men on the scene were hoping that you would be taken along with El Rata. It would have been a more elegant resolution."

"I almost wish they *had* taken me. I never got to talk to Watkins, and if I want to find some answers, I'm going to have to get inside New Life Ministries eventually."

"Perhaps it is better not to enter your enemy's den unconscious and alone?"

"I said *almost*. I am definitely grateful for the rescue."

"So that is two favors you owe me, Adam. One for the Rat's location and another for rescuing you. May I ask why you are so interested in this homeless shelter?"

"It just keeps coming up in several cases I'm working on. And something's not quite right with it – or with the Pastor lady who's in charge."

"People speak quite highly of both the shelter and its director. How is it involved with the Bell murder?"

"He volun – why do you ask? Why do you think it has anything to do with Bell?"

"You have been contracted by the police to assist with the Bell murder, so it only makes sense. It was a tough call between you and Claire Voyant, I understand."

"Yeah, you can imagine my pride at being chosen. Why are you interested in Bell's murder, anyway?"

"I'm not, particularly. I like to stay informed, and one of my friends in the department passed along that information."

"You have police informants?"

"I wouldn't put it quite in those terms. I have friends among the police, and friends have conversations. Friends also watch out for each other. Like I did for you tonight. Success is all about building and maintaining relationships, no matter the particulars of one's business."

"I wouldn't know. Success is not an outcome with which I have a lot of familiarity."

"Then you probably suck at relationships."

"I probably do. But I'm glad you're good at them. Otherwise, I might have woken up in that crack house, naked and afraid."

"I wouldn't want to see you afraid." The implication by omission was both arousing and somewhat disconcerting. I wouldn't have minded seeing her naked, either. But I was well aware of the stories that her lovers had a habit of disappearing. Her nickname in Brown Town was "La Viuda Negra," or "The Black Widow."

I have a normal male libido, by which I mean I imagine having sex with virtually every non-related, age-appropriate woman the first time I see her. All it takes is a momentary glance, and my imagination takes off. It doesn't matter what she looks like, what she's wearing, whether she is with someone else or alone. It is a basic instinct reaction. I don't act on it in any way. I don't even really watch the mental peep show, but I can't stop it from grabbing my consciousness for an instant.

It usually only happens once, which makes it much easier to deal with co-workers, other people's spouses, and nuns, to name just a few of the potentially awkward targets for recurring lustful fantasies. With Maria, however, it is pretty much an every-time thing.

As I adjusted my position on the couch, I felt – or, at least, imagined that I felt – a little relief from the pounding in my head as the blood rushed from there in answer to the call from another part of my body. Then I remembered the whole *Viuda Negra* thing, and the flow reversed directions.

Sex and death. Yin and Yang. Balance.

The awkward moment was rescued by young Alex, who appeared in the room carrying two large bags. He put them on the coffee table and disappeared. Maria opened them, and the smell of Chinese food filled the room.

"I hope you don't mind. Curiosity got the better of me and I re-dialed the last call on your phone." She took the phone out of her pocket and placed it on the table beside the food.

"Very brave of you to call for take-out when faced by armed thugs." Her face was expressionless, and I wanted to think that she wasn't secretly laughing at me. I sure would have been if I was in her position.

What the hell, I can handle a little ridicule – as long as it comes with Lee Fong's spicy noodles.

I left Maria's light-headed and heavy-bellied. My legs were overmatched in trying to keep my body upright and perpendicular to the ground, but muscle memory from my years as a drunk kept me moving in a generally forward direction until I reached Old Yeller, which Maria's people had parked just down the block.

I didn't seem to draw the same amount of attention from the neighborhood as I had on my way in the day before. Maybe people were getting used to me. Or maybe folks thought it better to not stare at the crazy gringo with a bandaged head and a blood-stained shirt.

On my way to the office, I tried to make sense of what had happened. Four different clients were paying me, and I was definitely feeling like a fraud for taking their money.

As I drove by Claire Voyant's shop on Burnham Street, I found myself thinking that they *all* should have just hired her instead. I'm sure her famous "fortunaura" readings were more intelligible than the collection of coincidences and speculation that I had accumulated in two days.

I swerved to the curb and pulled into an open parking space. If all I had was suspicions and intuition wrapped in disassociated facts, I might as well go to someone fluent in mumbo-jumbo.

Claire's place was in a former barber shop. The mechanical barber pole still worked, but the red and white striped insert had been painted over with stars, yin/yang symbols, rainbows, peace signs, glowing crystals, reverse swastikas, and – strangely – the black and yellow propellor-like symbol for radiation.

I'd have to ask Claire about that sometime. Some other time. The symbols climbed up the pole and disappeared, only to start again from the bottom. In my state at that moment, it was mesmerizing, and I stood there for a minute just following the movement of the pole.

"I had a feeling you were coming." Claire stood in her doorway smiling at me.

"I bet you say that to everyone."

She laughed. "Of course, I do. You're late, though. I got the feeling hours ago, and my prescience is usually more punctual."

"You may want to check your tuner, then. I stopped just now on a whim, when I saw your sign."

My head still hurt, but I couldn't help noticing – not for the first time – how pretty Claire is. She wasn't wearing any visible makeup, and her short, blonde hair was a bit askew. Her sweat shirt and yoga pants hung straight off her frame, showing no curves. When she laughed, lines appeared in her forehead and around the corners of her mouth, and they didn't go away completely when her face relaxed. She smelled more of laundry products than fancy perfume.

Maybe her lack of effort to make herself attractive was what made her attractive to me? Or maybe that pistol-whipping hadn't only restored my sense of smell but also supercharged my libido? I shook my head to clear it and was rewarded with a stabbing pain.

Claire withdrew into her studio, and I followed her, zipping up my jacket to cover as much of my bloody shirt as possible. She led me through a small waiting area with a simple metal desk and three padded folding chairs. There was a vanity wall, covered with diplomas and photos of Claire with local celebrities.

In the main room, the front window was curtained, and the walls were covered in shelving. They held books, bric-a-brac, small pictures and sculptures, cloth dolls, crystals, piles of fabric, and who knows what else. In the middle of the room, there was a circle of five barber chairs surrounding a bar table.

"Have a seat."

"Which one?"

"It doesn't matter. Which one calls to you?"

I climbed into one of the chairs. It was very comfortable, and it smelled like Old Spice aftershave.

Claire worked the controls on the chair to raise it slightly and tilt it backward until I was almost horizontal.

"Are you comfortable?"

"Yes, actually." I felt like I was floating.

"What can I do for you, Adam?"

"Just a trim. Leave it a little longer in front. Shorter on the sides and back."

"Ha, ha. Never heard that one before. Look, it doesn't take psychic powers to know that you think I'm a charlatan, or crazy, or a little of both. But I didn't reach out to you. You came to me."

I wanted to sit upright and look at her, but it felt too good where I was.

"Like I said, it just occurred to me. I'm working on a case, several actually, and nothing about them makes sense, so I thought...."

"... That since I don't 'make sense' from your perspective, I might be able to help?"

"Well, yeah. I mean it sounds kind of silly, but —"

"No, I get it. If you had a note written in Chinese, you'd go to Lee Fong's and ask someone to translate it. You see me as fluent in nonsense, so you come to me."

"Nonsense is a little harsh. I consider you fluent in the mysterious and incomprehensible." I was struck that she had used Lee Fong as an example. There were more than a dozen Chinese restaurants in town, and I had no idea how she knew which one I preferred.

"Okay. Well, you know it doesn't just all 'make sense' to me, either. That's what the rituals and tools are about. I use cards, or your aura, or the lines in your palm, or whatever to help me identify and articulate the messages in the energies surrounding and emanating from you.

"Energy straddles the physical and the extra-physical planes. It is here and now, and never and always – all at the same time. When the receiver – that's me – is tuned right, the past, the future, and the present can all come into focus."

"That almost makes sense."

"For you. For someone else it makes sense that…" She adopted a movie-style Romany accent. "*Zee future ees written in the lines of your palm!*" She shrugged. "Everybody is different."

"What do we do now? Which ritual will work with me?"

She laughed. "We're already doing it."

I opened my eyes and looked over at her. She was perched on the edge of another barber chair with a notebook and a pen in her hand. On the bar table was a digital voice recorder.

"Psychology is mysticism for the doggedly rational. You talk. I listen. Maybe I ask a leading question now and again. In the end, you'll think you figured it all out on your own – which is the only way you'll accept it."

"I feel like Toto just pulled back the curtain and exposed the Wizard of Oz."

"Everyone in that story got just what they wanted from the Wizard in the end, didn't they? Even though he was a fraud. What is it that you really want, Adam?"

I sighed and decided to just roll with it. I usually worked by talking things out with Julia or Squire. Why not try it with Claire?

"I can't believe I'm asking this, but is there such a thing as medium/client privilege? This needs to be confidential."

"I am a licensed therapist, Adam. As long as you don't pose an imminent threat to your own life or that of others, our conversation is privileged. I'm also certified in Tarot, Reiki, hypnotism, homeopathy, and half a dozen other things that you don't believe in. These are powerful tools, and I'm not so irresponsible as to use them without training."

Cracks of respect were starting to appear in the previously smooth wall of disdain that I kept between myself and Claire. What the hell. I edged a toe into one of the crevasses.

"Okay. A con man has been murdered, possibly due to stealing folks' money, but also possibly because of some ancient antiquities. Homeless people keep disappearing, and someone who works at the veterans' shelter has also vanished. No one really cares about the homeless people, except for Trent Argent – the guy at the VAC who's disappeared."

"And you."

"What?"

"And you. You care about the homeless people, don't you?"

"Well, yeah. But I don't really count. I'm being paid to find them."

"Aren't the police and city staff paid, too? Shouldn't they be concerned about citizens disappearing?"

"Yeah, right. Look some of my best friends are cops – okay, really just one – but disappearing homeless people are like dead drug dealers: professional curiosity requires looking into it, but there's little motivation to work the case very hard. As for City Hall, fewer homeless people isn't a problem, it's a campaign platform."

"Tell me more about the con man. Is he the financial advisor that's been in the news?"

"Yeah, Ellis Bell. The one who had his hands cut off. I'd like to see you read his palm!"

"If you find me one, I'll give it a try. Tell me the names of those who are missing. Names can be important."

"Well, there's Bell, Trent Argent, Michelle Rathborn, Sean Ryan, and – as of today – Sam Watkins. Ryan may not be missing, though, after all. He may be in Montana. Same difference."

"Interesting that you listed Bell among the missing, rather than the dead."

"Well, his *hands* are missing."

"And you believe that all these things are related in some way?"

"I don't know. Maybe I'm the only thing they have in common, that someone hired me to look for them, or in Bell's case, his murderer. But one thing does keep coming up in all the cases: New Life Ministries."

"What is New Life Ministries?"

"It's a homeless shelter over in the Old North Quarter. Strange place. The woman who runs it seems to be very well-connected. Ellis Bell was a patron. The chief of police and the mayor seem to love her, too. Supposedly has an extraordinary success rate. Sean Ryan has been transformed from an Orman derelict into one of Billings' solid citizens in a matter of weeks."

"And what's the name of the woman who runs New Life?"

"Jan Shelley."

"No, her real name?"

"How do you know it isn't?" It was one thing to accept that Claire wasn't completely crazy, but quite another to start believing that she really was clairvoyant.

"You dare question the mighty Oz?" she roared with a laugh. "Relax, nothing mystical going on. When you said her name, I could hear the finger quotes in your voice."

"We don't know her real name. We just know that the real Jan Shelley is dead."

127

"We?"

"Julia, my assistant, and I."

"Full name, please. Always give me full names, okay?"

"Julia Waters."

"Okay, so who is paying you to look for whom?"

"Well, the Rathborn heirs retained me to find Michelle, who they're hoping I won't find."

"Whom."

"What?"

"*Whom* they're hoping you won't find. Not *who*. Go on."

Aura-cleaning and auto-correct. Truly, Claire is a woman of many talents.

"Lieutenant Squire with the police is paying me to look for Bell's murderer. Gayle Forris, Trent Argent's partner, hired me to look for him. He disappeared while looking for Sean Ryan, who apparently has resurfaced in Montana. David Levant wants me to find the antiquities that he thinks Bell was trying to fence before getting murdered. And I'm looking for Sam Watkins on my own, because he can tell me about New Life Ministries."

"And all these cases are related?"

"Yes. I don't know. Maybe. That's what I want you to tell me. They're all connected to New Life Ministries in some way. I just keep coming back to that."

"I see."

"What do you see? A tall, dark, handsome stranger?"

"Hmm. Possibly. Give me your hand. Don't worry. I'm not going to read your palm. I just want a physical connection with you."

I reached out and she took my hand in both of hers.

"You know more than you think you do. We all do. All the time. The conscious mind is only capable of taking in a limited amount of information at a time. And, unlike our subconscious, it insists on order. If something doesn't fit, it will make it fit or pretend it isn't there. Something doesn't fit in what you've told me. When we find it, you'll have a way forward." She massaged the back of my hand.

"Two things strike me. You listed both Bell and Ryan among the missing. In Bell's case, you're quite certain that he's dead. But in Ryan's case, you used words like 'apparently' to describe his reappearance in Montana."

"Well, all Julia and I have are second-hand reports that Ryan is in Billings. I saw Bell murdered with my own eyes."

"You think it's possible that someone in Montana is pretending to be Sean Ryan?"

"Why not? Someone in Orman is pretending to be Jan Shelley."

"Yet you're certain you saw Bell murdered with your own eyes?"

"Well, I saw *someone* murdered. I'm sure of that."

"Ms. Shelley is not Ms. Shelley. Mr. Ryan may not be Mr. Ryan. Is it possible that Mr. Bell was not Mr. Bell? If you are looking for his murderer, then you may be looking for someone who doesn't exist. That would explain things not quite fitting into place."

"The police got a positive ID from his wife, and he had Bell's wallet and driver's license on him. "

"How did his wife identify him? Wasn't he also shot in the face?"

"Yeah. I don't know. I think there was a tattoo or a birthmark, or something."

Claire let go of my hand, and we sat in silence for a minute.

"There is one other thing. Before Bell was killed, I got a good look at him, and he seemed familiar to me. And I think he recognized me. But I've never met Bell."

"Hmm. Tell me more names. Tell me the name of everyone you have seen or spoken to in the last 24 hours."

"Well, some of the ones I mentioned already. There's also a Ms. Sanderson – no first name known – who mans the front desk at the vets' shelter. Maria Santos –"

"Tell me about Ms. Santos. No, never mind. Strong energy there. You'll want to watch your step with her, Adam."

"You've heard of the *Viuda Negra*, the Black Widow? She's not as dangerous as her reputation."

"It's not about that. She and you are, or will be, entangled in some way. Her energy clings to you like the perfume of a woman you've just spent the night with."

To which I cleverly responded, "Uh...."

"Anyone else?"

"There's another homeless vet, goes by the street name 'Captain Hook.' He's been helping me out."

"Okay, I have to ponder all this for a few minutes. Go out to the waiting room. There's a bottle of tequila in the bottom drawer of the desk. Help yourself, if you've a mind to." She worked the lever on my chair and nearly flipped me out it.

I walked to the waiting room easily, feeling more stable and clear-headed than I had all day. That felt wrong, somehow, so I took Claire up on her offer. Don Julio Silver. Two shot glasses. I filled them both, downed one and re-filled it. I placed the two shots on the desk and waited for Claire, savoring the burn of the tequila.

Claire sat on the edge of the desk and drained one of the glasses.

"Okay. Here's what I've got." She drained the other glass and raised her eyebrows. I re-filled. "Bell's not the one you watched die. All your cases *are* connected, and New Life Ministry is at the center of all this. Janice

Shelley is dangerous. Maria Santos is dangerous in an entirely different way. Bell is the key."

"What makes you so sure that Bell is alive?"

"I didn't say he's alive, just that he wasn't the man you saw murdered. And I'm not sure of anything. You are. You just can't get out of your own way for long enough to see it."

"So, what else do I know?"

"That's all you've got. Run with it."

We finished off the Don Julio.

"So, what do I owe you for, uh, your services?"

"The mumbo-jumbo is on the house. The tequila shots are $50 a piece, though. So that's $250. A gal's got to live."

Tuck's smelled of grease, sugar, and coffee. Being able to smell again was still a novelty, and it was a little disconcerting to have this extra element added to familiar places. It made Tuck's seem like someplace I'd never been before.

The waitress delivered my usual, a cheddar cheese omelet with Texas Pete hot sauce, as I waited for Squire. I wasn't sure what I was going to tell her, but I knew that she wasn't going to be happy. Anything short of the name and present location of Bell's murderer wasn't going to cut it. That's why I had already ordered pie.

Pie hath charms that soothe Squire's savage breast.

"Look, Mommy, it's Santa!" The cry came from a young boy in the booth behind mine, the same boy who had been kicking the back of my seat for the last five minutes. A man who did look a lot like Santa had entered the diner and stood at the register.

"Shh, honey! And don't point. It's not polite."

"But it's Santa!"

The man picked up a to-go order and paid, while the boy continued to fuss. Before he left, the man turned to the child and said, "Now, you be a good boy and stay off my naughty list. Ho, ho, ho!" He laid a finger beside his nose and winked before turning toward the exit. When he pulled open the door, the bell mounted on it rang.

"Mommy, it *is* Santa!" The boy was thrilled.

I was stunned. I knew where I had seen the murdered man before. He was a Salvation Army bell ringer. He had worked the exit of Fallow's grocery store for the month before Christmas. I usually put whatever change I had in my pocket in the kettle, but on Christmas Eve I had dropped in a five-dollar bill and been rewarded with a wink.

Squire dropped into the seat across from me, and immediately tucked into the pie. No comment about the bandage on my head or the bruising on my face, just straight to the pie. Claire, too, had said nothing. I couldn't help wondering if it wasn't a bad sign when people stop being surprised to see you looking like death warmed over.

"What have you got? All the City's seen for its money so far are some angry calls to the mayor's and the chief's offices. Not that I don't find that worthwhile, but the auditors would probably disagree."

"Bell isn't dead. Or at least, it wasn't Bell who I saw killed. It was a Salvation Army Santa. His name's Larry, I think."

Squire took another bite of pie and nodded, like this was just the news she was expecting. I felt a moment of concern that I could say something that off-the-wall to her and have it taken in stride so easily. Then I realized that it was just the awesome mellowing power of pie.

Once she had chewed and swallowed, she looked at me the way a lepidopterist looks at a butterfly that she has taken great care in pinning, only to conclude that it is an inferior specimen.

"Seriously? That's what you're going with, Adam?"

I pushed the food on my plate around. The eggs were too spicy and the potatoes were too salty. I guess I had gotten in the habit of over-spicing my food to compensate for the dulling of taste that had accompanied the loss of smell.

"It came together for me just before you got here. There was a guy picking up takeout who looked like Santa, and the bell on the back of the door went off, just as he winked at that kid behind me, and I suddenly remembered why Bell, or whoever, looked so familiar to me that night. I saw the guy every day for a month when he was stationed outside Fallow's Grocery. And that's the guy I saw get run over, shot in the face, and mutilated."

I might have been talking a little too loud.

"Mommy, what does 'mute a plated' mean?"

"Don't eavesdrop, son. You don't want to end up on Santa's naughty list, do you?" She gave me a glare as she marched him out of the diner.

"I don't know when I've heard so much talk about Santa in April. You do know how ridiculous this sounds, right?" Squire was still in her pie-eating happy place, so I was getting amusement instead of rage.

I'm going to have start carrying pie around with me.

"Of course, I do. But I told you and Woody that night. I knew I recognized the guy, and I have never met Bell. Think about it. Bell had embezzled millions, and he was involved in some black-market antiquities stuff. It's pretty convenient for him to die right then."

"The widow's identification? Bell's wallet?"

"Disfiguring his face? Taking his hands? If Bell wanted people to think he was dead, he could plant the wallet. And if the police tell a distraught widow that her husband is dead and then show her a messed-up body the right general size and weight, it's pretty easy to make a mistake."

"Do you think we're the Keystone Cops, Adam? Bell's wife identified him by two tattoos, one of which was in a place even the coroner hadn't looked."

"Tattoos can be faked. And this explains why they took the hands. Even with the wallet and the wife's ID, you would have taken fingerprints, and I'm betting that a financial advisor has to cough up his prints at some point, even if he's not in your system."

"Brokers' fingerprints are on file with the Department of Financial Services. I've got Bell's."

"But nothing to compare them to. Pretty convenient, huh?"

"I thought so, too. That's why we did a dental records check. The vic's mouth was pretty messed up from the shot to the face, but we got a solid match from his dental records."

"What about DNA?"

"This isn't a TV show, Adam. My DNA request got turned down flat. No money in the budget. Not when we've got a dental match, ID found on the victim, and a positive identification from next of kin. Just not going to happen."

"You asked for DNA testing?" Squire nodded. "*You've* got doubts that the vic is Bell!"

"I just like things all nice and tidy. Can't have too much evidence."

"Bullshit. You *do* have doubts. What doesn't fit, besides my eyewitness identification, of course?"

"Your identification of a Santa named Larry?"

"Don't dodge."

"Okay, you *can* have too much evidence. Here we have evidence of efforts to obscure the victim's identity: taking the hands and blowing the guy's face off. At the same time, we have lots of evidence that the identification was solid: the wallet, tattoos and the dental records."

"C'mon. Spill. What's the problem?"

"The dental records. Usually, we just get a pile of X-rays from the vic's dentist and have a guy at the state do the analysis. But after he sent over the records, Bell's dentist gave me a call. He wanted me to know that Bell had a lot of work done sometime in the last six months at another dentist's. He saw him for his regular cleaning and annual X-rays a couple of weeks ago and noticed the work. He said the work wasn't up to his quality, and he didn't want anyone looking at the X-rays to think he did shoddy work. Struck me as strange."

"So, can you get DNA testing now that your only eyewitness is certain it wasn't Bell?"

"Is he certain?"

"Pretty certain."

"Pretty certain that it was a Salvation Army Santa who might be named Larry is not going to cut it. Get me a full name and confirm your guy's dropped off the map. Talk to the dentist. Then submit an affidavit. *Maybe* I can get DNA then."

I wanted to pursue it further, but saw that she was done with her pie. Time to change directions.

"Whether the vic is Bell or Larry or someone else, I know one thing for sure: there's something funny going on at New Life Ministries." I filled her in on the events of the last day and Julia's research. I may have conveniently forgotten to mention my visit to Claire.

"You know that both the mayor and the chief are big fans of Pastor Jan, right? They'll go ape shit if I pick her up. And what you've got isn't enough for a warrant, even from Judge Easy."

Judge Thomas Easley is a DA's best friend. He is the go-to guy for warrants when evidence is slim. Thus, the nickname.

"Yeah, I know. Besides, I don't think we should show our hand just yet. She doesn't know that I know she's a fraud. I'd rather keep it that way for now. I'm just letting you know. If I disappear like everybody else involved with New Life, I want you to know where to look."

"Hey, if you disappear, the first place I'll look is passed out at a bar – or maybe Lee Fong's in an MSG coma. But after that, I'll check out New Life Ministries."

"What about Montana? Can you make some calls and try and find out if their Sean Ryan is our Sean Ryan?"

"I could. But what's the point? Even if it isn't, what does it prove?"

"I don't know. But no one is who they seem to be. Hey, make a call, okay?"

She said nothing.

"Then check in with Julia. She's been poking around about Montana Sean, too." That did the trick.

"If I find some time. Now, get the hell back to work. The city and, as I understand it, another half dozen people, aren't paying you to sit in Tuck's. You pick up the pie." She stalked out of the diner.

Apparently, pie is the crack cocaine of comfort food. Huge rush right out of the box, then a big crash.

The waiting room at Dudak Dentistry was clean and bright. The receptionist behind the glass frowned when told that I didn't have an appointment, and her frown deepened when I handed her my card. Dr. Denny Dudak, DDS would see me *if* he had a few moments between appointments.

I caught up on celebrity gossip while I waited. According to one of the magazines, a boy band singer I'd never heard of was heartbroken over the end of his relationship with a young woman whose claim to fame rested on being the half-sister of a starlet I also hadn't heard of. They were both very cute, and I was grateful for the caption that identified which was which.

"Mr. Perdue?" Dr. Dudak stuck his head into the waiting room. "I have five minutes, now."

I followed him to an examination room.

Dr. Dudak leaned against a counter. "Sit, if you want." The only place to sit was the dental chair. What the hell. I'd sat in a barber's chair and been psychic-analyzed, so why not sit in the dentist's chair?

"I understand you had some concerns about Ellis Bell's dental records, doctor."

"Not about the records. We keep meticulous records here. I only thought it worth mentioning that Mr. Bell had a lot of work done very recently, and that there was no indication of any need for it six months ago."

"What do you mean by indication of need?"

"There were two very deep fillings in molars that had not shown any sign of decay on his bite wings six months ago. It is unlikely that they would have deteriorated so quickly."

"Bite wings?"

"Radiographs. X-rays."

"Was anything else odd?"

"The fillings themselves were amalgam, which is not unusual for molars. But Mr. Bell always insisted on resin composite, even in the back of his mouth."

"What's the difference?"

"Amalgam are what you probably think of as 'silver.' They are very obvious. Resin composite looks just like regular tooth enamel. Mr. Bell was quite vain."

"Anything else?"

"He also had an incisor pulled where – again – there had been no indication of decay previously. Of course, he could have damaged or lost the tooth in an accident. But I would have expected him to get an implant rather than a bridge. That is what *I* would have recommended. More expensive, of course, but an altogether better solution from both a practical and an aesthetic viewpoint."

"Is the resin stuff more expensive than silver, too?"

"Yes. I suppose that may have been why he went to someone else for the work. He was quite sensitive when I asked about it. Of course, I understand from the papers that he embezzled quite a bit of money, so I wouldn't have thought cost to be a problem."

"Anything else you can think of?"

"No. Now, if you'll excuse me...."

"Just a couple more questions, Dr. Dudak. Do resin and amalgam look different on X-rays?"

"Of course. Amalgam appears much brighter."

"You wouldn't mistake one for the other on an X-ray."

"*I* certainly wouldn't."

"And could you also tell the difference between an old silver filling and a new one?"

"On a radiograph?"

"Yes."

"No. They would look the same."

I thanked him for his time and left, receiving a final disapproving glance from the receptionist.

My next stop was the Salvation Army. It was time to see if I could uncover the identity of "Larry the Santa."

"What brings you here today, Mr. Perdue? I haven't seen you in a long time." There were twice weekly AA meetings at the Salvation Army, and Major Tom Danker was nearly always there. I hadn't been in over a year. "Staying sober, I hope?"

"As a judge, Major Tom."

"Most of the judges in Orman are drunks."

"Afraid that's true."

Major Tom looked disappointed but not surprised. "I take it this is a business call?"

"It is. I am trying to find one of the bell ringers from last Christmas. I think his name was 'Larry.' He worked outside of Fallow's Grocery for most of the season."

"We had a ringer there, but I don't think his name was 'Larry.' Let me see what I can find." He typed away at his keyboard and split his glances between me and the screen. "Ah, here's what I'm looking for. Yes, his name was not Larry. And he was a resident of the shelter at the time, which makes the matter of releasing his name to you a bit more delicate. May I ask why you are seeking him out?"

"Well, I believe that something bad may have happened to him."

"Something bad has happened to most everyone who stays with us."

"It's a case I'm working on for the police. I can't give you any details, but I can assure you that the bell ringer I formerly thought was named Larry is not in any trouble with the law. All I want to do is make sure he is alive. If he is, then a very wild theory goes out the window, and I can get back to following slightly less crazy leads. Is he still staying at the shelter?"

"You know I can't tell you that." As he spoke, though, he held my gaze and shook his head. "If you are working for the police, could you have them issue a formal request for information?"

"I told you, it's a wild theory, Tom. I'm the only one who has any faith in it. And maybe Squire. Squire is at least willing to consider it. But I've got to be honest with you, I couldn't get the drunkest judge in the county to issue a warrant, or subpoena, or whatever it would take to cover you."

"I'm not worried about being covered, and I answer to just one judge."

He stared at the screen for another moment, then at me for slightly longer.

"His name is Gary Carson. He was a top ten ringer for us this past Christmas. He left the shelter a month ago. There is a notation that his employer called twice looking for him. He still has a credit in his room account, which means his departure was not arranged in advance."

"His employer?"

Major Tom smiled and pressed a button on his phone. "Miranda?"

"Yes, Major?"

"I'm sending Adam Perdue down to you. He is looking for one of our past guests. Please assist him in any way you can."

"Sure."

"Do you know Miranda?" I nodded. "She is a wonderful person, with a wonderful heart. Do you agree?" I nodded again.

Miranda is one of the case managers at the Army. She combines genuine compassion for everyone she meets with an unerring sense for bullshit. She knows everything that goes on in the shelter and most of what happens out on the street. Sending me to Miranda with his request for her cooperation provided me with access to more information than giving me the administrative password to the shelter's computer system.

"Hey, Randi! How've you been?"

"If you want my help, you ought to know better than to call me 'Randi.' Only my mother gets to call me that. You can call me Ms. Cooper or just plain Miranda."

"Just Plain Miranda is a mouthful, but I like it better than Ms. Cooper."

"Whose life are you looking to ruin today with an insurance settlement, a family reunion, or maybe divorce papers?"

"It's a little different kind of case this time, Miranda. His name is Gary Carson. He was a bell ringer and was staying here until fairly recently. All I'm looking for is proof of life. I don't even need to talk to him."

"I remember Gary. Good guy. He lost more battles than he won with his demons, but he kept on trying. Did a great job with the bell and kettle, as I recall."

"Major Tom says he was top ten."

"I don't doubt it. Abe Green, the manager down at Fallow's, liked him enough to hire him on to manage the loading dock. He worked there for a couple of months, everything was going smoothly, then he dropped off the face of the earth. Didn't come back to the shelter and never showed up for work again."

"Major Tom said he had money in his room account. What about his locker? Did he come back for his things?"

"Nope. He's past thirty days, and his stuff's due to get boxed up and moved to the warehouse."

"I don't suppose..."

Miranda slid a clipboard across her desk. "Sign in. We get volunteers to help with this job a lot. There are ten other lockers on the list, though. You've got to do them all."

"Fair enough."

Miranda produced a volunteer badge, which I pinned to my jacket. Five minutes later, I was in the locker room with a list of names and numbers and a pair of bolt cutters. I spent the next forty-five minutes packing up the left behind belongings of left behind people. I kept Gary's locker for last, so I wouldn't be tempted to run off chasing after a lead without fulfilling my end of the bargain.

Based on the first ten lockers, the only lead I'd have is to the county dump. I found myself regretting the return of my sense of smell, courtesy of Pastor Jan's thugs. It wasn't that the contents of the lockers reeked. It was more subtle than that. It was a mix of sweat, mold, and cheap synthetic clothing left for too long in the dryer. It's a familiar odor to anyone who has ever spent time in a homeless shelter.

Most of what was in the lockers could easily be classified as trash: ancient magazines and paperback books with loose pages, rummage store clothes, toys from fast food kid's meals, plastic plates and cutlery, used plastic bags. But there were also artifacts of better times: family photos, watches, packets of letters, and jewelry. I packed everything up into boxes and marked the boxes with names, dates, and an ID number.

Gary's locker wasn't very different from the others. There was a pair of old tennis shoes, a few sweaters, reading material. In the bottom there was a shoe box. Inside was a passport. I opened it to the picture page. There was Gary, wearing the smile of a man about to embark on an adventure. It had expired five years ago. I flipped through the pages and saw colorful visa stamps, for Thailand, Indonesia, Malaysia, and several I couldn't make out.

His social security card was there, on top of a Cross pen box. Inside the box, I found a needle, spoon, cotton balls, and a lighter. Gary may have been fighting his demons, but they were still winning some rounds. There was a box of condoms with an expiration date that was still in the future, and a receipt from St. Martin's Medical Clinic, dated February 23rd, a week before he'd disappeared. It was clipped to a piece of newsprint with an advertisement for women's shoes. I turned it over. It was an article about New Life Ministries.

A paragraph about their free medical and dental services was circled in red. There was also a picture of Pastor Jan and the Mayor cutting a ribbon. I laid the appointment slip and the clipping on the counter and photographed them with my phone. I rummaged through the rest of his stuff, but found nothing else of interest. Before I sealed the box shut, I put in a twenty-dollar bill and one of my cards, with "Call me" written on the back. Cast your bread upon the waters....

Julia wasn't picking up on the office line, so I called her personal cell.

"Listen, Julia. I need you to try and find Squire. She's not answering her phone and I just keep getting her voicemail at the station. I've got to go to St. Martin's Free Clinic, but then I need to see her. Tell her that the Salvation Army bell ringer I was talking about disappeared a month ago, and that I found a connection to New Life Ministries. That place is the Grand Central station of missing persons. Oh, and the Santa's name is Gary, not Larry. Gary Carson."

"OK."

In the silence that followed, I realized that I hadn't had a chance to update Julia on my revelation about Bell and the Santa. She should have been mystified by my message and asking lots of questions. As the silence grew longer, I remembered that I had suggested that Squire touch base with Julia a few hours before. And that neither of them had been answering their work phones.

"Put her on the phone, Julia."

"What? Who?"

"Squire. Just put her on."

Squire came on the line. "So, what have you got, Adam?"

"Besides bad timing?"

"Yeah, besides that."

"I've got the name of the bell ringer."

"The one who's a ringer for Bell?"

"Yeah. A dead ringer. His name's Gary Carson, and he disappeared from the Salvation Army shelter and his grocery store job about a month ago. Left money in his room account and all his belongings in his locker. I think he went to New Life Ministries."

"Why?"

"It's a little thin just yet, but that's where it's leading. He had an article about the place in his locker, and he had an appointment at St. Martin's Clinic just before he vanished. I think they referred him to New Life. Let me talk to the folks at St. Mart's and see if I can firm it up. Can I meet you somewhere in an hour?"

We made arrangements to meet at the station, and I took off for St. Martin's. I was conflicted about Julia and Squire. They both deserved any happiness they could find, but they were also the closest things to friends that I had in the world. Plus, Julia worked for me, and right then I was working for Squire. There was the potential for things to get very messy.

Time enough to worry about that after I reduced my client caseload a bit.

My confidence that I might finally start getting some answers grew when I saw that Linda was manning the front desk at St. Mart's. She was one of those special people who made it a point to know the rules backwards and forwards – and then broke them without hesitation when she thought it was the right thing to do.

"How's the L-lovely Linda today?"

"I'd be better if I had some L-lovely flowers for my hair."

I flung my arms out with my hands wide open, like a magician about to make a bouquet suddenly appear in one of them. Nothing, not even a bent playing card.

The only magic trick I know is how to make myself disappear. I've only pulled it off once, but it lasted for years.

"I'm wondering if you can help me, Linda."

She gave me an eye roll that said, "Nobody can help *you.*"

"I'm trying to find Gary Carson. He had an appointment here about a month ago, and I wanted to see if he ever came back for follow-up, got a referral to someplace else – or anything you might be able to tell me. He hasn't been seen since."

"You know that patient information is confidential." She looked around the waiting room, where the only other people were two elderly men who appeared to be sleeping. She started tapping away at her keyboard.

"I'm not looking for anything personal. I don't care what he was treated for or anything like that. I just need to find him. Shortly after his appointment here, he disappeared off the face of the earth – left a good job at Fallow's and money in his account at the Salvation Army. Is there *anything* you can tell me?"

"He had an appointment on February 23rd. There wasn't any follow-up appointment made. That's all I can tell you. Sorry."

"OK. I appreciate your help, Linda." I turned to go.

"We don't make follow-up appointments if someone needs a service that we don't provide." I turned back. "I'm not referring to Mr. Carson," she explained, "just saying that's how it is in general."

"What sort of services?"

"Oh, dental work, for example. We have a donated dental X-ray machine, and we'll use it to help diagnose issues. But we don't have a licensed dentist to do any treatment."

"If someone had dental X-rays done, you'd still have them, right?"

"Sure. If someone had them done, we would have their X-rays on file."

"Even if you referred that someone for further treatment?"

"If they have Medicaid, yes. Then the dentist they went to would want to do the X-rays themselves. If they don't have Medicaid, we'd try and get them in at the Free Dental Clinic. In that case, we'd send the X-rays over with the patient. But appointments there run about two months out. If you've got a toothache, that's a long time to wait."

"What else would somebody do? How could they get treatment earlier?" It was killing me not to ask her about New Life directly, but I wanted it to come from her.

"Beg, borrow, or steal fifty bucks and go see a street dentist. There are a couple of people in town who trained in other countries and aren't licensed here – but they more or less know what they're doing and keep their instruments relatively clean. Sometimes folks come in here with bleeding problems after a street pull. We pack their gums, give 'em some antibiotics and send 'em on their way. We're not licensed for extractions, but we are licensed to provide first aid for botched ones. It's an imperfect system."

"You think?"

She shrugged. "The only other option would be New Life Ministries. Word is they have a dentist on staff. But as far as I can tell, that place is by invitation only. Which is pretty strange for a homeless shelter."

"How would Gary Car – uh, how would *someone* with a dental issue know about New Life?"

"Word gets around. And there have been articles about them in the paper. I remember posting one on our board a while back. I think it specifically mentioned the dental services. Check out the board. It's probably still there. I don't remember the last time we cleared it out. A future archeologist's Dead Sea Scrolls, that board. Layers and layers."

"Like an onion."

"Or parfait. Parfait's got layers, too."

I looked at the items tacked to the board. The oldest thing I found was a five-year-old poster announcing a Veterans Stand Down event. No articles on New Life Ministry.

"I know I posted it. Sometimes people take stuff, though."

I took out my phone and showed her the photo of the article from Carson's locker.

"February 15th. Yep. That's the story. Hell, that could be the one I posted. See how the one section is circled in red?" She opened the drawer of her desk and pulled out a red wax pencil, the old-fashioned kind that you peel. "I like these better than Sharpies."

"So, you think Carson could have taken this from the bulletin board?"

"That would be my guess. I can't swear to it, of course. I must not be the only person in the world who uses a wax pencil, since they still make 'em. But Carson was in here a week after I posted it, and you found it in his locker. Hey, you're the detective. You can put two and two together, right?"

"Sure. I just wish they added up to four more often. But this is good, Linda. This helps a lot. I definitely owe you some lovely flowers for your hair."

"Promises, promises."

"Primroses, primroses. Next time, for sure."

A scruffy young man burst in the door, blood flowing from a head wound above one eye. I got out of the way and let Linda do her thing.

At the station, Squire was not quite as impressed as I was.

"Look, Adam, it's worth following up on. For you. But you've got nothing here that would justify me opening up the identification issue."

"So, don't open it up publicly. Just quietly request the DNA testing from the State Bureau of Investigation. You've got to know someone there who would get it done for you on the down low."

"I told you, it's not like a TV show. I can't just make a call and get a DNA test. I've got to file requisitions up the wazoo – and every one of them has to be signed by the Chief. And that is not going to happen with what we have."

"OK. What about the dental records? Can you request Carson's dental records from St. Mart's and ask the folks at SBI to look at them?"

"What for?"

"To see if they're also consistent with the body."

"Is that even possible, for two people to have the same teeth?"

"I don't think so. That vic's mouth was shot up pretty good, though. I'm betting that they used the records of the dental work, more than the teeth themselves, to make the ID. And two people *can* have the same dental work done."

"Not by chance."

"Right. Not by chance."

"Shit. What am I supposed to tell SBI? 'I know you already made an ID for us here, but how about looking at this other guy, too?' That's going to go over like a stale doughnut."

"Just ask them whether it's possible that the vic could have been either Bell or Carson, based on their dental X-rays. Tell them you're writing an article or something. Everyone knows you're an egghead. They'll indulge you."

"If the Chief gets wind of this, I'm toast. You better be onto something here, Adam."

"Trust me, I am."

With great self-restraint, I resisted saying anything about Julia, and Squire followed my lead. I felt bad asking her to go out on a limb, but not too bad.

Squire's not one to cling in fear to the tree trunk. She lives her life out on the thin branches. Besides, I had a plan for helping her out. If all went as planned, the Chief would be grateful that Squire was out in front on the ID issue.

It had only been a few days, but it seemed like I hadn't seen Gayle Forris for weeks. Julia had been making the daily reassurance phone calls, which hadn't been very reassuring as there was almost nothing to report. Gayle buzzed me into her building immediately, without using the intercom. I made a mental note to tell her to be more cautious about letting people in without checking them out. I started up the stairs to her apartment only to meet her on her way down – in quite a hurry. She went right past me without a glance. The downside to having a forgettable face, I guess.

"Ms. Forris?" She turned her head and stopped mid-step.

Recognition dawned. "Mr. Perdue. Was that you who rang the buzzer? I was expecting someone else. Do you have an update on Trent's disappearance?"

I could tell from her tone that she was disappointed not to have heard from me sooner. I can't blame her. I should have been the one giving her daily briefings. That's what I do when I have one client. With four, it's not as easy. I realized that I really hadn't updated anyone except Squire and resolved to contact Al Rathborn and David Levant as soon as possible.

"Yes. I believe that his disappearance is linked to another case I'm working."

"A photographer is picking me up downstairs for a story. I thought it was he who rang the bell. You can fill me in before he gets here."

She continued down the stairs, and I followed a step or two behind her, trying to maintain a safe and respectful distance while bending over awkwardly so I could speak quietly in her ear: Quasimodo faithfully falling in behind Esmeralda as she descended the cathedral stairway.

"You're aware of the Bell murder?"

"I am a reporter, Mr. Perdue."

"Right, of course. Well, there may be some doubt as to the identification of the body."

She paused, and I stopped a little too late to avoid sticking my nose in her ear.

"What sort of doubt? I thought the police had positively identified Bell."

"They're becoming a lot less positive," I lied. "Another man with a strong resemblance to Bell is also missing. Remember there were no fingerprints to check."

"What about DNA?"

"The results aren't back yet. I don't think they're in a hurry to make themselves look bad."

"Interesting story, but what does it have to do with Trent?"

159

"It's all connected. Bell, Trent, the man Trent was looking for, and the missing guy who I think has been misidentified as Bell – all of them are connected in one way or another to New Life Ministries. The last anyone saw of Trent, he was on his way there."

"Then what are you doing talking to me? You should be at that New Life place, looking for Trent."

"I have been there, and I'll be going back. But the woman running the place is very secretive, and she has friends in high places."

"Secrets are your business, are they not, Mr. Perdue?"

We had reached the sidewalk. A town car was pulling up.

"That's my ride. I have to go. Keep me informed by telephone." She opened the passenger side door.

"Wait. The stuff about New Life Ministries was way off the record. But the possible misidentification of Bell is not. It might benefit the Bell investigation and Trent if that story got some attention."

"Gayle, we have to go *now*," came a frantic voice from inside the car.

"Big story?"

Gayle shrugged as she lowered herself into the leather seat. "A strangled corpse washed up down by the docks. I'll try to get something out about the Bell ID, but I don't think any story but this one is going to get much attention for a while. The cops are already referring to the victim as the Wharf Rat, because of the tattoo on his neck."

When I got back to the office, the local news sites were already rolling out stories about the Wharf Rat, complete with pictures. OrmanOnline had a particularly gruesome photo of the victim. Yep, it was Watkins. The coroner estimated that he'd only been in the water for half a day and set a preliminary time of death half a day previous to that – right around the time the goons from New Life grabbed him from the shooting gallery. When I was re-discovering my sense of smell, poor Watkins was losing his sense of everything.

Gayle had also managed to get in a blog post about the Bell investigation, which she must have written and posted while in the car. News does travel fast in the internet age. Her post said that the identity of the body in the Bell case was no longer rock solid, citing a confidential source "connected to the police department." According to that source, anomalies in the victim's dental records were causing some involved in the investigation to question the certainty of the identification.

It was vague as hell, and the idea that I was "connected" to the COP made me a bit queasy, but it would justify Squire reaching out on the dental records. It also might get her in trouble with the chief, who'd figure her for the leak, but the chief's doghouse was a second home for Squire.

Why strangle Watkins? What did he know that was so damning? It's not like anyone other than me was likely to

162

listen to anything he had to say, even if he did know something. Gayle Forris was right: I needed to be at New Life Ministries unraveling some of these mysteries.

I left a note for Julia on the back of the note I'd found when I got there. Hers said: "Call David Levant." Mine said: "Gone to NLM."

I called David on my way.

"Mr. Levant, I'm sorry for not keeping you updated. Things are moving fast, and they're all centered around that homeless shelter where Bell was volunteering. I have reason to believe that Bell is not dead – or, at least, the body identified as Bell's isn't his. I can't prove it yet, but I'm close. I don't really have anything on the antiquities, but I'm sure that they're somehow linked to New Life, too." I finally took a breath.

"Adam, Lieutenant Squire was just here."

"She can't still be looking at you as a suspect."

"No, actually she was asking about you. About our arrangement."

"She knows about it. I told her right up front, like I said I would have to."

"Yes, but that was before she pulled a body out of the river."

"What does that have to do with anything?"

Levant paused, long enough that I glanced at the phone to see that we were still connected, then he finally

163

continued. "Apparently, you were looking for this man with the rat tattoo before he ended up in the river. According to witnesses, you found him somewhere in Brown Town. Then he turns up in the river, strangled. There have been two murders in Orman this week. Both involved a strangled rat… and you. I guess the authorities –"

"Are you fucking kidding me? Squire thinks I had something to do with Watkins' murder?"

"No, I don't think she does. But she may be the only member of the police force who doesn't."

"She could have called me directly and asked about it, or asked me to come in." I immediately realized that she probably was trying hard NOT to find me, to give me a chance to keep working before getting wrapped up in red tape.

"Thanks for the heads-up, David. I'm on my way to New Life now. Watkins claimed that he was being held prisoner there, two other people I'm looking for were last seen there, and Bell – a very unphilanthropic man – was volunteering there. That's where the answers are." My phone buzzed. Then it buzzed again. "I've got to go now. I hope I'll have some answers for you soon."

I had two new texts. The first one was an automatic message thanking me for signing up for breaking news text alerts from the Orman Times Gazette. The second was a breaking news text alert: "Warrant issued for arrest of private detective in connection with the Wharf Rat Strangling." I clicked on the link. During his examination of the victim's body, the coroner had found a private detective's business card clutched in Watkins' hand. Mine.

The card I had given to Sanderson at the vets' shelter had found its way to Watkins. He must have been at the shelter when I gave it to her. If she had just let me talk to him....

According to the article, my buddy Woody Wales had declared me "armed and dangerous." The public was advised not to confront me but to call 911 if I was spotted. Great. I held the button down on my phone until it turned completely off.

I pulled a U-turn and drove in the opposite direction from New Life Ministries for as far as my nerves would let me. I pulled into a parking space at Walmart and then backed into the opposite space, much to the annoyance of the driver behind me.

Backing in provided cover for me as I swapped out the license plate. The new plate was registered to Walter Pritchard for a vehicle with a VIN that was one digit off from the actual one. I renewed it every year faithfully with the registry, and no questions had ever been raised.

I tossed my original plate, wallet, and phone into the glove compartment and reached under the seat. After a little groping around, I found what I was looking for: my gun, another wallet and phone bound together with a thick rubber band, and a pocket-sized bolt cutter that looked like industrial-strength toenail clippers.

I left the key in the ignition and the door unlocked. If someone stole my car now, they'd be doing me a favor. I opened the other wallet to find a picture of myself staring back from a driver's license in the name of Walter Pritchard. It was a fake, but a good one, complete with hologram. Walter also had a couple of pre-paid debit cards. The cards and burner phone had been purchased at Target months ago, along with the backup battery charger that I plugged into the phone.

There was a car service app on the burner phone. I had never used it before, but had signed up as Walter in case I ever needed to travel incognito. I had passed over the national companies in favor of a local one called "Riders on the Storm."

Hey, I'm a Doors fan, and it wasn't like I had expected to use it a lot. I input my location and an intersection near New Life as my destination. In ten minutes, the car arrived and a bored driver took me to my destination, without conversation or any apparent curiosity. Better than a Chatty-Cathy cab driver.

There was no going in the front door at New Life Ministries this time. That would only result in some very happy guards and a quick trip downtown cuffed in the back of a cruiser. The sun had set, but there was still enough light to find my way along the high fence to an area far from any of the buildings. While I waited for it to become completely dark, I tried to make sense of the latest twists and turns.

I had to be a lot closer to figuring it all out than I thought I was. Otherwise, why kill Watkins and pin it on

166

me? Okay, sure, it could be just because Pastor Jan didn't appreciate my manners. But that didn't seem likely. What did she think I knew that I didn't know I knew?

At this point, all I had was a growing certainty that New Life Ministries was a front for something, and its founder wasn't whom she claimed to be. And that the body identified as Bell was really a Salvation Army Santa whose life had been coming back together until he met Pastor Jan. It was time for me to see if I could pull Pastor Jan's life apart and get to the bottom of the whole mess.

It took fifteen minutes to cut a gap in the fence. The mini bolt cutter was convenient but not quick. It also seemed prudent to let varying amounts of time lapse between the sharp pops of the links being sheared. I looked around for something to mark the spot. If I needed to make a fast getaway, I didn't want to be running along the fence looking for the gap. I picked up a white plastic grocery bag that was stuck against a bush and tied it to the fence about halfway up. It would have to do. I stashed the bolt cutters under a bush and went through the fence.

I made my way to the side of the main building without seeing anyone, or more importantly, without being seen. It seemed that Pastor Jan counted on the fence to keep out the curious – and what kind of idiot would want to break into a homeless shelter, anyway?

The only windows were narrow horizontal slits about ten feet up. I could see light coming out from them, but I couldn't hear anything, and there was no way I could get a peek inside. I walked along the outside until I came to a wing with no light coming out from the windows and what looked like a service entrance. I grabbed the door handle. To my surprise, it turned, and I was able to open it a crack. There was a dimly lit hallway and no one in sight. So far, so good. The lack of security, though, made me doubt that I was going to discover anything useful.

As I eased the door closed behind me, I tried to turn the handle. It was unyielding. Once I closed it, the door wouldn't open from the inside again without a key. They weren't worried about anyone breaking into New Life Ministries. They were worried about someone breaking out. I held it open with my foot while I fumbled in my backup wallet. I took out a one-dollar bill, folded it into a square, and let the door slide shut with the paper wad over the latch bore, keeping the bolt from engaging. It's always a good idea to have an emergency exit plan.

There were two doors on each side of the hallway, and one on the end. The side ones were locked. The one at the end opened, and I peered through the crack at another hallway. This one was brightly lit, and I could hear something muffled, voices or a radio maybe. There were doors every eight or ten feet. They had glass in the tops, reinforced with metal mesh, like you'd see in a jail or a mental hospital.

There was no place to hide in that hallway, but I wasn't going to learn anything cowering where I was. I figured I could try to pass as a lost client if challenged. I stepped into the hallway and let the door close behind me, sacrificing a five this time to keep from being locked in. I approached the first door and peeked into the window.

There was a woman lying on a bed with ear buds on. Her lips were moving, as if singing along to something. She was dressed in white hospital scrubs and had two large bandages on her face, one just over and one under her nose. She was the right general age to be Michelle Rathborn, but short of poking my head in the door and asking, there was no way to know for sure. That would be Plan B, after I'd had a good look around. The room looked like it could have been in a college dorm. It was carpeted and contained a bed, dresser, wardrobe, and desk.

I moved down and checked out three more rooms. Only one was occupied, by a man who appeared to be meditating. He was dressed in blue scrubs. All the doors had bolts on the outside, but none were locked.

At the far end of the hall, the rooms were different. In one, there was a full array of dental equipment, including one of those X-ray machines that looked like a security camera mounted on a mechanical arm. No doubt, this was where Gary Carson's teeth had been altered to look like Ellis Bell's – before someone squashed him with a car, put a bullet in his head, and chopped off his hands.

Another room looked similar, but without the X-ray machine. Lots of drill-like tools surrounding an examining table. It didn't seem like they would have enough volume to justify two dental surgeries. Then I saw the racks of little plastic bottles in every color of the rainbow – actually, way more colors than that. More like the colors of a rainbow on acid. I squinted and looked more closely at the instruments. It was a tattoo and piercing studio.

The last room had all kinds of equipment along the walls and hanging from the ceiling, with a single platform in the very center. It was surrounded by plastic curtains. There were drains in the floor, and electrical cords running in all directions. It looked like a mini surgical theater.

It finally hit me, like I had just walked into a plate glass door with a full head of steam: Pastor Jan was running some sort of human chop-shop, customizing the bodies of the homeless so they could die for clients who wanted to disappear.

Then it hit me again, like I'd gotten up off the floor and walked into the door again. Not only were homeless people's bodies standing in for those who wanted to die, but they were also being disappeared so that the same folks could claim their lives. That's probably what had happened with Sean Ryan.

I was as stunned as an idiot who had walked into a glass door twice.

Loud voices approached from somewhere, and I ducked into one of the empty rooms, leaving the door slightly ajar. There was nowhere to hide. The bed was low to the ground, and the wardrobe was too small. I pulled back the bed covers and got in. I brought the sheet up under my chin to cover for not wearing scrubs.

The voices got louder as they approached. A man and a woman. They paused several times as they made their way down the hallway, perhaps looking in on their guests. I closed my eyes and forced myself to breathe slowly and steadily, like someone asleep.

Their footsteps stopped outside the door to the room I was in. I heard the woman laugh and then say something to the man. He laughed, too. Then I heard the bolt slide shut on the outside of the door, sealing it and cutting off the sound of their laughter.

I opened my eyes and saw Pastor Jan and Ellis Bell on the other side of the door. Even through the metal mesh in the window, I could see their broad smiles.

Several minutes later four men entered the room. I offered no resistance, which seemed to disappoint them, and my wrists and ankles were bound to the bed frame. They left and bolted the door shut again. When the light in the hall went out, it was pitch black.

I had a sudden and urgent need to urinate – something that always seems to happen to me when there's zero chance of relief. To take my mind off my bladder, I tried to figure out what Pastor Jan had planned for me. I shuffled through dozens of possibilities, none of them pleasant.

Everyone I know hates having dental work done, but I've never minded it. The chairs are comfortable, the staff have beautiful smiles and smell like peppermint, and I don't have particularly sensitive teeth or gums.

It's different, though, when the chair has leather straps binding you at the wrists, ankles, and neck. And it's *really* different when the person hovering over you is a war criminal who used to be Saddam Hussein's personal dentist. Ali Bayram smelled like sandalwood and sweat.

He fiddled with a device that resembled a miniaturized version of the jaws-of-life, the sort of thing you'd use to get Malibu Barbie out of the twisted wreckage of her dune buggy after it had been t-boned by a Tonka truck. Or at least that's what came to the twisted wreckage of my mind when I saw it.

After a week of twice-a-day dental work, imagining the mutilation of toys was one of the milder manifestations of my delirium. The nights spent in a heroin-induced daze didn't help, either.

"I need to get this in while you are still awake, if you don't mind. Or, I suppose, even if you do. Hee hee. Open wide now."

I clamped my jaws shut and shook my head. Well, I told my head to shake, but it didn't move much. The leather band binding my head to the back of the chair may have had something to do with that. My stomach cramped and bile seeped upwards into the back of my mouth, but I willed a calm and determined expression onto my face.

Being a private detective involves its fair share of acting. Given my particular niche, I mostly get to play characters like Ratso Rizzo in *Midnight Cowboy*, slapping car hoods and shouting, "I'm walking here!" I never expected to end up portraying Babe in *Marathon Man*, the clueless captive of a sadistic dentist with no answer to the question, "Is it safe?"

"Truly, Adam, you do not want to fight me on this. I can insert it once you are asleep, but it could do much more damage to your lips and gums that way."

Like it mattered. My expiration date couldn't be more than a day or two off, at best. I supposed there was no need to make things any worse, but it *is* one of the few things I truly excel at doing. I kept my mouth clamped shut and bared my teeth at him in what I hoped was a terrifying grimace.

"Whatever you prefer." Bayram rolled the "r" at the end, making a sound like the purr of a cat. "Perhaps you'll feel more cooperative in a few minutes. May I compliment you again on your fine oral hygiene? To reach your age and have only three fillings and no other major work speaks to excellent brushing and flossing habits."

In reality, my oral hygiene habits weren't much to brag about. There had been a couple of years when I rarely touched a toothbrush. Of course, my teeth were getting regular sterile rinses then, as long as cheap whiskey counts as sterile, and a brief pass-through on the way to my bloodstream counts as rinsing. The one winning ticket I'd received from my father in the genetic lottery was a nearly indestructible set of choppers.

"And your wisdom teeth were removed before any significant impaction." He turned his attention to the light box on the wall where five sets of X-rays were displayed side-by-side. The one on the far right was marked "D. Stevens" and had been there when I was first strapped into the chair. It had a dozen or more bright spots of different shapes and sizes. On the left end was the first one he had taken of me, with three irregular blobs of metal where my fillings were. The ones in between showed the steady progress of Bayram's work.

He rolled a large metal canister next to the chair, placed the attached mask over his nose and mouth, twisted a knob on the tank, and breathed deeply for about ten seconds. He took it off and rocked gently for a minute, eyes closed and humming softly. He strapped the mask onto me.

I considered holding my breath but knew it was pointless. What's done is done. That's a lesson that I've learned the hard way. Hell, I've learned it the easy way, too. You can't move on until you let go. So, I let go. I felt little bubbles fizzing in my temples and spreading to the back of my head.

Bayram pulled my mask down just long enough to maneuver the apparatus into my now compliant mouth. He looked back and forth between the X-rays and me, talking to himself. His voice faded in and out like an AM radio station on a country road. "So much to do today before the work is complete! How does one know where to start? Well, I guess one must start at the beginning, eh?"

My head was enveloped in soft, crackling bursts and seemed to be detaching from my body. "Mrs. Robinson, you're trying to seduce me!" I giggled.

I came out from under the laughing gas the same way I had gone in, little bubbles bursting in my head as if my brain had been carbonated. Only on the way back to consciousness, as each bubble popped there was a piercing pain instead of a euphoric tickle.

"Yes, you are coming along nicely, Mr. Perdue. Only one session to go, and your mouth will be the spitting image of Mr. Stevens'. Truly, the *spitting* image!"

Bayram laughed at his own pun. I said nothing. The less I talked, the more Bayram did. I already knew that I was being set up to be the body of a guy named Darren Stevens, who had paid a tidy sum to be relieved of the burden of his past without sacrificing his future. The timing, though, had not been clear before. I would have to accelerate my escape plan.

Right after I came up with it.

Spending all day high on nitrous oxide and every night in a heroin-induced haze made planning just a bit challenging. But it suited Pastor Jan's plans perfectly. Darren Stevens, or, rather, me standing in for him, was going to die in a car accident while overdosing on heroin. Apparently, Mr. Stevens had never gone face first through a windshield before, so I was going to have to do it again so that my fractured facial bones wouldn't be a giveaway. A dead giveaway.

Multiple needle marks and previous use would make my accident seem more plausible, and a high-on-heroin prisoner was a docile prisoner. Win/win. I wondered if Stevens had been out buying heroin to firm up the story. Probably. Pastor Jan didn't leave much to chance.

I had no idea how she had found a client who I would be a useful stand-in for on such short notice. Was there a Tinder for people who wanted to find a double to kill? Swipe right if you'd like Adam Perdue to take the fall for you.

"Yes, Mr. Perdue, you may be my finest creation." He beamed. "Perhaps, though, I should be calling you Adam?"

I got where he was going, but didn't bite. That seemed to disappoint him. But only a little.

"Yes, it is right that I call my creation Adam. Don't you think?"

The popping in my head had subsided enough to think reasonably clearly, and the anesthetic hadn't worn off so speaking wasn't painful. "Seems like that might be a sin of pride there, Doc. I thought you were a good Muslim."

"Oh, my. Heavens no, sir. I am a very bad Muslim. But I am a very good dentist. It is fortunate for you, I think, that it is not the other way around!"

"I'm not sure anything about my current circumstances is fortunate."

"You are not in pain. You have food and drink and a comfortable bed. There are quite literally billions of people in the world who would trade places with you."

"Knowing that they might die tomorrow?"

"Even so. But you may not die tomorrow. It may be a week, or a month. Who knows? Just because your teeth are ready doesn't mean it will happen immediately. This is not all about you, you know. Other plans must be put in place, and the time must be right. Pastor Jan is a kind woman. She gives comfort and ease to troubled souls."

"By killing them?"

"By honoring them. The men and women who come here have nothing in their lives. Most were dead long ago, on the inside. Just empty husks dragging themselves from place to place, like the zombies in your films. Pastor Jan gives them the serenity of knowing that though their lives may have lost all value, their deaths will have meaning."

"You're both out of your fucking minds. She's a psychopath and you're a sadist."

"Calling names does not become you, Adam. And you know nothing of insanity and sadism. Saddam was a psychopath. I detested what I did for him, torturing his enemies – sometimes even their children right in front of them! I took no joy in it. But I knew that there were many who would gladly take my place and torture me and my family. He was truly a sadist. Even when he had everything he wanted from a prisoner, he would not allow them to die quickly. Pastor Jan is not like him. And I am not, either."

"You are torturing me now. You and Pastor Jan. I don't want to die. No amount of laughing gas and heroin is going to make me okay with it, either. Knowing that you are going to be killed and being denied the opportunity to save your own life is torture. No matter what you call it."

"It is different for you, I know. You do not want to be here, and you do not die willingly. But you have chosen your bunk and now must sleep in it."

"No one wants to die. Do you think Gary Carson wanted to die?" Bayram looked confused. "Carson. The guy you fixed up to die in Ellis Bell's place."

"Oh, yes! I remember him. And you are wrong. He did want to die. He knew that was part of the bargain. For weeks, he had everything he wanted: prostitutes, liquor, and drugs. He was out on his own every night. He could have walked away anytime but came back, always.

He knew that one night it would be finished. And he was grateful for the time he was given to indulge his desires. Even more grateful, I think, to know that when he died it would help a man who matters in a way that he did not. A man like Ellis Bell."

I wasn't sure if I was still feeling the effects of the nitrous, or if Bayram had already started the valium drip I always got before being carted back to my room. I sure hoped I wasn't lucid. Bayram was telling me that most of Pastor Jan's victims were volunteers.

"Now, it is time for you to return to your room. Sweet dreams, Adam." He turned on the drip, and I felt the cool rush of medication into my forearm. I embraced unconsciousness like a drowning man grabbing onto a life preserver.

I awakened to find Coo sitting on the side of my bed. "Awakened" might not be the right word for it. Coo is a delusion, or hallucination, or some other sort of mental manifestation who has appeared to me ever since the accident, when I'm very high and particularly stressed or depressed. I hadn't seen her in quite a while. But there she was at my bedside, seeming as real as the concrete walls of my room. I could see her, hear her, and – for the first time – smell her.

Coo didn't really look like anyone. Her face was like one of those police Identikit drawings, with no details filled in. Her voice reminded me a bit of my mother's but had a more musical tone to it. She smelled like flowers, Windex, and wood smoke.

"Hello, Adam. Long time, no see!"

"Coo."

"I hope it's not an inconvenient time. You do seem a bit tied up at the moment!"

"I figured you'd be showing up soon, Coo. You're the very opposite of a good time girl."

"I'm here when you need me."

"What I *need* is for you to undo my restraints so I can get out of here."

"You know I can't do that. But I'm here for you. Always."

"Always has a pretty short horizon, right now."

"It seems that way, but you can change it. Unless you don't want to. Would you rather join Sarah and Elise? It wouldn't be giving up, really. Just accepting the reality of your circumstances. Stop fighting a hopeless battle and embrace being with your family again, at last."

As real as she seems, I know that Coo is just a creation of my own subconscious. She can't have thoughts that I don't have. That's what made it so disturbing that she was counselling surrender. She had never done that before. No matter how deep and foul the gutter I was wallowing in, she had always urged me to keep fighting, to never give up.

Of course, my circumstances had never been quite this bleak. Getting sober and accepting help when you're down isn't easy. But it doesn't compare to what I was facing at that moment.

"I'm not sure I like fatalist Coo. What happened to pep talk Coo?"

"It's not like you're just down a couple of points with time on the clock. You're getting buried and the buzzer is about to go off. It might be time to give up, dear."

"Fuck off, Coo!" I didn't really want her to leave, but she never does what I tell her anyway.

To my surprise, she shimmered like a desert mirage and vanished. I took a deep breath and relaxed on the bed.

Heroin is nice. There is a reason that people become addicted to it. It makes the world all soft and fuzzy, like a forties romance movie – or a sixties porno. And you don't have to be present to win. Being conscious without being present is heroin's finest gift to its users. Things still happen. Thoughts still occur. But none of it really matters.

"I understand you were more of a cocaine guy, back in the day. But heroin's the white man's drug of choice these days." I opened my eyes. It was no longer Coo sitting on my bed, but Pastor Jan.

"I thought we should have a little talk, as your stay with us is nearing its end. Can you imagine my surprise and joy when you put yourself into this room, just waiting for me to flip the deadbolt? I felt like a deer hunter who has spent the day without a glimpse of my quarry only to return to camp and find that an 8-point buck has strapped itself to the hood of my car."

She pulled the drawstrings at the neck and waist of my hospital gown and ran her hand down across my chest, nails lightly scratching my skin. I tried to grab her arm before remembering that my arms and legs were zip tied to the bed rails.

"It was a good enough solution to have the police arrest you for Watkins' murder, or at least drive you underground or out of town until I could wrap up some open orders. It was so much more elegant for you to make a gift of yourself, and just as I was beginning to despair of finding a match for the eager and well-resourced Mr. Stevens! When you first came to my office, I recognized that you would be suitable. I couldn't see how I would ever be able to use you, but circumstances change – and now so have you."

Pastor Jan's hand moved lower.

"Shooting up coke may be a great rush, but it does have disadvantages, doesn't it?"

She was massaging me and I was responding the way that men respond to a massage in that region. "The problem with cocaine is that it increases a man's desire but limits his ability. Very frustrating for the ladies, you know.

"Heroin, now, has the opposite effect. Diminishes interest but no negative impact on capacity." Her massaging continued.

"Stop it." It came out even more weakly than I meant it.

"What's that? I guess we should have established a safe word back when we first met in my office, huh? How many times did I tell you to stop? To stop pushing, prodding, and violating me? But you just kept coming. No safe word."

She bent over me and punctuated her point in a way that cut through the heroin haze. Possibly there wasn't enough heroin-drenched blood reaching my brain, now that demand had increased so sharply elsewhere.

I tried to recall obscure sporting statistics, to calculate the area of an irregular triangle.

Her head moved up and down. "It's not nice... when you want someone to stop... and they won't... is it? Hmm... based on your reaction... though ... it *can* be kind of nice."

I was hardly the first man to be betrayed by "the little head." Some guys give their junk a nickname, like "Biggie D" or "Anaconda," or they just go with the classic, "John Thomas." I call mine Benny, short for Benedict Arnold. At that moment, Benny was having a grand old time with the psychotic lady who was planning to kill me.

I thought of Carson's body lying on a slab at the morgue, face shattered and hands cut-off. Pastor Jan started moving faster. Then I imagined myself on the slab, charred beyond identification, except for the beautiful dental work that Doc Bayram had been doing on me. I saw Squire and Julia standing next to my body. Julia was crying. Benny finally surrendered and stood down.

"Bah!" Pastor Jan sat back up and slapped me hard in the groin. That definitely cut through the heroin haze. The pain was so intense I thought I was going to curl the bed into the fetal position with me.

She opened her purse and took out a lipstick. While I grunted in agony, she carefully applied it to her lips. She popped a piece of gum in her mouth and stared at me while her jaws worked.

"Okay, Adam. You want to do this the hard way? Or, the 'not hard' way? We can do that. There's more than one way to rape a man, you know. Next time I visit, maybe I'll bring some friends. But I think I've made my point, anyway. It's not nice to have things done to you against your will, is it?"

I said nothing. She raised her hand and held it over my crotch.

"No, it's not."

"You have been doing a lot of things that I didn't want done. I wasn't done with your little town, and now I'm going to have to leave. That means *much* more work for me and *much* less money – for a while, anyway. And I don't appreciate it. Orman is a perfect place to work. Off the beaten track, small enough to be manageable yet big enough to provide an excellent client pool. Yes, I will miss it here. And Orman will miss my work. The mayor will be devastated."

"The mayor doesn't have enough brains or character to be devastated."

"You're probably right," she laughed. "Nonetheless, I was performing a necessary service and no one will take it up once I'm gone."

"Oh, I bet there will still be people helping criminals escape the consequences of their actions. Only they'll be doing it with fake IDs, or by arranging travel to countries without extradition – you know, old school."

"Of course. But who will help the homeless? This place will close, and dozens will be back out on the streets, dead to themselves and a deadweight on society. My model works."

I was stunned. Pretty much every piece of scum I've ever encountered was the hero of their own story, but this was insane.

"You really think that killing homeless people is a model that works?" I did finger quotes when I said the word "model," but with my hands strapped down I doubt she noticed.

"For those who want to die, of course it is. For those who want to live, we help them find their way back into society. You keep talking about me killing people. It is more a case of assisted suicide. You will be the first person in Orman I have actually murdered. Everyone else has been a volunteer and I have just facilitated their last wishes."

"What about Watkins?"

"Well, that's on you. A direct consequence of your interference. Collateral damage. Fitting, in a sad way. Mr. Watkins' entire life was a case study in collateral damage."

"How's that?"

"His parents divorced when he was a teenager and used him to punish each other. They subjected him to their own personal Procrustean bed: stretching him beyond his limits, cutting him down to size – whatever suited their battle needs in the moment."

"Fancy reference there, Pastor. I guess the Bible isn't the only book you've read."

"I've read many books, Mr. Perdue. I could compare his childhood to Dr. Doolittle's pushmi-pullyu, with his parents pulling on the reins in opposite directions – if Procrustes is too high-falutin' for you."

I said nothing. What was there to say? I doubt she was interested in my my musings on whether a psychopath can also be a savant.

"Speaking of falutin', Fallujah was another place where he became collateral damage. He was captured by Al-Qaeda in Iraq, at the very beginning of the US effort to take the city from insurgents. His unit had received instructions that if anyone was captured, they should try to stall for two hours and then tell their captors anything they wanted to know. Two hours was long enough for any information an individual soldier might possess to be made useless by changes of positioning and battle plans.

"Unfortunately for Mr. Watkins, the insurgents who took him were well aware of the standing order. They employed a Burdizzo, a crushing instrument used to bloodlessly castrate sheep and goats. He told them everything he knew within fifteen minutes of being captured. Once again, collateral damage."

"Is there a point to this story?"

"You imagine yourself to have been a hero, when you forced us to release Mr. Watkins. In fact, though, you were just the latest in a long line of people who used him for their own purposes, oblivious to his real needs and desires. You don't even know why he wanted to leave, do you?

"When we first brought him into the program, he was a candidate for replacement, in which a client would take over his life. Other than the tattoos, he was an excellent match. His fingerprints wouldn't be the same, of course, but that wouldn't pose a problem as long as our client didn't try to access VA or other government services.

"Mr. Watkins was very excited at the prospect of having a month or more of everything he desired before being replaced. He was already enjoying regular doses of heroin. We didn't know about the injury he had sustained in Iraq until he was well into his counseling sessions.

"Our client was willing, though reluctant, to have rats tattooed on his neck, but he drew the line at having his testicles crushed. So, we shifted gears and transferred Mr. Watkins to the rehabilitation program. I'm afraid it was all a bit confusing to him. He was in an irrational state when he decided to leave."

"Are you saying that everyone in here is a volunteer? They're all just lining up to be killed so some crook can disappear?"

"Of course not. Most of them just receive our services and get on with their lives. Like Watkins would have, if you hadn't interfered. He was sober, getting free dental care, and we were removing those awful rat tattoos. In another month or so, he probably would have had a job and his own place. But *you* interfered. It is very rare that someone matches my other clients' needs and also is ready to stop pretending to live.

"In the year I have been here, we have only been able to make ten matches. Eleven if I count you. We had been seeking a physical match for Mr. Stevens for several months, and then you walked in here and put yourself in a room. All we had to do was throw the bolt! That was pure serendipity."

"You don't think the police are going to be a little suspicious when I disappear and Stevens' body – whoever Stevens is – just happens to show up? Squire knows about the dental work dodge. She'll put two and two together."

"I'm insulted, Adam! I didn't start this enterprise yesterday, you know. You haven't disappeared. You left town. Just the way you came into it. Quietly, and with a bottle of liquor in your hand. You are wanted by the police for murder. You are depressed and wracked with guilt.

"Mr. Stevens has been drinking and drugging his way across the state, driving your car and using the ID and credit cards that you so helpfully left in the glove compartment. Oh, he switched the license plates back, by the way, just so there wouldn't be any confusion. He's been captured on a dozen grainy security videos wearing the jacket and baseball cap he found in the trunk. Not that anyone is going to check.

"You don't have any family anymore, do you? And no real friends. The only people who care at all are a whore turned office assistant and a cop you met in group therapy. I understand that they are much more interested in each other these days than in the whereabouts of an addict on the lam for murder. Squire won't be getting anywhere near the case, anyway. She's getting a promotion to deputy chief and heading up the mayor's new community policing initiative. Not everyone rebuffs my attentions, you know. Of course, the mayor *asks* to be tied to the bed!"

The only positive thing I can say for the combination of racked balls and a heroin hangover is it makes for a pretty good poker face. The depth of her knowledge about me – and the people close to me – was a shock, but I don't think it showed on my face. That the mayor was into submissive sex wasn't really a surprise, just a private room that I had never needed to peak into.

"Pretty thorough. But there are a lot of loose ends and just enough suspicion about Bell's murder – "

"Yes, but loose ends take time, and I will be long gone by the time anyone ties them together. For now, the police will be happy to pin Watkins' murder on you. They'll follow your bar-storming trail until it peters out, and Ellis Bell will become a cold case that never leaves the freezer. I'll find another town like Orman, and get back to making dreams come true."

"There are more people that will wonder what happened to me than just Julia and Squire," I said with a lot more confidence than I felt. David Levant would still be looking for his antiquities and might smell a rat. I owed Maria a favor, and she wasn't one to let a favor go uncollected. Claire might wonder what had happened to me. They might look for me.

For a little while.

Maybe.

"If you say so. Why do you care anyway? You've been dead for years, the same as the street corner Santa and Watkins. Just like all the people I've helped to move on. Some of them had a lot more to leave behind in this life than you do. Stop putting up the brave front. It's the only way you'll ever see them again. You may be afraid that there is no afterlife, but you also have to be holding out hope that there is. It's your only chance. You're sure never going to see them again in this life."

I remember once when I had been just a little tipsy and gotten pulled over by the police. My giggles disappeared, and I became stone cold sober in an instant. Well, after a week of steady drug abuse, I was more than a little tipsy. But invoking my dead wife and daughter was a lot more sobering than blue lights in the rearview mirror. For the first time in a week, my head was completely clear.

"Manipulative bitch, aren't you? That's what you did with Carson, Watson, and the others? Dug into their past, found their vulnerabilities, and then exploited them. What you can't find through internet searches, your psychiatrist pulls out in therapy. Based on your dentist, I'm guessing he was Idi Amin's shrink?"

"No," she laughed. "Close, though. Actually, *she* ran psyops for Baby Doc Duvalier's Tonton Macoutes. If I ever tire of identity replacement as a career, I may turn to dictator staff outplacement. It's so hard for amoral professionals to find meaningful employment after the fall."

She paused and looked at me for a long second. "So, what's your pleasure? Do you want to know or not?"

"Know what?

"Why, when you are going to die, of course. You may mock me, but I am genuinely a compassionate person. If you would rather not know, you will simply not awaken from one of your heroin dozes. But if you'd rather face the moment, I'll let you know when the hot shot is coming. Your call."

It was the sort of riddle that college students bat back and forth while passing around a joint. Would you like to get hit by a bus, without ever seeing it coming? Or would you rather get a terminal diagnosis and know you would die within a few weeks? One spares you from fear and contemplation and the other provides you with the opportunity to get your affairs in order.

"Fuck you. That's my answer. I have no choice here, and we both know it. So, fuck you."

"*Now* you want to fuck me? Too late, I've moved on. Have it your way. I'll decide when you die, and whether or not to tell you. Dr. Bayram assures me that his remaining work could be reasonably accomplished post mortem, so it could happen at any time."

She stood up. "I'll be sending someone in later with a nice little bump for you. You'll feel wonderful for a while, fall unconscious, and then you'll either die or wake up." She paused at the door and smiled. "It's a *mystery!*"

There was no way to know what Pastor Jan's plans were for me, whether the next shot would be the last or not, but I was never going to be more clear-headed. If I was going to make an effort to escape, this was the time. Both my ankles and wrists were zip tied to the metal frame of the bed. The only chance I had was to actually break the bed frame apart.

I moved my body as far away from the wall side of the bed as I could and tried to throw myself out of it. The bed tipped a little, but the legs next to the wall had nowhere to go. I rocked again, and the bed went up on two legs for a second until the wall again stopped it from going over. But it moved away from the wall by a fraction of an inch. I kept at it, tipping and rocking, until my wrists and ankles were raw from struggling against the restraints.

Once I made a little progress, the whole process became more violent, as the bed legs tipped further and further up before crashing to the floor again. Finally, the legs scraped along the wall, and the bed flipped over.

Then I was on my stomach, with the bed on my back pinning me to the floor. It was hard to see how my situation had improved. I still couldn't get my hands or feet free. But I had decided to flip the bed over, worked at it, and accomplished my goal. As Claire might say, I was *visualizing*. If only I could visualize myself all the way out and far away from New Life Ministries.

I had been completely wasted for the last week or so, but my time hadn't been. I knew exactly what was in the room and where it was. Not that it took a lot of effort to memorize. There was only one other piece of furniture, a wardrobe, and no windows. There were no adornments on the wall. It was a smooth cube with a single door that was bolted from the outside. But it did have one flaw in its design as a cell.

The mattress had slid part way off the bed when it flipped, and I worked it with my back and hips as a I crab-walked on my palms and toes. Eventually, it slid out from between me and the bed frame. That provided a little more range for my arms and legs. I had hoped that the frame itself would have broken enough when it flipped to pry a hand or foot loose, but no such luck.

I scuttled my way over to the wall where the door was, inch by excruciating inch. When I felt the frame of the bed above my head hit the wall, I arched my back and shoved upwards with my hands as hard as I could. The bed frame jumped a couple feet up the wall and then slid back to the floor, gouging the drywall. I tried again, this time also pushing forward with my legs. The front of the bed frame hit the wall and stayed. I hung from it as it formed a triangle with the wall and the floor, my hands and feet dangling at the ends of the zip ties, with my toes just able to reach the floor.

I tip-toed forward while jerking my shoulders back, and the bed frame slid and gouged its way up the wall until it was almost vertical. At that point, my hands could touch the wall. I knew I had to be careful to not go all the way vertical, or my feet would be lifted off the ground and I'd be stuck hanging on the bed with the wall just out of reach. Or, worse, I'd flip all the way over and end up back on the bed right where I had started only without a mattress. I inched my way over to the door frame to try and exploit the one mistake: the door hinges were on the inside.

Using the edge of the bed frame, I forced the pin from the highest hinge up a couple of inches and then a couple more. Finally, I was able to grab it in my hand and wiggle it free. Armed with a six-inch metal bolt, I went to work on the bed frame at the junction where the zip tie was secured. The metal first resisted, then twisted, and finally sheared. With one hand free, it was relatively quick work to disengage from the bed frame. Thanks to the nearly soundproof concrete walls, the racket I made hadn't attracted any attention.

My first stop was the wardrobe. My street clothes and even the wallet with Walter Pritchard's driver's license and credit cards were there, but no shoes, phone, or gun. I got the logic of not leaving a gun or phone, but taking my shoes seemed like pure spite. I changed out of the scrubs and put the bed back together, after prying off a nice jagged piece of stiff metal from the frame. With the blankets and pillow gathered into a plausibly human lump, it might be enough to fool someone who glanced in the window. I used the piece of metal to pop the bolts from the other two hinges and pry them apart.

I pulled on the hinged side of the door. The deadbolt on the other side bent but didn't shear off. Still, I was able to pull it open just enough to squeeze out. The hallway was empty. I jimmied the door back most of the way, but I couldn't get the hinges back in place. It was the best I could do, and I was much more concerned with getting the hell out of there as fast as I could than with delaying the discovery of my escape.

I retraced my route from over a week ago, praying the whole way that the folded cash was still keeping the door locks from engaging. As a general rule, I don't pray for help. It's not that I don't believe in God, necessarily. The jury's out on that, as far as I am concerned. But praying seems too much like negotiating. "Please let me live, and I promise I'll be good." That kind of *quid pro quo* deal-making seems more up the Devil's alley than God's.

Still, I prayed the doors would open. I didn't offer anything in return except to keep on being me. It would be God's call whether that was something valuable enough to be worth an intercession.

The first door opened, and I retrieved the five-dollar bill. As I walked quickly down the hallway to the outside door, I was relieved to see that there was no light coming in from the high windows. My watch said 6:30, but I had no idea whether that meant 5:30 AM or PM. It was either just getting dark, or about to get light. Either would do. Good fortune seemed to be smiling on me. I walked to the door and pulled on it confidently. It didn't move. I turned the handle. Nothing. They must have found my handiwork and removed it. Or maybe it just fell out. Didn't matter.

I stared at the door standing between me and freedom. These hinges were non-removable – no pins to pull. I leaned against the wall and closed my eyes. Game over. Eventually, someone would see that I was gone and come looking for me. I thought of the windows and opened my eyes to check them out, momentarily encouraged.

The ledges were out of reach, and there was nothing I could use to boost myself. At my youngest and most athletic, I couldn't touch the rim of a basketball basket, and these ledges looked at least that high. I was suddenly so tired that I almost fell down. If I hadn't been leaning on the wall, I probably would have.

My body ached, my brain had put up a "Do Not Disturb" sign, and my soul – well, my soul had pretty much folded its tent when the door didn't open. I had not felt so beaten, empty, and exhausted since I heard the news in my hospital bed that Sarah and Elise had died in the car accident.

Like then, I was ready to join my wife and daughter in whatever came after this lousy excuse for a life. Like then, though, I knew that killing myself or even letting myself die would really piss them off. Instead, I had let the doctors heal me and then gone on a five-year binge of drugs and alcohol, doing everything I could to dull the pain, but always stopping short of anything that would actually kill me.

This time, it was going to be up to other people whether I lived or died. Or, really, just *when* I died. Pastor Jan probably had half a dozen contingency plans, but I was damn sure none of them included me living very long

As if responding to the thought of her, like a demon being summoned by a spell, I heard her voice. It was coming from outside and approaching the door. Well, it was going to happen sooner or later, so why not get it over with? A key turned in the lock.

"We don't have to be in a huge rush, but we need to start gearing down."

The door opened, and I flattened myself against the wall behind it.

"We won't be taking in any new clients, and you need to finish your other business. I figure we have a couple of weeks at least."

Pastor Jan and Ellis Bell breezed past as the door started to swing shut. Bell's left arm had a huge bandage on it, and he was holding it out to the side gingerly.

"It's not so easy to move the antiquities," Bell replied. "Levant thinks I'm dead, I don't have anyone I trust enough to use as a go-between, and the FBI is still sniffing around. But I may have something in the works. Two weeks should be enough. What are you going to do with the nosy guy from the vets' shelter?"

"I haven't found a match for him, so there's really only one option. Such a waste, though. On the bright side, I think we can kill two birds with one stone. His colleague has outlived her usefulness and knows far too much to be left behind. Perhaps a murder suicide? Or a simultaneous accidental overdose?"

Well, that confirmed that Trent Argent was still alive, though with a rather short shelf life. Sanderson was pretty insufferable, but that didn't rate death at the hands of the way less sufferable Pastor Jan.

As the door swung shut behind them, I was completely out in the open. If they turned around, they couldn't miss me. I moved quickly and quietly on my bare feet, and caught the door as their footsteps and voices began to recede down the hall. I eased my way out and let the door shut behind me with a click. I leaned against it and breathed deeply with my eyes closed against the glare of an overhead security light for at least a minute. When I opened them, I saw one of Pastor Jan's goons not more than thirty feet away, walking along a lighted gravel pathway.

I could see his face clearly, and it seemed impossible that he hadn't seen me, but I'm not one to look a gift horse in the mouth. When he passed out of sight, I took off and found my way to the hole I had cut in the fence. It hadn't been discovered, or they hadn't bothered to fix it yet. In either case, I was free.

ON THE RUN

Escaping New Life Ministries was definitely good news, but I wasn't exactly ecstatic. I had no money, no phone, and no shoes. Not a new experience, alas, but during my previous times in that condition I hadn't wanted to accomplish anything more than finding another drink – and I hadn't been wanted for murder. The same basic strategy applied, though. I needed money, and the first place you go when you need a buck is someone who owes you.

There is a lively economy among the destitute. Money, liquor, drugs, and favors of one kind or another are traded freely on a variety of exchanges. Of course, a bum who owes you money is less likely to dispense cash than a broken ATM. But someone may owe him something, and she may have an EBT card with a few bucks still left on it, and so on.

I was moving with a better-resourced crowd these days. David Levant, Michelle Rathborn's Uncle Unctuous, Gayle Forris, and Squire all owed me money. I was definitely charging all my clients the daily rate for my stay at New Life. All of them owed me for about a week's work – unless Julia had been keeping up with collections despite my disappearance.

Squire was out. We might be friends, but I was wanted for murder and giving money to folks on the lam is generally discouraged at the police department, even in Orman. Uncle Unctuous might give me some cash, but

201

he'd be on the phone to the police the minute I left. That left Forris or Levant.

I mentally flipped a coin in my head, which came up tails. Levant. If a mental coin flip seems a bit flippant for a potentially existential decision, well it probably is. And I definitely cheated. Levant's office was about two miles away, while Gayle's apartment was twice that. I have a high threshold for pain overall, but I'm also a true tenderfoot. My soul was feeling better than it had in a week, but my soles were screaming with each step.

Upon arrival at Levant's office, I was ushered into his inner sanctum within seconds of being announced – setting a new record for speed of access by a non-family member.

"In exactly five minutes, you will be officially announced to me and I will call the COP to let them know that you are in my waiting room. I appreciate that you are almost certainly being set-up, but I cannot harbor a fugitive."

With his planned speech over, he looked at me for the first time.

"You look terrible. And no shoes? According to the COP, you've been drinking your way across the state, but you look more like you just flunked out of hobo boot camp."

"Let's stick a pin in your plan to tell the police I'm here. I think I have a better option, and you may be willing to go for it once you're up to date." He inclined his head, noncommittal. He glanced at my dirty, bloodied feet that were dangerously close to one of his oriental carpets. I stepped back a little further onto the hardwood.

"I have been enjoying the hospitality of New Life Ministries for the last week or so. I need to tell you what's going on, and I need money. Cash. As much as you're willing to give me."

He nodded.

"First off, Ellis Bell is alive."

"The police don't think so. Especially not after one of his hands arrived at COP headquarters in a freezer container via UPS. It actually displaced the story about the missing private detective suspected in the Wharf Rat murder for a whole news cycle. No worries, though. You were back on the front page this morning, having been tracked to a bar outside Lincoln. On the bright side, at least no one expects you to be around here."

"Well, I've seen Bell. And now I understand about the bandaged arm. He may be missing one hand but is otherwise alive and well. He wants to get rid of the antiquities he tried to sell you. Is the FBI still sniffing around about that?"

"No, they determined that Bell's death meant the articles would either never be found or would leave the area immediately. They never seemed very interested, frankly."

"Look, you hired me to find the antiquities. I don't know where they are, but I do know that Bell needs to move them, and he needs to move them fast. He wants to get out of town before crazy Pastor Jan decides that the police need his other hand to really close the case.

If you have someone you trust who Bell wouldn't connect to you, you should have them express an interest that gets back to Pastor Jan somehow. At this point, I get the feeling that the first reasonable offer will make the sale."

"I can do that."

"I don't want to put you in a bad position, but someone else needs to know what I know before the police catch me – or Pastor Jan's goons kill me." I brought him up to date, which took a while, because he hadn't known anything about the Trent Argent and Michelle Rathborn cases.

"If I might summarize... New Life Ministries is a front for a criminal operation that alters the appearance of homeless people and then kills them so that the people they resemble can disappear. Then they provide their clients with a new identity, sometimes that of one of the dead homeless people. Is that right?"

"Yeah, though it sounds a lot more antiseptic when you leave out the details like the war criminal dentist drilling folks' teeth, a client having his hand amputated to protect the operation, and stuff like that."

"Yes, details are important. So, we have a Salvation Army Santa named Gary Carson whose appearance was altered so he could pass as Bell. He was then murdered, which got Bell out of a jam over embezzling from me and others. But you don't know what Bell's new identity is meant to be?"

"No. He might be replacing another homeless person. Or they could have built him a new identity the old-fashioned way, with forged documents. Hell, he may be leaving for Brazil once he monetizes the antiquities. He's going to be a lot harder for Pastor Jan to place with one hand missing."

"True. Your teeth were altered and several tattoos added so that your body could take the place of someone else who wants to disappear, a Darren Stevens."

"Correct. It's possible the police could figure it out from the prison tattoo database, if he has spent time in prison. Otherwise, you'd have to subpoena every dentist in the area and try to match my new mouth to someone else. And, of course, he might be from out of town."

"You still have no idea where the convenience store heiress, Ms. Rathborn, is – or even if she is still alive."

"Also correct, unfortunately. I may have seen her at NLM, but the woman I saw was not being restrained in any way, so it's fair to assume that if it was her, she isn't currently under duress. While her siblings certainly have motive for wanting her dead, her disappearance actually hurts their cause. I suspect there's a deeper game going on with her."

205

"And you believe that at least one person whom the nefarious Pastor Jan has supplied with a new identity has replaced another homeless person, a Mr. Ryan, and is starting a new life in Montana."

"Nefarious Pastor Jan. That would make a great hip-hop name."

"I don't know if it is admirable or horrifying that you retain a sense of humor about all of this, Adam."

Levant took out his wallet and started laying bills on the table. "I assume that twenties and fifties are more suited to your current circumstances than hundreds?"

I nodded and pocketed the money, just under a thousand dollars. "My first stop when I leave here is Target, where I can buy some new shoes – heck, I guess I need new everything. I'll also pick up some burner cell phones. I'll give you a call, and we'll leave the line open for a few minutes. Then you call Squire and tell her I've just told you my story over the phone. That will cover you."

"I will record your call and provide the recording to Squire, so remember that when we talk. That will certainly cover me. But wouldn't Squire possibly be able to trace the call to the burner? You would then lose the advantage of them searching for you in Lincoln instead of here."

"Good point. If you ever tire of falafels and philanthropy, you'd make a good PI. I think I know where I can get a burner that will be much harder to trace. It may take me up to an hour, but you can expect a call from me around then."

"In the meantime, I will have a friend put out some feelers and see if we can't lure Mr. Bell out into the open. I assume that Squire will believe your story, but at this point I don't think she will be able to re-open the matter of Bell's ID. We need to produce Bell himself."

"Agreed. But Squire can start digging really hard into the Nefarious Pastor Jan and at least keep her under surveillance so she can't skip town – or murder his prime suspect. If she could get a warrant for New Life, she might even catch Bell and Doctor Bayram and start the whole thing unraveling."

"And what will you do next?"

"I still need to find Michelle Rathborn and Trent Argent. And I only know one place to look."

"You're not going back inside New Life Ministries?"

"No way around it. Subtlety and stealth didn't work, so I'm going to go with my strengths this time."

"Which are?"

The mild sense of insult I felt at being asked that by a former and present client dissipated when I found myself unable to immediately bring any to mind. But I kept thinking about it.

"Persistence for one."

"Stubbornness, yes."

"Tomato, tomahto… Improvisation for another. Oh, hell. I don't really know how I'm going to handle it, OK?"

"Just be careful. NPJ is not likely to pull any punches."

"NPJ?"

"Nefarious Pastor Jan. Isn't it traditional to describe rappers with long names by their initials?"

"Yeah, rappers and select Supreme Court Justices. I guess that makes me SAP - Stubborn Adam Perdue. Not the best name ever, but you can call me by any initials you want, as long as they aren't RIP."

After outfitting myself at Target, I paid Maria another visit. Too bad I didn't have a watch with one of those exercise apps. I was definitely getting my steps in today.

"My, you do get around. According to the police, you're currently on a statewide pub crawl, staying one lurch ahead of them. Now, here you are in my house looking fresh as a daisy – well, not so fresh, actually, and paler than usual. Are you okay?"

Something that might have been genuine concern crept into her voice. Between that, the way she crossed her legs while reseating herself on the couch, and the scent of *Le Chevrefeuille*, something that might have been genuine desire crept into a different part of my body. "I'm fine. Just been spending a lot of time indoors lately."

As I said it, I realized that I wasn't feeling fine at all. My hands were clammy and my stomach was cramping. "Actually, I don't remember the last time I had a proper meal."

"That's easily addressed." Maria pushed a button on her phone, and Alex appeared.

"Please have the cook prepare something for Mr. Perdue. A sandwich and some chips?"

She looked at me, and I nodded. "Now, what brings you here, Adam?"

"I have a favor to ask, I'm afraid."

"Another? And I haven't collected on the last one yet!" Her expression went from playful to serious. "I do hope you don't plan to tell the police how you found El Rata Flaca. Growing and selling an almost legal product is easily overlooked, but accessory to murder is something else altogether."

"That's not a conversation that I hope to have anytime soon. I certainly don't want to cause you any trouble, but your men can attest that I was unconscious on the floor when Pastor Jan's goons took Watkins away. I'm guessing that his time of death will correspond to when I was lying on your couch unconscious. You and your people are my alibi."

"I am no one's alibi." She fixed me with a glare. "You *will* want to find a way out of that mess without dragging me into it." She smiled again. "You really don't know how to butter up a girl before asking her for a favor, do you?"

"It's not an area of expertise for me, I admit." My stomach hurt and I was getting light-headed. Right on cue, my food arrived. Maria waved at it and nodded. I ate it all in under a minute, washing it down with a Mexicoke. My stomach felt a little better and my head wasn't quite as fuzzy.

"I need to borrow one of your burner phones. I have to make some calls without letting anyone know I'm in town. About the only thing I have going for me right now is that the police think I'm on the other side of the state."

"The burners aren't magic, you know, Adam. If they run a trace on a call, it will show them that you are accessing local cell towers. They won't need more than a few seconds to get that much information. The system isn't set up for hiding your location but for separating your identity from the number when it shows up in phone records and avoiding calling patterns that attract attention."

"Oh, I guess I don't need another favor from you, then." How was I going to manage to contact Squire or Julia – without letting the police know I was back in town? Even if they thought I was far away, they'd surely have someone watching my office and Julia's apartment – never mind trying to drop in at Squire's place of business.

"No, you still need a favor. It's just a bigger one than you thought." I didn't even see her summon him this time, but Alex was back in the doorway. "I need a rover set up." He nodded and disappeared.

"This may take a few minutes. While he is gone, why don't you catch me up on where you have been for the last week, if it wasn't the bar-storming tour that the police are following?"

I gave her a pretty comprehensive description of my time as a guest of Pastor Jan's: imprisonment, dental work, tattooing, the regular shots of heroin and valium, and how I managed to escape. I left out Pastor Jan's aborted sexual assault. At times, she probed for more details, but mostly she just let me talk.

It felt good to tell someone everything that had happened to me, especially someone close enough to care at least a little about me, yet distant enough for me to expose myself without shame. If it hadn't been Maria, it probably would have been Claire. Not Squire or Julia. Good friends have a duty to spare each other the more squalid details of each other's lives, whenever possible.

When I finished, we sat in silence for a couple of minutes. I thought about next steps in my various investigations. I don't know what Maria thought about.

Alex returned, carrying a small laptop and a phone, connected together by a cable. He placed them on the coffee table in front of me and looked at Maria. She nodded.

"Keep the phone connected to the computer, and the computer connected to Wi-Fi. Open this program, select 'map view,' then 'search.' Put in the location where you want the call to come from. Give me an example."

"A bar in Lincoln."

"Any bar?"

I nodded. "Wait, no. It needs to be a downscale place."

Alex nodded and typed. A selection of bars in Lincoln came up. I actually had drunk myself across the state once, and one of the bars jumped out at me. "Use that one, 'Paddy's Place.'" He clicked enter and a blue dot appeared on the map hovering over Paddy's Place in Lincoln.

"Any call you make right now will appear to be coming from Paddy's Place. But you have to stay on Wi-Fi. If you lose the wireless signal, the phone will default to the cellular network and use the nearest tower."

"Can't the wireless signal be traced?"

"Sure," Alex smiled. "But the laptop is set up to use a VPN that connects to a server in Canada. The FBI or the CIA could probably trace it back, given enough time, but the local cops won't even try. Everything they see will indicate that the phone is at Paddy's Place. They're not going to dig deep enough to find anything else."

I nodded like I knew what a VPN is. "This is pretty neat shit."

"Oh, this is nothing! If you want, I can send your phone for a walk around downtown Lincoln and have it drunk dial your exes from a new location every ten minutes or so. Do you want me to show you?" Alex was excited.

"No, Alex. That is more than Mr. Perdue requires. Thank you."

Alex left, and I stashed the phone and computer in the small case he had provided.

I stood up to say my goodbyes and had to grab the arm of my chair for momentary support. I realized that even after the meal, I was still feeling off.

Maria gave me a look that was a mix of sadness and something else. The "something else" made me uncomfortable. It was somewhere on the pity/contempt scale, and there's no spot there that I want to be.

"It's the heroin, Adam. It's only been a week, but you were using it daily. You may be experiencing withdrawal."

"Shit!" I hadn't considered that possibility. "I don't have time for this right now."

"Then you need to find some methadone, or something similar. That is not something I am prepared to help you with. Do you know anyone else who can help?"

I nodded. It wasn't going to be Maria *or* Claire who heard my story, but both of them. Claire worked with recovering addicts. She would be able to help.

Maria stood up and saw me to the door. "Mark your calendar, Adam, for next Friday: The Founders' Ball."

I look at her, confused.

"Your first favor in return. You will be my escort to the Founders' Ball."

I laughed. The Founders' Ball was the highlight of the social season in Orman. "Sure, why not? If I'm not dead, in jail, on the lam, or too strung out to stand... it'll be my pleasure."

I used one of the Target burners without the fancy computer hookup to download the Riders on the Storm app and called a car. No more walking for me.

Claire finished up with a client while I cooled my heels in her waiting room. I thought about where the tequila was stashed a few too many times for comfort. I'd been a drunk for a few years, but alcohol had never been my primary addiction. Numbness was. With a lot of effort, I had gotten to a place where every drink wasn't an attempt to check out mentally and emotionally.

Heroin is the ultimate numbing agent. Alcohol produces intense feelings before bringing on numbness, but smack bypasses all feeling and goes straight to the place where nothing matters.

I told myself that it hadn't been my choice to use it, that I hadn't so much fallen off the wagon as been tossed off. In any case, the tequila in Claire's drawer was singing me a very seductive song.

A door shut from somewhere inside Claire's inner sanctum. The door near the tequila drawer opened, and she beckoned me inside. I settled into one of the barber chairs which was a little too reminiscent of being back with Dr. Bayram, and endured a long, probing visual examination. Eventually, Claire nodded.

"Well, you certainly look rode hard and put away wet!"

I couldn't help but laugh. That's exactly how I felt. "Well, it's been a rough week…"

Again, I recited the only slightly sanitized version of my stay at New Life. Claire asked no questions and took no notes.

When I was done, she spoke. "You were correct, then, that Ellis wasn't dead."

"Well, it was you who told me that I didn't think he was."

"You knew that you knew. You just didn't know it. Well, it seems like you have the big picture in a little clearer focus now, so you must be here about something else."

"I think that I am experiencing withdrawal symptoms. I'm light-headed, nauseous, and can't think straight. And I need to think straight right now. I thought maybe you could help."

"I could teach you some breathing exercises that might help."

"I was thinking about something that requires less effort on my part. Like a pill, or a shot."

"I don't have prescribing privileges, Adam. With your history of addiction, it's probably not the right approach anyway."

"Unfortunately, I don't have time for the right approach. I'm wanted by the police, and by Pastor Jan and her goons. I need a silver bullet."

"You seem more worried about the New Life crowd than the police."

"The police think I'm on the other side of the state, while Jan knows I'm right here. Plus, the police *might* ask questions first and shoot later. Jan's goons are likely to do the opposite."

"I would think that she wants you alive more than the police. You were being groomed to die as someone else. You're worth a lot of money to her. The police, on the other hand, would find their job much easier if they were to simply eliminate you. 'Save the public the expense of a trial,' as they say."

In my addled state, that hadn't occurred to me. I wasn't so addled, though, that I couldn't use Claire's logic against her.

"See, that's why I need a quick fix. I should have realized that."

Claire gave me the look that my wife used to give our daughter when she used a naughty word correctly: disapproval tinged with pride.

"It wouldn't hurt your long-term recovery to rely on methadone for a week or two, to alleviate the symptoms. But, as I said, I do not have prescribing privileges."

"Well, you wouldn't want to be writing prescriptions to fugitives anyway, would you? No need to create a paper trail. Maybe you know someone who knows someone?"

Claire sighed. "Give me an hour or two. I have a client who is making great progress in his recovery. He has reduced his need for methadone considerably. My guess is he's selling his extra doses on the street. I suppose a good citizen would try and divert them...."

I gave her a handful of bills from the wad provided by David Levant. She raised an eyebrow, and I peeled off some more. She took the money from me, then grabbed my hand. "There is a condition, Adam."

I waited, self-conscious of how clammy my hand must have felt in hers.

"When this is all wrapped up, I need you commit to a minimum of six sessions with me, one a week. We can address whatever you want: the heroin addiction, your past issues with alcohol, the death of your wife and daughter, or anything at all. Pick one thing that you'd like to stop running away from and work with me on it. No charge."

"Okay."

I don't know which of us was more surprised to hear that simple assent come out of my mouth. She nodded and let go of my hand.

It's a good thing that my chances of having a future were so bleak, because it now looked like that future included putting on a monkey suit for Maria and having my head shrunk by Claire.

My fingers hovered over the keypad of my phone as the cursor blinked in the destination field of the Riders on the Storm app. I needed somewhere with a wi-fi signal and a little space for me to set up the phone/computer thingy, without attracting too much attention. It didn't seem smart to go somewhere public, but I couldn't go to my office, Squire's, or Julia's – and Old Yeller's whereabouts were unknown.

When I want to lay low, I usually just check into a shelter for the night. No one pays any attention to homeless folks. But the whole computer/phone thingy would definitely draw attention.

David Levant? He might be willing, but I had no idea where he lived. His office had too many people around, and I had already been there once that day. Gayle Forris? Would she turn me in? Throw me out? Only one way to find out.

The car dropped me a couple of blocks from Gayle's apartment, just to be safe. Walter gave the driver a generous enough tip to get a good review but not so generous as to be memorable. It wouldn't do for Walter to be very memorable. Fortunately, he was using my face, which is the very definition of forgettable.

Gayle was not at home, or at the least not answering her buzzer. I sat on the stoop with my little computer case, trying to think of my next move. I could try camping out in a coffee shop with free Wi-Fi and hope not to be recognized. Before I could dream up and dismiss another stupid idea, a minivan pulled to the curb. Pre-adolescent children exploded from every door, all of them in dirty baseball uniforms. There might have been enough for a whole team.

A woman emerged much more slowly from the driver's side and went around to the back, where a hatch was opening. The kids ran all over the sidewalk and the stairs in front of the building, in a frenetic pantomime of a baseball game. They ignored me, and none of them offered to help the woman as she tried to lift three bags of groceries out of the back of the van.

"Can I give you a hand?" She straightened up, surprised but apparently too tired to be really taken aback.

She considered me carefully. "Are you selling something?"

I realized that the computer case gave me a look of legitimacy that I otherwise would have lacked, if a door-to-door salesman could be considered legitimate. "No, Ma'am. Just waiting for my friend Gayle up in 4B."

She gave me a hard look and shrugged. "Oh, well. I don't suppose you'll murder me in front of the Mudville Nine – and I'm not sure that's a worse fate than what's in store for me with them, anyway. Their victory ice cream is melting." She grabbed a bag, stepped back and waved at the other two.

I gathered the bags and started up the steps. She opened the security door and held it for me. "Straight down on the left. 1A. Just leave them outside the door." As I returned to the vestibule, a flock of grimy and happy kids flowed around me.

"Thank you. Feel free to sit inside the lobby and wait, if you prefer."

I did prefer. "That would be great. Say, could I ask you for a small favor?" I held out my phone. "I don't seem to have a cell signal here, and I'd like to call and check on Gayle. Do you have a Wi-Fi network you'd be willing to share?"

She looked doubtful. Chants of "I scream, you scream, we all scream… for ice cream!" were coming from inside her apartment. She shrugged. "The network is, 'Mom's All In' and the password is 'Boyz2Men:' Capital "B" boyz with a "z," the number "2," capital "M" in men."

I smiled. "I'm familiar with the name."

"Don't say a word. I'm changing the password as soon as the monsters have their ice cream, so make your call quick."

"Yes, Ma'am. And good luck in there."

She sighed, picked up the bag with the ice cream and strode into the apartment, girded for battle.

Once the program on the laptop verified that my cell phone was currently coming from Paddy's Place in Lincoln, I placed a call to David Levant. After identifying myself to the receptionist and waiting on hold for a minute or so, David came on the line.

"Mr. Purdue. It has been some time since you reported any progress. Before you do so, however, I must advise you to turn yourself into the police immediately. As you must know, you are a person of interest in the murder of a homeless man."

"Pershon of interesht or prime shushpect?" Maybe I was laying on the drunken slurring a little bit too thick. I dialed it back. "I didn't kill Rat Neck, and the poleesh should know better. Things will cool down soon. Not much to report on the antique-… uh, anti-quite… the stolen old stuff. But I'm getting closer. Bell is alive! I just have to figure out how to draw him out into the open."

"The police don't think so. His hand –"

"The police are idiots! Except maybe Squire. Sometimes. I saw Bell, uh, a few days ago – before I skipped town. He was rockin' a mongo bandage on his left arm but was otherwise the picture of good health! Tell Squire she was right about that from the start." I assumed that the call recording would wind up in the case files. Might as well have some kudos for Squire on the official record.

"You should tell her yourself. Turn yourself in and tell her the whole story."

"That's not gonna happen. Not today. I'll be in touch when I know more." I disconnected.

That was sufficient cover for Levant and Squire. And enough misdirection to keep the cops looking for me in Lincoln.

I put the cursor on the little phone icon hovering over Paddy's Place and clicked on an icon of a hiker. A box appeared asking, "What is your destination?" I moved the cursor to the middle of Memorial Park, by the fountain commemorating the Vietnam War. Another box asked, "Duration?" It was about a ten-minute walk, but I put in four hours. A winding path through and around downtown Lincoln appeared and the little picture of my phone began to blink.

Every few minutes, the location services on the phone would ping a nearby cell tower and lead anyone tracking my burner phone on a merry goose chase. This little program was threatening my commitment as a technophobe.

The next call was to Julia at the office. The police were certainly monitoring that phone by now. "Hi, Julia. I have to make this quick. I'm in Lincoln tracking down a lead about Pastor Jan at New Life Ministries. Do you have any more information on her?"

I realized that I hadn't slurred any of my words, and hoped that the COP had only been able to get a warrant for phone records and not a full tap. Screw it, anyway, if they had. It was way more fun trying to talk sober for the police when drunk that it was trying to talk drunk for them when sober.

"Boss, where the hell have you been? Everybody is looking for you. The cops, your clients, a guy called Captain Hook…."

"I was the unwilling guest of Pastor Jan for a week. And she was not the perfect host. I needed to get out of town for a while to clear my head and keep from getting arrested for something I didn't do."

"I know you didn't do it, Adam. Squire knows it, too." There was a muffled snort in the background that didn't sound much like affirmation. Squire and Julia seemed to be spending a lot of time together. "In fact, you should talk to her right away. I could –"

I cut her off, knowing that she was about to offer her the phone. "No, I'll talk to Squire when I'm ready to. The very last thing I'm going to do is call her right now." Julia and I used a set of codes that were pretty simple. The more adamantly we said something, the more likely that the opposite was true. When I said that calling Squire was "the very last thing" I'd do, she knew that it was the very next thing I was going to do.

"Okay, Boss. I really haven't gotten too much more on Pastor Jan. I've tracked her back through two more identities – both missing or dead people she appropriated. But I don't have her real name. I know a bit more about New Life Ministries, though. They are leasing their premises from an LLC…."

I heard papers being shuffled in the background and pictured Julia at her desk, surrounded by her usual organized mess of files and sticky notes. Squire was sitting comfortably in the worn leather visitor's chair in the reception area. In my mind's eye, she was smiling as she watched Julia rummage through papers, humming happily. DK the cat was curled up on a chair.

That's the scene I wanted for them. A little sadly, I realized that if I had been in the room, Squire would have been scowling and pacing, Julia wouldn't be humming while she worked, and DK would be howling for food.

Maybe Pastor Jan was right, about them at least. Maybe I was just an obstacle to their happiness that they would forget quickly if I disappeared.

And maybe I was really strung out and letting my imagination get the best of me.

"It's called Marsan Enterprises. The building has been leased to half a dozen different companies over the last decade. Nobody stayed long. New Life Ministries signed the lease just over a year ago. By the way, Marsan also appears on the list of Ellis Bell's clients."

"Marsan doesn't ring any bells for me. Have you got the names of any officers, or the registered agent?"

"Not yet. The Secretary of State's online system is down for maintenance. Hey! Since you're in Lincoln, you're a lot closer to their office than we are. You could go ask for the paper records."

"Yeah, I suppose. I will if I get the time. You keep trying the website. I have another call I have to make now. I'll see you soon, hopefully not in a holding cell. Keep working on the Pastor Jan puzzle."

"Will do, Adam. Please be careful." There was a murmur in the background. "And, oh yeah. You should turn yourself in to the police. I really, really think you should. Bye."

I disconnected and immediately dialed Squire's personal cell. Even Judge Easy wouldn't authorize a tap on a police lieutenant's phone, just because she was a little friendly with a PI who was now a murder suspect. At least I sure as hell hoped he wouldn't.

"So where are you, really?" Squire sounded bored.

"Nice to hear your voice, too. Have you heard from David Levant?"

"Yes, just now. So where are you? If you're in Orman, you're going to get caught. By us or Pastor Jan. You better be in Lincoln."

"Okay, good thing I am in Lincoln, then. But I might come back to Orman in the not-too-distant future. I need to pay another visit to New Life Ministries."

"Uh-huh. You know if you end up across the desk from Woody Wales again, there won't be anything I can do for you."

"Roger that. In case Levant didn't make it crystal clear to you, though, Bell is alive."

"Uh-huh, I got that message. But Rat Neck is dead. Proving Bell is alive won't get you off the hook for that."

"But proving that Pastor Jan and Bell are part of a criminal enterprise and that Rat Neck and I were in their way would go a long way toward clearing me. I'll do what I have to do. Just do me a favor and see the Bell case through. Bye." I cut the line.

To the untrained ear, it might have sounded like Squire wasn't exactly thrilled that I was still alive, probably in Orman, and definitely going into New Life Ministries. But those 'Uh-huhs' were filled with poignancy and betrayed just how relieved she was to hear from me and how supportive she was of my efforts.

Uh-huh.

There can be a fine line between "tried and true" and "stupidly obvious." Climbing through a hole in the fence and dashing to the nearest building had gotten me into New Life once, and I didn't have a better plan for my return trip. Assuming that Pastor Jan had tightened security since my last visit, I needed a way to fatten up that narrow line just a bit. I had an idea. It wasn't a good idea, but time was short and it would have to do.

Using Walter's pre-paid credit card, I got a ride to the Super Walmart. Nothing beats Walmart when you're looking to make a bad idea work. They have everything, of course: food, hardware, clothing, electronics, etc. But more than the specific items on my list, I needed a shot of Walmart's unique energy.

Sam Walton's "Magic Kingdom" puts Walt Disney's to shame. It may not be "the happiest place on earth," but Walmart is a thumbnail sketch of America.

It's an icon of corporate greed that swallows small businesses whole and turns real life Main Streets into Disney-like props. It also welcomes homeless families living in their cars with free, safe parking and bathroom sinks large enough to wash a few essentials or to bathe a baby.

In its aisles, stay-at-home parents in sweat pants mingle with morning-after clubbers in leather and glitter, next to construction workers and bankers sharing the frustration of trying to figure out if the "value size" really is cheaper.

You can get your eyes checked, open a bank account, buy a cell phone, purchase insurance, have a medical exam, send and receive cash across the globe – and you can do any or all of these things in a ball gown or your pajamas, with people who are exactly or nothing at all like you. All the weirdness and the ordinariness that is America come together at Walmart.

After getting a cash advance of five hundred dollars from Walter's pre-paid credit card, I purchased a few essentials for my not very good idea: a compact 24V cordless multi-tool with drill-driver and saw attachments, a crowbar, zip ties, poster board and paints, half a dozen air horns, two 36-packs of toilet rolls, and duct tape. I wasn't sure what the duct tape was going to be used for, but you can never have enough duct tape.

Rushing through the aisles and standing in line at the register with all the other shoppers vaulted me back in time momentarily. I had been buying supplies to build a playhouse for Elise in our backyard in another suburb, a long time ago. She had been four or five and had squatted next to me as I put it together, playing operating room nurse to my surgeon, handing me tools and pieces as needed. Sometimes, they were even the right ones.

"Is that everything?" The harried cashier's voice broke through my reverie, and I nodded.

"Yes." That *had* been everything. Long gone, now. My eyes misted, and my hand shook as I tried to swipe Walter's card. The cashier shot me an impatient glance and then her face softened. She took the card from me and swiped it.

My hands continued to shake as I placed the bags and boxes into my carriage and walked out of the store. I drove the memory of Elise out of my head, an effort that for many years had required a pint or more of hard liquor. It made me sad that it only took an effort of will now. Still, my hands continued to shake, and I sat down heavily on the bench at the bus stop.

My hope of riding out the heroin withdrawal was fading fast. Where was Claire and my methadone? As if in answer to my thoughts, Walter's phone rang. It was Claire. Punching her address into the phone app, I was informed that a car was five minutes away, and an animation with confetti and streamers congratulated Walter on becoming a Frequent Rider on the Storm.

Claire raised her eyebrows at the large volume of toilet paper when I put my purchases down in her waiting room. The magical acceptance of any and everything as normal doesn't last once you leave the store. A man carrying around 72 rolls of toilet paper was bound to raise a few eyebrows once outside of Walmart's judgment-free zone.

Claire handed me a half-full pill bottle. The prescription label identified the medication as methadone, but the name of the doctor and the patient had been scratched off.

"Take one a day, and don't crush or chew them. They're on a time-release. They should ease the withdrawal without incapacitating you. Do NOT overuse them trying to get a buzz. You can overdose just like on heroin, and you won't really get high no matter how many you take."

She held out a small box. "This is Naloxone. Keep it with you. It could save your life or someone else's. Anyone who is around opioids should have it with them at all times."

I swallowed a pill and washed it down with water. My request for a shot of tequila had gotten me only a stern look.

"And, remember, we have a deal. As soon as you get things under control, you're back here for weekly sessions."

I nodded, unworried. It's not like I ever get things under control.

Just knowing I had taken the drug made me feel more relaxed, and I got the shaking down to a mild tremor. "Uh, do you mind if I leave my things here for about an hour? Not having my own car makes storing things a little inconvenient." Claire gave the toilet paper a long look while shaking her head, let out a sigh, and nodded.

I wondered what had become of Old Yeller. Had my doppelganger, Darren Stevens, ditched her behind some dive bar where he had been leaving a trail of my downward spiral toward an overdose? I assumed that the COP had put out a BOLO on her, and I really hoped Stevens hadn't torched her.

After about half an hour, I felt great. No more shaking, no more anxiety. I didn't feel as good as I did on the heroin. My brain still worked, and as long as I was thinking, there was always the potential for pain. For the moment, though, I had become, as Pink Floyd sang, "comfortably numb." Next stop, the vets' shelter.

The plan for getting into New Life Ministries had come to me when I remembered something that Julia had mentioned on the phone. It had gone past me at the time, but eventually sank in. Among the obvious people looking for me, clients, police etc., she had also mentioned Captain Hook. I didn't know why he was looking for me, but thinking about the bit of misdirection he had done in the donut shop made me realize that what I needed to get into NLM was a distraction. To create a distraction, though, I would need help. Who would be willing, or oblivious enough, to help Orman's most wanted fugitive?

Hook was relaxing in a beach chair set in a beam of sunshine that had fought its way into one of the alleys behind the vets' shelter. "I heard you were looking for me?"

Hook glanced up and down the empty alley before replying. "Yeah, me and whose army?" he chuckled. "Everybody is looking for you, man."

"Well, you're the one who found me. What's up?"

"Sanderson has disappeared. Thought you might want to know that. First the night desk guy disappears, and now the day desk gal. I figure that's not a coinkydink, you know?"

Jan must have already snatched Sanderson. There was no time to waste.

"You're right. No coincidence at all. She and Trent both are in serious trouble." I took a deep breath. "And I need you to help me get them out of it."

"Don't care much for her, but Trent's a good guy. As to helping you... I dunno, man. The cops want you really bad. What do you have in mind?"

"Trent and Sanderson – and probably Michelle Rathborn – are all being held at New Life Ministries. Pastor Jan plans to kill Trent and Sanderson. I'm not sure what she has in mind for Rathborn. I have to get in there to rescue them, and I need you to create a distraction." No back story, no context, just cut to the chase. Anyone in their right mind would dismiss me as crazy. That's why I had come to Hook.

Hook nodded. "That place never felt right to me. They flat out wouldn't talk to me when I tried to get a bed there when the VAC tossed me for drinking. Folks said that Sanderson could get you in, but she wouldn't talk to me either. Who ever heard of such an exclusive shelter? Pisses me off. What kind of distraction do you need?"

"They've got security there, lots of it. I need them all looking one way while I get through the fence and into the building another way."

Hook sat up and moved the back of the beach chair upright. "How many?"

"I don't know for sure. We need something that will get and hold the attention of all of them for half an hour or so."

"Hmm. No bombs or gunfire, then?"

"No."

"Good, I'm not a fan of either one. I'd give my right arm to never have had an encounter with an IED." He chuckled.

"What I have in mind will require about a dozen people, and it's not dangerous. It might even be kind of fun. Do you think you could round them up? I'll pay $100 each for an hour's work. I'll cover transport from here to New Life Ministries and back. There's $500 in it for you, if you can do it ASAP."

"Give me an hour. I'm going to need to show folks some money, though. I'm not known for having that kind of cash."

I counted out a thousand dollars. He handed half of it back. "Not that much, man. People see that kind of money, they start getting ideas. I'll give everyone $20 up front and the rest when the job's done. Any special requirements or anyone will do?"

"Just willing and able to walk around a bit."

"Too bad. The Wheelies are always looking for something to do."

The Wheelies are a group of disabled homeless veterans. They won the state wheelchair basketball title a few years back.

"The Wheelies are still around?"

"Sure. Some new guys, some slicker wheels. Still around."

"Actually, they would be great. Transportation may be a problem, though."

"Nah, the shelter's got a tricked-out bus that can carry them all. For $100, the driver will find something to enter in the log. Who's gonna question her, anyway, with stiff britches Sanderson not around?"

"Perfect. You gather the Wheelies and meet me on Railroad Street a block from New Life Ministries' main gate tomorrow about an hour before sunset, say 5:00 PM."

"You got it, boss."

I was reluctant to overuse Walter's good name and credit, but there really wasn't much choice. I needed a place to crash for the night, and I couldn't risk going to a shelter or staying out on the street. I would also need a car for the next day. I caught a Rider to the airport and got a rental from a bored clerk who barely looked at me.

Her lack of interest was shared by the check-in clerk at the Waystayer Motel. A half hour in the mildewy shower seemed like a day spent in a fabulous spa, and the coarse sheets felt like the finest silk against my skin. I slept like a baby – a baby who has nightmares about dentists, rat tattoos, and spooky-eyed women.

In the morning, I helped myself to a rubbery waffle from the complimentary breakfast buffet and washed down a methadone pill with my coffee. When I went out to the parking lot, I realized I had absolutely no idea what my rental car looked like.

I didn't remember the model, the color, or anything about it. The key showed the plate number, so I walked around pushing the unlock button and squinting at license plates until I found it. A white Honda Accord. The Adam Perdue of automobiles, immediately forgettable.

With six or seven hours to kill and unable to go anywhere I might be recognized, I drove around the Orman Metropolitan Area, as the Chamber of Commerce proudly referred to the city and its near suburbs. I kept the speedometer at 5 mph below the limit on every road and obeyed all traffic laws. Getting busted now while just sight-seeing would break the irony meter.

Orman isn't beautiful, quaint, or particularly prosperous. But it isn't ugly, cut-from-a-mold, or destitute either. The Orman River winds through downtown, with walking and bicycle paths on both sides. On a nice summer day, canoes, kayaks, and small sail boats glide along its course, under the three main bridges: two for cars and one for the railway.

Most of the people who grow up in Orman seem to want to stay, and even flotsam like me that washes up there by accident isn't in a hurry to to move on. That qualifies it as an urban success story in 21st century America.

I bought lunch at the food court in the Orman Heights Mall, so named to distinguish it from the older Orman Mall. The neighborhood isn't called Orman Heights, and the area is actually in a bit of a depression and prone to flooding. The developer apparently just thought that the "Heights" gave it a bit of class.

I stood out a bit in the lunchtime crowd, where the average age was about sixteen. I took my pizza slices and fountain drink out to the car. I was more in the mood for Middle Eastern, but I figured my picture behind the counter at the Baba Ganoush franchise might have "call 911" next to it these days. My free meal might come with a free ride to Woody Wales' interrogation room.

After lunch, I parked the rental car under the Front Street Bridge and walked along the river. The path was crowded with walkers, runners, bikers, and dogs. The only ones who paid me any attention were the dogs, and I didn't think they'd rat me out to the authorities.

Almost every person who strolled, sped, or rolled past me on the path had ear phones in and stared resolutely at the ground or at a cell phone – except for one young woman who was wearing virtual reality goggles, waving her arms, and laughing. I have no idea what she was looking at. The president, the Pope, and a gaggle of A-list movie stars could have walked that path naked and not have been noticed.

While I had started out the day wishing that it was already 5:00 PM, I actually felt some regret when I realized it was time to get back to work. It was an extraordinary thing for me to enjoy an ordinary day.

I drove to Claire's, collected the supplies, and headed out to Railroad Street. The van from the shelter was parked on the shoulder, with the Wheelies already out on the tarmac. Two of them were jousting with the red-tipped white canes that the vehicle carried as spares for sight-impaired riders. The others lined the side of the road. The van driver was working the crowd and collecting bets on the outcome.

"Down he goes!" shouted the triumphant jouster as he scored a strike directly to his opponent's chest, tipping him and his chair over. He waved the broken cane around in triumph. The driver passed out cash to the winning bettors then went to help the toppled contestant, who waved her off with a cheerful, "Fuck off, Walker!"

He righted his chair, locked the wheels, pulled his legs up until his knees were tucked against his chest, placed his right arm onto the chair seat and his left against the ground and heaved, raising and turning his torso enough to slide back into the seat. He threw a glare in the driver's direction and a much longer, harder one at his opponent, who was still doing a victory dance in his chair.

I walked up to the driver and extended a hand. "Hey, Walker. I'm Adam Perdue. Thanks for helping to pull this together."

"Who you calling Walker, walker?" She shook my hand with a firm grip. "My name's Parks. Lisa Parks. George there calls everybody with working legs, 'Walker.' He cracks himself up."

"Pretty impressive move, getting back into the chair by himself."

"Yeah, these guys are athletes. You ever seen 'em play ball?" I shook my head. "You need to come out and watch sometime. They flat out compete. So, what have you got in mind for our afternoon entertainment? Hook just said to bring everyone here."

"You know the shelter just up the road, New Life Ministries?" She nodded. "Well, among their many sins, they don't take anyone who is physically disabled. The Wheelies are here to make a little noise about that. Would you mind giving me a hand with the signs?"

We walked to my car, where Hook leaned against the fender. He held a cigarette in his left hand. Taped to the metal prosthesis on his right arm was a sign scrawled in drippy red poster paint, "Crips are out for Blood!"

"Made that up myself. Probably get shit from the Thug Pride folks for appropriating gang names!"

Lisa and I grabbed more poster boards and paints and distributed them to the Wheelies, who got to work making protest signs that leaned heavily on four letter words and pictographs of genitalia.

The one female member of the Wheelies, Ellie, had a sign that read, "Fuck me! You know you wanna!" and featured a Kama Sutra style sketch of exactly how it might be accomplished.

We gathered into a tight circle, and I explained what I wanted.

"Why do you want to get in there, anyway?" The question came from the winning jouster, nicknamed "Galahad" because of his perfect record in street jousts.

"And why can't you just walk in. You got legs, don't ya'?" This was from Ellie. Everyone chuckled.

I remember reading once that Mark Twain said something along the lines of, "I try to always tell the truth. It's so much easier to keep my story straight." I follow his advice as much as possible. Besides, these folks were risking arrest and deserved to know why what they were doing mattered.

"Here's the short version. The people at that shelter are running a huge con and have killed at least two people that I know of, Gary Carson and Sam Watkins. Both homeless folks. Full disclosure: the police want me for the murder of Watkins. So, if anyone gets arrested, you don't know my name or why I paid you to protest. Otherwise, a public nuisance charge could turn into aiding and abetting a fugitive."

Lisa Parks spoke up. "Anybody who wants out, now's the time to say. We'll get in the bus and drive away."

"And you still get paid," I added.

No one spoke or moved. "I'm pretty sure they've killed one more person, Sean Ryan, and I know for damn sure that they plan to kill at least three more: Michelle Rathborn, Trent Argent and Ms. Sanderson from the vets' shelter. The point of your protest is to distract them so I can get in there to rescue those three and take down the bad guys and gals."

There was a lot of murmuring, and I heard a couple people mention "Herb" and "Sergeant Argent" with concern in their voices. Galahad spoke up. "Do you have to rescue Sanderson? Sure, Trent's a good guy, but..." There was awkward laughter in agreement. I decided to treat it as Wheelie wit, rather than a serious suggestion, though I took their point.

It was time to get the show underway. The sun had just hit the horizon, and dusk was the perfect time for what we had in mind. "Hook, can you go grab the toilet paper?" He nodded. "OK, I've got four sets of chains and padlocks. Who's up for chaining themselves to the fence?"

The protest outside of New Life Ministries' front gate started quietly. Five of the Wheelies rolled up to the entrance and blocked the gate, with their signs wedged between them and the arms of their chairs.

Lisa, Hook and three others paraded behind them letting off short bursts from air horns. The same guard who had been there when I first visited, Ned, came out of his box and waved at them amiably. He didn't go for either his radio or his phone.

As distractions go, it was underwhelming. I needed every guard in the place and as many staff as possible rushing to the front to check out what was going on while I tried to slip in through the fence at the back. Two of the Wheelies with chains wrapped around their waists moved up to the gate and padlocked themselves and their chairs so that the entrance couldn't be opened.

That got a reaction. Ned shouted at them and pulled out his radio, talking rapidly into it. He went back into his booth and came out with a pair of bolt cutters. He cut first one padlock and then the other. "Please don't obstruct the entry and exit to the property. It is a safety hazard." No one came running to help or observe. This was not going well at all.

I pulled out a fresh burner phone and dialed the "breaking news" number for WORM TV, Orman's local Fox affiliate. "There seems to be a disturbance at New Life Ministries out on Railroad Street." I waved at Hook, and he and Lisa let out some longer bursts with the air horns. The rest of the group started chanting, "NLM Deals Death to Disabled!"

"Yes, a group of people in wheelchairs are having a protest and the guard at the shelter is threatening them with some kind of weapon." I hung up. In fact, the guard had returned the bolt cutters to his shed and was leaning against the wall, scanning the crowd.

When he eyed Ellie's sign, he turned bright red. She saw it and started pantomiming oral sex, moving her open mouth up and down above her curled fingers and pushing out her cheek with her tongue.

I dialed 9-1-1. "Something's going on out at New Life Ministries on Railroad…" I caught Ellie's eye and gave her the thumbs up. She let out a blood-curdling scream.

"Get him off of me! Somebody help!" She added one more scream that trailed off into a gurgling moan. Someone was going to have to help that woman come out from her shell.

I cut off the 9-1-1 dispatcher in mid-sentence as she asked for my name.

The WORM studio was only half a mile away, while the nearest police station was a couple of miles. Barring a patrol car happening to be close by, I figured the TV folks would beat the cops to the scene. I needed to be far from the action by the time Orman's finest arrived.

Ned's continued lack of interest or attention was getting to me – and apparently to the Wheelies, too. They upped the volume of their chants, and re-chained themselves to the gate with new padlocks. He shrugged and came toward them with the bolt cutters.

"Hey, Screw!" Galahad waved at the guard, who paused. "You've got a delivery!" Galahad tossed something over the fence, and Ned instinctively dropped the bolt cutters and raised both arms to ward it off. It was Galahad's colostomy bag, and he had cut a slit into it before launching it toward the guard. It sailed in a beautiful arc and hit Ned's upraised hands.

Liquified feces spilled out of the bag and all over the guard's head and hands.

"You fucking son of a bitch!" He pulled out his radio and barked into it. Doors began to open in the buildings, and guards and staff rushed toward the gate. At the exact same time, a TV truck rounded the corner on Railroad Street and screeched to a halt in the intersection, just barely beating two patrol cars, with lights flashing and sirens blaring.

"Ready, aim, throw!" Gallahad shouted. A volley of toilet paper rolls flew over the fence, draping trees and roofs, and unrolling along the ground. A couple of the rolls just hit the ground and bounced without unraveling. "You've got to start the roll before throwing it, folks! C'mon, another volley!" The next fusillade flew over the fence, to the delight of the TV cameraman.

I slipped away with a final nod toward Hook, who lit up a cigarette and wandered away from the crowd. The Wheelies continued tossing rolls of toilet paper over the fence. I made my way around to the back of the property, where I hoped the hole I had cut was still there. It was. Staring at it, I asked myself what the hell I thought I was doing.

I had no real plan, no backup, and my last visit to NLM had not gone well at all. And then there was the heroin withdrawal. I was sweating, and when I held my hand out, tremors were clearly visible. The methadone tablet I had taken with breakfast didn't seem to be having any effect, and I wondered if resistance could develop that quickly.

Two loud booms sounded. Hook had set up fireworks tubes with Silver Salute mortars – the loudest ones available. By poking a hole in the base of a cigarette and threading the end of the fuse through, then lighting the cigarette, he had created timed fuses. He'd be in plain sight and far away by the time the cigarettes burned down and hit the fuses.

"You just gotta make sure and use proper cigarettes like 'Boros or Camels," he had explained. "Those natural, hippie brands will go out if you don't keep sucking on them. Real smokes burn nice and clean until they hit the filter – or a fuse!"

Two more booms shook the area. What the hell. I took the Methadone bottle out of my pocket, dry-swallowed another pill, and crawled through the fence.

I had no idea where Argent, Sanderson, and Rathborn were, but I did know where they weren't. I'd been able to peak in the windows of all the rooms in the block where I was held on my way out the last time. I made my way as quietly as possible to an exterior door on a wing of the building opposite the one where I had enjoyed Pastor Jan's hospitality.

I carried a knapsack with a crow bar, battery-powered multi-tool, two batteries, and an assortment of attachments: "the B&E package," as the clerk at Walmart had called it. The tools would probably get me through any barrier to entry, but they were heavy and awkward to haul around. They also could be quite loud when in use, though at that moment the noise being generated by the Wheelies could probably provide cover for a jackhammer and a truck engine with timing issues.

The door had a handle lock and a deadbolt, and both were engaged. I pulled out the angle grinder from my bag. I had already attached a wheel head onto it that the guy at Walmart had said would cut through anything other than some material called "Proteus." He assured me that I would only run into that if I wanted to break into a federal facility of some kind. NLM did not use Proteus for their door locks. It only took about thirty seconds to cut my way through.

The corridor had rooms on both sides, all with windowed doors and outside bolts. Some of the bolts were thrown and some weren't. Ms. Sanderson I would easily recognize, but I pulled up the photos of Trent Argent and Michelle Rathborn that Julia had texted to Walter's phone and gave them a long look before approaching the first window.

The bolt was open, and there was no one in the room. I went to the next one, again with an open bolt. There was a middle-aged man squirming on the bed, watching TV through squinting eyes. Not one of mine. Before moving on, I glanced at the television. It was showing hard core porn.

Better to first check only the rooms where the bolts were engaged. The first one I came to held Ms. Sanderson. She was tied to the bed as I had been and was staring at the ceiling. She must have caught movement in the window, because she turned her head and stared at me.

I don't think she could really see me, as the corridor was dark and her room was bright with fluorescent lighting. Just in case she could, though, I held up my index finger, indicating that she should wait. First found, last to be freed – as she would be on the way back out.

The next locked room held an elderly woman who seemed to be sleeping. She didn't appear to be restrained in any way. Not one of mine, but in the spirit of "Free Willy!" and "One Flew Over the Cuckoo's Nest," I quietly eased the bolt open and moved on. There was only one more bolted door. Inside, Trent Argent was tied to the bed. He was staring blankly at the empty wall opposite the bed. A string of drool reached from his beard to the pillow.

Great. He was zonked out on heroin, despair, or both. Presumably my arrival as rescuer would counteract the latter. For the former, I had the shot of Naloxone that Claire had given me.

I threw the bolt and opened the door. Trent didn't move a muscle. I cut his restraints and lifted an arm. It flopped back onto the bed. His head did turn a little and he might have been staring in my general direction. I lifted his arm again and pulled up the sleeve of his smock. Ugly needle marks pocked the inside of his elbow area. Using the bed sheet, I tied off his upper arm and gently slapped the inside of his forearm.

Claire had explained that the life-saving drug could be delivered intramuscularly or intravenously, but that the latter was faster and more effective. I slapped his arm a little harder and tightened the tourniquet until I saw a decent vein standing out.

My hand shook as I took the cap off the needle. Preparing Trent for an injection had given me a rush of adrenaline and anticipation, just like when they had prepped me for another dose of heroin.

I flashed back to one of those public service ads they used to run showing the horror of drug addiction with a big close up of a bruised and pockmarked arm tied off with a rubber cord and a scary needle about to pierce the skin. They may have been effective at keeping people who were scared of needles from trying heroin, but they also made every junkie or former junkie who saw them feel the same rush I was having at that moment. Smack porn.

I shook off the gnawing desire in my gut and poked at Trent's vein with the needle. Pulling back on the plunger slightly, I saw the rush of red into the syringe that indicated I had hit the target. I slowly injected the Naloxone.

I ran back down the corridor and burst into Ms. Sanderson's room. She looked confused by my sudden appearance but more or less clear-headed. I went to work on her restraints.

"When I get you loose, I need you to come help me with Trent, who doesn't look like he's going to be able to walk by himself. Then we're getting you both out of here. I assume you're OK with that plan." She nodded.

By the time we got to Trent's room, he was pretty much conscious.

"OK, Mr. Argent. There's no time for even a Reader's Digest version of the whole story, but we're here to rescue you. Is that OK with you?"

"Hell, yesss." He swung his legs over the side of the bed and hopped out. Unfortunately, his legs had continued swinging well past the vertical position, so he landed on the floor in a heap. He laughed. "That's gonna hurt in the morning!' he mumbled cheerfully.

With one of his arms around each of our necks, Sanderson and I walked him down the corridor. By the time we got to the door, he was mostly holding himself up. "Do you think you can handle him by yourself?" I asked Sanderson.

"If I have to," she replied in the hoarse voice of someone who hadn't spoken aloud in a while.

I opened the door and pointed through the darkness in the general direction of where the hole in the fence was. "There's a way through the fence there. Look for a plastic bag halfway up." I handed her a flashlight. "Try not to use it unless absolutely necessary. I think the guards should all still be engaged by the main gate, but I'm not sure."

Two more Silver Salutes went off, their flashes now visible in the night sky. Air horns rang out, and loud but unintelligible chanting could be heard in the distance.

"What the hell is that?" Sanderson asked as I slipped out from under Trent's arm and leaned him against her.

"The Wheelies are providing a distraction. Don't waste it. Get moving." I handed her a burner cell and a wad of cash. "Call a cab and get the hell out of here. My number is already in that phone. If you run into trouble, give me a call."

Walter's phone buzzed in my pocket. I glanced at it and saw a string of recent calls and texts from Claire. Whatever it was, it would have to wait.

"It would be a lot easier to handle him if you came as well."

"Sorry, you've got to manage. I still need to find Michelle Rathborn and get her out."

Sanderson gave me a long look, and it was obvious there was something she wanted to say to me. But she just sighed and nodded. I guess gratitude can be a tough emotion for some people to handle.

"Make sure Trent gets home." I gave her the address. "You might want to make yourself scarce. It isn't going to take the cops long to figure out who was recruiting folks from the vets' shelter for Pastor Jan's chop shop."

She did at least have the good grace to flush in embarrassment. "I didn't know what they were doing. Not at first. By the time I had an idea of what was really going on…."

"Tell it to the chaplain, Sanderson. Just get Trent home. I have other fish to fry."

Sanderson and Trent made their way off into the darkness and I turned back into the corridor. Facing me in the hallway was the old lady whose room I had unbolted, wearing nothing but a smile. The smile was coming from a set of dentures held in her upraised hand.

"Eyes up here, pervert!" She clicked the upper and lower half of her dentures together as she talked, like a ventriloquist manipulating a dummy's mouth. She stood in the middle of the hallway, blocking it.

I kept my gaze resolutely on the clicking teeth. "Uh, Ma'am, I'd love to talk with you, but I'm a little busy right now. Maybe you could go back in your room and we could continue this conversation later?"

"OK," she clicked. Then she turned and went back into her room, pulling the door closed behind her.

I slowly and quietly slid the bolt back into place. I was relieved but not too surprised by her compliance. One lesson I had learned while living on the street is that being polite and reasonable with people whose grip on reality was a bit tenuous often defused potentially volatile situations. Of course, it could also go exactly the opposite way.

I gave each room another glance and concluded that Michelle Rathborn wasn't in this wing. Of course not. That would have been too easy. I was just going to have to go room by room until I found her. Or until Pastor Jan and her goons found me.

Despite the withdrawal jitters, I was starting to feel just the littlest bit of confidence. I figured that I had more or less completed two of the four jobs I was being paid to do: Trent was on his way home to Gayle Forris, and I had solved the murder of Ellis Bell by proving that he wasn't murdered at all, even if Squire was being a stick in the mud about accepting it. Now, all that was left was to find Michelle Rathborn, recover some antiquities, and clear myself of Watkins' murder. Easy peasy.

When I got outside, it was quiet. Too quiet, as they say in the old cowboy movies just before a flaming arrow hits the side of a covered wagon. The demonstration must finally have broken up. I was going to have to make a lot less noise. There was one more wing to check, and I made my way to the door, hoping against hope that it would open. It didn't.

I'm not much good at picking locks, even after taking a few weeks' worth of lessons from a locksmith. If it's a simple lock and I have plenty of time and no pressure, I might get it open in ten or fifteen minutes. Given the way my hands were shaking, this one was going to take a lot longer than that.

An alarm bell sounded, so loud that it rocked me back on my heels. The old-fashioned red metal fire bell just above the door was clanging, and it was soon joined by other alarms from other parts of the complex.

I pulled out the angle grinder and went to work. Even standing right there, I could only barely hear it over the alarm bell. The locks cut easily and I slipped into the relative peace of another corridor lined with doors.

Emergency exit lights blinked above the door I had come in, and the one at the end of the hall. I saw the back of someone wearing pajamas disappear through the other door as I entered. Otherwise, the hallway was empty.

Weaving from one side to the next, I checked on the rooms. I came to one that was bolted and opened it. A man ran out and by me without a glance or a word. The rest of the rooms were empty. There was no sign of smoke or fire, and I wondered if the alarms had been set off because Trent's and Sanderson's escape had been discovered.

I cracked open the door that pajama man and the silent runner had gone through. Across a short courtyard, flames were crawling out of the window of what I recognized as Pastor Jan's office in the main part of the building.

As I eased the door closed, I heard the sound of running footsteps and turned just in time to see a flashlight coming down in an arc that ended abruptly at my forehead. The sound of the alarms receded as I hit the floor.

When I awoke, I was sitting in a chair with my arms tied behind me and my legs bound to the chair – with the zip ties that had been in my bag. Before I could really savor that irony, my attention was seized by Pastor Jan slapping me hard across the face.

"You are a very meddlesome and aggravating man! And a crazy one at that. Three times now you have come into my house meaning to do me harm. Trust me, this is not a case of 'Third time's a charm.'"

The zen master I sometimes aspire to be would have remained silent. The real and present Adam laughed maniacally. "Sister, your number is up. You're going down on multiple counts of kidnapping and murder."

"Being wanted for murder and actually 'going down for it' are two very different things, as you well know, Mr. Perdue. In an hour, I'll be far away from here inhabiting a new identity. You'll be found dead, victim of an overdose. It will be interesting to see if the police play it as accidental or suicide out of remorse for the murder of Watkins.

"Given the competence level of the COP, and the mayor's natural desire to sweep all this unpleasantness under the rug, they may even blame any and all unexplained deaths on you, not to mention the arson of my office."

How much did the police really have on Pastor Jan? Enough to hold her and find out more, but was that enough for them to decide not to just blame everything on me and close the books?

Squire wouldn't go for it, but it wouldn't be up to her. Bell would get to stay dead, and Pastor Jan would start all over somewhere new. Bravado continued to strut on my smiling face, but in my heart it was starting to stagger.

"While I consider myself second to none in the contempt in which I hold most of Orman's finest, they are not all as stupid and venal as you think."

"Your friend Squire? She's certainly due for a promotion when she ties this all up in a neat bow for a grateful mayor, maybe even to chief. You really think she values your friendship enough to throw all that away?"

With a start that caused my reeling bravado to steady itself, I realized that I actually did believe that our friendship – and a stubborn insistence on doing the right thing – meant much more to Squire than being chief of police.

"Even if she does, though, you won't be here to know it." She turned to the two goons at the door, shook the bottle of methadone pills that had been in my bag, and tossed it to Thug One. "It's time for Mr. Perdue to take his meds."

Thug Two grabbed my hair with one hand and my chin with the other, forcing my mouth open and tilting my head back. Thug One emptied the bottle into my mouth and poured a 32-ounce, unnaturally blue

Gatorade in behind it. I had no choice but to swallow. It was horrible.

I hate Gatorade.

Pastor Jan smiled, as I coughed and spluttered. "I looked it up on the internet. Taking 150 mg. of methadone at once is nearly certain to cause a fatal overdose in someone relatively new to opioid use, and you've just taken 21 pills at 10 mg. each. By my math, that equals... uh... dead detective! Quite ironic that you're to be killed with your own pills. And with an empty box of Narcan in your bag, to boot! Are you a fan of irony, Mr. Perdue?"

"More of a detached observer, really, than a fan *per se*." I used my very best William F. Buckley, Jr. impression so that intellectual superiority and boredom dripped off each word, positively oozing from the sibilant "*per se*" finish. I figured that I was going to be too sleepy for clever banter soon, not to mention dead shortly thereafter. I wasn't going to go out crying.

"I do rather admire your spirit, Mr. Perdue. But I have things to do, people to be – you know: busy, busy, busy!" She turned to the goons and pointed at one, then the other. "You, come with me. You, watch him until he passes out and then untie him and leave him on the floor, with his head near the bed frame where you smeared his blood. Rub his wrists and ankles with this." She tossed him a pocket-sized bottle of skin lotion. "We don't want any obvious signs that he was recently bound."

"Hey," Thug Two complained. "I got stuff to do, too. The fire department is gonna be here any minute."

"Don't worry, he'll be gone in a minute or two. I just don't want him making some last ditch effort to escape before going down."

I let my eyelids drop and nodded my head before straightening up with a jerk. I wasn't really feeling that sleepy, but I wanted to convince the goon that I was already nearly out. I repeated the nod and jerk as Jan and Thug One left the room. One more time with the nod, then I kept my chin on my chest. I snored lightly. Thug Two was pacing and staring at me. The faraway sound of sirens could be heard over the alarm bells.

"Fuck this!" Thug Two cut the zip ties and shoved me roughly out of the chair in the direction of the bed. I landed like a sack of flour and my head bounced on the floor right where the flashlight had dented it. I managed no reaction other than a brief interruption of my snoring.

"Fucking stupid babysitter is what I am," he muttered as he rubbed my wrists and ankles with lotion. It felt nice. The floor felt nice. Everything felt nice. But I was still conscious, and Thug Two was leaving the room.

I didn't think I had much of a chance of escaping, but maybe I could make a call to 9-1-1 before passing out and they could rescue me with Narcan. I heard Thug Two's footsteps receding down the hallway, and rolled to my feet – rather elegantly. I really did feel the best I had since escaping from Pastor Jan the last time, and not all that sleepy. They had left my bag, and I retrieved

Walter's phone. Time to call 9-1-1 and hope there were some EMTs nearby with Narcan. The missed calls and texts and a new voice message from Claire blinked at me.

It would be nice to hear Claire's voice again. Vaguely aware that I had grabbed the phone for some other reason that was really important, I played Claire's message.

"Adam, we have a problem. The client who sold me the methadone told me today that most of the pills are fakes. He only had three or four left so he got some fakes from a friend to fill the bottle. The good news is they aren't fentanyl or anything else that could be deadly. The bad news is he thinks they were pressed from laxative powder. So, you may not get the relief from withdrawal that you were looking for, but you're going to be extremely regular. Come by when you get a chance, and I'll replace them with the real thing."

Claire's client had ripped us off – and saved my life by doing it! When I stopped laughing, I still felt as good as I had in weeks. The few real methadone pills were doing their job. I tried to ignore the ominous rumbling coming from my stomach.

I emptied everything from the knapsack except for the duct tape and zip ties. When I left the room, I realized that I was in the main part of the building, the part that was on fire. Black smoke ran along the ceiling, and there were flames licking at the walls down at the end where Pastor Jan's office was. Not sure whether I was looking for Michelle Rathborn, Ellis Bell's antiquities, Pastor Jan, a way out, or a toilet, I paused in indecision. Instinct took over, and I ran toward the fire.

I have great instincts.

In this part of the building, the rooms were all outfitted as offices or examination rooms. I passed by the tattoo removal studio and a second dental surgery. It was starting to feel hot, and I moved in a crouch as the smoke began to get lower. The next room I looked in revealed Ellis Bell, struggling to get a large roller suitcase zipped shut. With only one hand, he wasn't having much luck.

"Need some help with that?" When Bell saw me, his look of frustration turned to one of rage.

"You! You are supposed to be dead – again! "

"Look who's talking. Bet you're having second thoughts about lending a hand to the police investigation. Am I right?" I was still in a crouch to avoid the smoke, and standing still in a squatting position was sending the wrong message to my laxative-overdosed bowels. Thankfully, I hadn't eaten anything since lunch many hours before, so there wasn't much grist for the mill to work with.

Bell thrust his good hand into the suitcase and came out with a gun. I moved quickly toward him and kicked him in the groin as he frantically pulled the trigger without results, growing increasing frustrated, like a contestant on a quiz show who knows all the questions but can't get their clicker to ring in first.

When the message I had sent got from his balls to his brain, he crumpled over and the gun fell to the floor. It's a well-known medical fact that while a man's brain is incapable of sending messages to his balls, it does work the other way around.

"Not familiar with handguns, Ellis? That might be the first nice thing I've learned about you. There's this little lever here, called a 'safety.' You need to slide it to off before the gun will fire. Of course, it's hard to do with only one hand." I pocketed his gun and threw open the suitcase. Clothes, toiletries, shoes – a ridiculous number of shoes, really – and antiquities.

"Well, well, well, what do we have here? Besides a touching tribute to Imelda Marcos' love of footwear, I mean?" There were dark stone statuettes, delicately-carved marble friezes, a gold vase, jewelry boxes, and several long plastic rectangles that I knew from my childhood collecting days were used to store coins. No sword, though. That was the only item that David had mentioned specifically, and it would be a shame not to retrieve it.

I took the duct tape out of my bag and wrapped Bell's elbows and knees together. "So, where's the sword, Ellis?"

"You can't tie me up! We have to get out of here!"

"Take it easy. Where's the fire? Oh, yeah – right down the hall! Well, Ellis, here's the thing. If I've got to go searching for the sword, I need to have you tied up. Now, if I had the sword, I could untie you and we could both get out of here. What do you say?"

"In the ski case, you psycho! It's in the ski case." He nodded his head at a corner of the room where one of those long hard cases that people use to ship their skis was leaning against the wall.

I checked it out. Along with skis, poles, and assorted other cold weather sporting accessories was a long velvet bag cinched at the top with a drawstring. I pried it open and pulled the sword out like young Arthur drawing Excalibur from the stone.

The glory of that imagery was spoiled somewhat by the fact that I was still squatting and just as I raised the silver-handled, two-pointed sword above my head, a loud, wet fart thundered from my butt. Not like a sharp clap of thunder, though. More like one of those long, low, rumbling peals that grows in intensity to a climax and then sputters out in a series of fading crackles.

"Jesus, man! What the hell was that?" My burst of majestic flatulence had caused Bell to momentarily forget his predicament.

I'm not tooting my own horn when I say that it was truly a fart for the ages. From somewhere in the great beyond, Joseph Pujol, Le Petomane – the world's most renowned practitioner of the flatulent arts – was looking down on me with pride. Somewhere else in that great beyond, hopefully far away from Le Petomane, my wife was shaking her head and suppressing a smile.

I was roused from this methadone and laxative induced reverie by the sound of loud voices and the smashing of windows. The fire department had arrived.

"You'll be fine, now, Ellis. The good people of the OFD will pull what's left of your chestnuts from the fire. Bye, bye!" I put the sword back in the ski case, zipped the other suitcase closed and headed for the door at the opposite end of the hallway from where the sounds of the fire fighters were coming, walking quickly with my rolling bags like a vacationer in the airport who was late for the flight to Aspen. I wondered if Bell and I had the same size feet. With his beautiful shoe collection, I would be the hit of any après ski scene for sure.

Keeping the building between me and the fire trucks, I made my way to the hole in the fence and rolled Ellis' bags to where I had stashed the rental car. I drove to a nearby Dunkin' Donuts that I knew would have Wi-Fi. I really wanted to grab a cup of coffee and some munchkins, but I was afraid of what would happen if my digestive tract had anything other than air in it to expel.

I stayed in the parking lot and got Alex's laptop setup from under the seat. I plugged my phone in. When the search box appeared, I entered the address of the COP headquarters and set it to take my phone on a rambling walk around it.

Stakeouts can be incredibly boring, and I imagine that monitoring phone calls from a desk makes a stakeout look like a Disney ride of fun and adventure. If anyone was still tracking me, at least my apparent proximity to my pursuers would provide a little excitement.

The first call was to Claire, to let her know that her miscreant client might have actually saved my life, and that I was sending her a referral. No answer. I left a message. The next was to Gayle Forris.

She was delighted to have Trent back and let me know that my description on the current police alert had been modified from "armed and dangerous suspect" to "material witness." Apparently, my status in the criminal world had taken a pretty big hit.

"By the way, I resent that you tipped WORM to your NLM demonstration instead of me."

"You're a serious journalist. I thought it was more up their alley. Were there any arrests, do you know?"

"I understand one man was initially cuffed and charged with assault and battery, but it turned out that the victim wasn't interested in testifying about his close encounter with a colostomy bag. It was all sorted out before the COP was able to come up with an accessible van to take the perpetrator in. The victim seemed quite eager to leave the scene, anyway. Perhaps he a had a prior commitment."

"Or had committed some priors.... What was the deal with the fire, anyway. That wasn't the Wheelies, was it?"

"The who – oh, your friends in the wheelchairs. No. That apparently was set in the office of Pastor Jan by person or persons unknown. There was a lot of damage and one of the shelter clients was burned quite badly, but her injuries are not considered life-threatening.

"Apparently, the fire fighters found Ellis Bell wrapped up in duct tape. I believe he is in police custody now, charged with fraud and embezzlement, with 'additional charges expected to follow,' as they say. You've had quite a busy day, especially for someone who had not appeared to be doing anything on my case for the last two weeks."

"It's like painting a room. All the time goes into preparation: scraping, filling, sanding, and taping. The actual painting part is relatively quick."

"From my experience, the clean-up can also be quite time-consuming."

"Yes, that's true. I have a few more calls to make, but I wanted to make sure Trent had gotten home. I entrusted him to a rather untrustworthy person – but I didn't have a choice at the time."

"Ms. Sanderson, his colleague at the shelter. She delivered him safe and sound and seemed to be in a great hurry to leave. Trent's okay, but very tired. We talked for a bit, but he kept nodding off."

"Uh, I'm sure he'll get around to telling you about his treatment at NLM himself, but having received similar hospitality for a shorter period of time, I think you need to know that he's probably been given quite a lot of drugs and may experience some symptoms of withdrawal. You will want to find him somewhere where he can get help. I'm going to text you my friend Claire's number. She should be able to recommend a good place."

"He already told me about the drugs, Mr. Perdue, and about a lot of other stuff that is going to give me nightmares. I appreciate your concern, however, and look forward to talking with Claire."

"OK, that's it for now, I guess. Once the dust settles a bit, I'll get you an exclusive with David Levant on the stolen antiquities. That should make up for missing out on the demo."

"Indeed, Mr. Perdue. That would more than make up for it. Goodbye."

It didn't seem like I needed extraordinary security measures any longer, so I disconnected the phone from the laptop and texted Claire's number to Gayle. My phone buzzed, and the screen showed that I had received a text from an unknown caller. The text read: "Take a close look at Mike Romeo."

I puzzled over the cryptic text as I drove to my office. There were few people who had the number of this particular cell, and even fewer with any reason to shield their identity. By the time I had arrived, I hadn't made much progress.

As I had hoped, I got a two-fer. Squire was there with Julia. "I don't care how much you hang out here, Squire, I'm not putting you on the payroll. I understand I am no longer a wanted man?"

Squire laughed. "As if you were ever wanted, Perdue." Julia punched her in the shoulder, hard. "Damn girl, you're stronger than you look."

Julia gave her a "there's more where that came from" look and turned to me. "Ignore her, Adam. I have been worried sick about you – and then we heard there was a fire at New Life Ministries. Are you OK?"

"I'm fine, Julia. And take it easy on Squire. She may look like she can take a beatin' and keep on bleatin,' but she's really quite the fragile flower.

"Squire, I heard that Bell was taken into custody, but what about Pastor Jan?"

"Disappeared. She was at NLM when the fire department arrived, but no one has seen her since. A couple of her security guys have outstanding warrants, and they're being questioned."

"Please tell me Woody is doing the interrogation?"

"Yep!"

"I hope he keeps asking them what happened to Gary Carson's hands. One of the guys you caught either did the hit or knows who did. I'm guessing that they don't know much about where Pastor Jan may have gotten to, though. She probably already has another identity set up in some other town that she can slip right into. Were you able to find out anything more about her, Julia?"

"I've tracked her back to her original identity, Laura Walker. She was busted for selling drugs at her Ivy League college and disappeared while out on bail, never to be heard from again. Interesting stuff, but nothing that's likely to help find her now. Where do we stand on our other cases, anyway? I want to send out some invoices!"

I gave her and Squire the rundown on Trent Argent. "You can send a final invoice to David Levant, too. With

Bell located, it'll be your job to find his money and the antiquities, Squire."

"Funny thing about that, Perdue. Bell claims that you took the artifacts from him and left him to die in the fire. I assured him that we were tracking your cell phone and you were a hundred miles away in Lincoln at that time. That was right about when his lawyer showed up and he stopped talking. I expect that the stuff he stole will find its way back to the feds, right?"

"Uh, yeah. I'm sure it will. I think Levant was making a deal to buy them from him. I'm sure his plan is to turn them over to the feds so they can be returned to their rightful owners overseas."

"I hope so. Then we could make a note in the file that Bell was just telling a crazy story to try and deflect blame."

"That's three out of four cases closed. Not bad. What happened to the clients at NLM after the fire, Squire?"

"There was one client who received burns on her arms and chest and a couple of cases of smoke inhalation. They're in the hospital. The rest were taken to other shelters if they wanted, or just walked away."

"Tell him the best part, Danny!" I had never heard anyone call Squire by her full first name of Danielle before, let alone Danny. I'm pretty sure her mother calls her Squire.

"The woman who was burned was the other person you were looking for, Michelle Rathborn."

"Make that four out of four. Pretty fine detecting, even if I do say so myself."

Squire snorted. "Eh, in fairness you can't really claim Rathborn. You didn't find her, the hose boys did."

"Well, let's call it three-and-a-half, then." I was glad to hear that Michelle had been located and a little disappointed that I hadn't been the one to find her. Belatedly, I also felt bad about her getting burned in the fire.

"How did Rathborn get caught up in the fire, Squire? As far as I could tell, clients weren't allowed in that part of the complex."

"No idea. She hasn't really been questioned yet. Her uncle has been down to see her, and while she has some nasty burns and a wicked sore throat from smoke inhalation, she's expected to recover. Hey, she's the heir to the Quickie Buy fortune. I imagine that money goes a long way in making the recovery process bearable."

She couldn't have been more wrong. I had received a ton of insurance money after Sarah and Elise died in the car accident, and it didn't help me recover at all.

Squire knew enough about my past to know that she had accidentally sent my mind down a bad path, and so she moved on quickly.

"Anyway, she's not really a police matter – unless she wants to press some kind of charges against Pastor Jan. Not that there is any shortage of those."

"Oh, Adam, I forgot to tell you the other good news!" Julia looked excited. "That ugly wreck of yours was recovered outside of Lincoln, and Danny had it towed back to your parking garage."

Old Yeller was back in her nursing home. Maybe all was going to be right with the world.

There was a knock at the outer door. Julia scooped up DK from his cat bed next to her desk, dropped him in my office and pulled the door firmly shut. When she answered the outer door, the sweet smell of Lee Fong's Szechuan filled the office.

Julia handed the delivery man some cash and brought two plastic bags over to her desk. "Sorry, Adam. We didn't know you were coming. Do you want me to call them back and get something for you?"

Yowling sounds started coming from my office. DK had smelled the food, too.

"Hey, there's always a ton. You can share with us." Squire definitely was feeling guilty about the "money helping recovery" remark. There were never any leftovers from Lee Fong's.

Clawing and scratching sounds came from behind my door and then what sounded like a furry body hurling itself desperately at the barrier.

"No, I – uh – I'm not really hungry." That was a lie. I was starving, and it took great force of will to not rip the bag open and tuck into that fragrant sweet and sour pork. While the influence of the methadone seemed to have waned, my intestines were still begging for something, anything, they could churn into a fiery discharge.

"I've got to drop by David Levant's anyway. Don't forget to invoice the COP, Julia – today counts as a full day."

Squire shrugged. "Seems reasonable." The combination of Julia and Lee Fong's food made Squire almost as amiable as when she had pie.

Old Yeller seemed none the worse for wear, and the drive to the Levant Foundation gave me a chance to reflect on Gayle's observation that cleanup was as hard as preparation. I had a lot of reports to write. Julia could send out invoices for my daily rate, but I had to provide some narrative to justify it and detail my expenses. I wondered who I could plausibly expense the air horns and toilet paper to?

Then there was Maria. I needed to return her hide-and-seek phone setup and then escort her to the Founders' Ball. And Claire expected me to start doing sessions with her. The great thing about crisis and chaos is that they allow you to postpone living the parts of your life that you're more comfortable ignoring.

Levant's receptionist told me that he was currently in a meeting. I insisted to her that he would want to be interrupted, and she used the speakerphone to inform David I was there. "Does he have anything with him?" he asked with more excitement in his voice than I had ever heard before.

"He looks like he's going skiing." That got a long pause.

"Send him in."

Levant was standing on a step stool in the middle of his office, and a tailor was chalking the cuffs of his tuxedo pants. He raised his eyebrows at my baggage. "You do look like you're going skiing."

I opened the large suitcase and started removing the items one by one and placing them on the coffee table. He jumped off the stool, knelt on the carpet, and picked up each as I put it down to inspect it. "Oh, my! Exquisite! How unusual!"

The tailor scribbled some notes and waited patiently. When I stopped placing items on the table, Levant looked at the suitcase in disappointment.

"Nice shoes, but I don't see the sword."

"Too long to fit in the suitcase." I unzipped the ski case and pulled out the velvet bag. He took it from me, loosened the top, and peeked inside. He took the handle and turned it around in his hands. He slowly drew it out and placed it carefully on the edge of the table. He looked up and down it with a reverence that he hadn't shown for the other items.

"Remarkable. I have no idea if it is what it is purported to be, but it is beautifully crafted and unlike any other sword I have ever seen."

"What is it purported to be, again?"

"Bell was selling it as the sword of the Prophet, Peace Be Upon Him."

"Mohammed?"

"Yes, and Ali after him. Before them, the blade, with a different handle, was said to belong to Ibrahim – whom you call Abraham. It was the sword he held to his son

Isak's throat – the sacrifice he was willing to make to God.

"At the very beginning of everything, it was gifted to Adam by the angel Gabril when he and Eve were banished from the Garden.

"For Shia Muslims, it is the Holy Grail and Excalibur all rolled into one. It is prophesied that it will be wielded by the Mahdi, a messianic figure who will arise before the end times and lead Muslims to conquer the world. The sword is called Zulfiqar."

"Meaning no disrespect, David, but that's a lot of mojo for one sword."

"Indeed it is, Adam." He laughed upon saying my name. "It has come full circle, from the first Adam to you!"

"And now, to you. Officially speaking, it would be better if I never had possession of these things, if you don't mind. Perhaps you can say you purchased them from an anonymous seller?" He nodded, lost in thought.

"How would you even authenticate something like that, David?"

"You can't really. The handle could be dated to the time of Muhammed, Peace Be Upon Him, and Ali, perhaps. But the chain of custody was broken in the 7th century, after Ali's death. There are many stories of where it went and contradictory depictions of it. Most show it with two points, like this one, but others with only one.

"The problem is that it doesn't matter whether it is real or not. If people believe it to be real, then the person who wields it will have great power over Shias, and many Sunnis, as well. Having it here in front of me, I confess to feeling like the dog who catches the car: I have no idea what to do with it."

"Just give it to the feds with the rest of the stuff. That's what you plan to do, right? Get them all back to the museums from where they were looted?"

"Yes, but I can assure you that this sword is not in any museum's official inventory. I'm not sure where it would be returned to."

"Maybe it'll end up next to the Arc of the Covenant in some vast warehouse, like in the Indiana Jones movie."

"It would be comforting to think that such powerful objects can be safely lost in the bowels of bureaucracy, but I don't know...."

"Well, that's way above my pay grade. As long as most of this stuff gets to the feds, my ass is covered. I leave the rest to you. Hey, what's the monkey suit for, anyway?"

He looked down and remembered he was having a tuxedo tailored. "I am so sorry, Ahmed Jan, I had completely forgotten!" He placed the sword in its bag and hopped back onto the stool. The tailor continued his work as if it had never been interrupted.

"My wife insisted I wear a new tuxedo to the Founders Ball next week. I have several that fit me perfectly, but she wants me in this one."

"So, it's formal, this ball?"

"Very much so." He saw the look on my face. "Are you going?"

"Yes, I owe a favor or three to Maria Santos and she chose to claim one by having me escort her to the ball."

"Well, you will be the envy of many there with Maria on your arm. Do you have a tux?" I shook my head. "We're about the same size." He jumped down off the stool again, walked to one of the closets, and came out with a tuxedo in a plastic dry-cleaning bag. Of course, David Levant would have a tuxedo in his office... in case a formal emergency arose.

"Put this on. Ahmed Jan can make any necessary adjustments. I will turn my back as you undress."

I have tried saying "No" to David Levant before, without success, so I didn't argue. I stripped off my clothes, which honestly were rather ripe. I stood with his tuxedo on, the jacket of which fit perfectly. The pants were good at the waist but just a little long.

"OK, you need to wear shoes for him to get the cuffs right – but not those nasty things. Let me see…" he pulled a pair of black brogues from Bell's collection and held them out. I pulled them on. Damned if he and I didn't wear the same size. I would never need to buy shoes again.

"Up!" he indicated the stool, and I took his place on it. It only took a minute for the tailor to do his thing with the chalk. Levant changed places with me, and I got redressed.

"Ahmed Jan will take care of the cuffs, and I will have the suit sent to your office in plenty of time for the ball. I look forward to seeing you there, Adam."

"Yeah, me too." If my lack of enthusiasm was obvious, he didn't acknowledge it. He started talking to the tailor in Arabic, Farsi or some other language I didn't understand.

Apparently, I was dismissed.

From Levant's office, I headed downtown to find Captain Hook. He was relaxing on a folding beach chair in the alley behind the vets' shelter.

"Hey, it's the private eye formerly known as Orman's Most Wanted!"

I tossed him an unopened pack of cigarettes with a disposable lighter rubber banded to it. "In the flesh. I wanted to stop by and thank you for pulling off our little distraction outside New Life the other day. And to see if you needed any more cash for the Wheelies."

He caught the cigarettes and opened them up. "It was my pleasure. All the excitement and intensity of battle without the killing and dying. Not a fan of that part. But sneaking around in the dark and making things go bang? That's a rare joy. And the Wheelies are fine. I think they'd pay *me* to do that again!"

"Hey, I got one more loose end I'm trying to tie up. You ever hear of somebody named Mike Romeo?"

"Heard of more than one. That would be the call sign of anyone with the initials MR, if you were talkin' on the squawk box. It's the NATO alphabet."

He sucked on his cigarette nervously. "Matter of fact, they're my initials. If we were on voice coms, I'd identify myself as 'Mike Romeo,' and you'd be 'Alpha Papa' – which is a pretty cool handle."

Why would anyone be warning me about Captain Hook? And who would know his real name? "Well, right now I'd have to call you 'Charlie Hotel' then, since I don't know your real name."

"I thought you were the luckiest or the smartest detective ever and had figured it out, asking about Mike Romeo. Real name is Mitchell Reardon. You use it or tell anyone, though, we're done. Mitch has done some shit that I don't need sticking to the bottom of my shoe. You just keep calling me Hook."

"OK, Hook. Help me out, though. Why would someone text me with a warning to look into Mike Romeo?"

"No idea. If they were pointing you to me, they'd have to know my name. That would mean the police, folks at the VA, maybe some shelter staff. But that would depend on you knowing my name, which you didn't. Doesn't make sense, really. You know any other people with the initials MR?"

When Hook mentioned shelter staff who would know his name, I immediately thought of Sanderson. And she would have had my burner cell number. When he asked if I knew anyone else with those initials, my coin finally dropped.

"Luckiest," I muttered.

"What?"

"Luckiest detective, not the smartest."

Orman's downtown area is almost completely deserted by midnight, and it was quiet under the River Street Bridge. I could hear the gurgle of the river that would have been drowned out during the day by the rumble of cars and trucks passing overhead.

Claire had gotten me some real methadone, and one a day was doing just what she promised: keeping me even. Soon, I'd cut it to once every two days, then three, and hopefully after that I could cope on my own.

Headlights swooped through the parking lot and went out. Squire descended the steps and joined me. Our regular running route was north along the jogging path on the east side of the river up to the Florence Avenue bridge, then back down the west side of the river and across the River Street Bridge. It was almost exactly five kilometers.

She took out her police radio and called in a "BCR" with our location. BCR stands for Black Cop Running. Even a respected police lieutenant, soon to be deputy chief, becomes just another "suspicious character" to the concerned citizens living in the riverfront condos, who see only a black face in sweats and a hoodie.

We started jogging. "That shit must get old for you."

"What? Oh, the Black Cop Running? Not really. It's like fastening my safety belt in the car. It's just something I do to increase my chances of survival while doing a routine activity."

"Really, you don't resent it?" We started to pick up the pace.

"Sure, when I think about it. Just like I resent the fact that if I vote for Ron Wiggins for City Council, I'm a race traitor, an Aunt Jemima, an Oreo – not to mention a self-loathing gay woman. But if *you* vote for Ron Wiggins, you're just a dumb ass.

"I guess it would be nice sometimes to just be a dumb ass. There's a long list of things about being black, lesbian, and a cop that I'd have to spend time resenting, if I thought about them. I just don't have the bandwidth to spare. C'mon junkie, let's see if you can still run." She picked up the pace and I matched her.

"You voted for Ron Wiggins?" I asked, incredulous.

"That corrupt cracker? Of course not. I'm not a dumb ass."

We did the first 5k in under 15 minutes and the second in 30. I begged off a third and sat under the bridge catching my breath while Squire did another lap in less than 20 minutes. Apparently, I had been holding her back.

She jogged up to her car and came back with a couple of beers.

"You didn't suggest a midnight run just for the exercise, Adam. What's on your mind?"

"Well, it's a delicate matter that I thought was better for us to discuss alone."

"This isn't about Julia, is it?"

"No. It's about Michelle Rathborn." I told her what I was thinking and how I thought it should be handled. She asked a few questions, made a few suggestions, and we had a plan.

"OK, now it's about Julia. You know that I'll have to kick your ass if you break her heart, right?"

She snorted. "Like you could." She took a long drink from her beer. "What if she breaks mine?"

It was all over but the shouting. There was plenty of that at the Rathborn family settlement conference. I had talked Albert, aka Uncle Unctuous, into letting me attend. None of the next generation of Rathborns seemed happy to see me, even when I placed a tray of Quickie Buy Slurries in the middle of the conference table. The frozen drinks come in a variety of flavors and fluorescent colors not found in nature. But they sure are refreshing on a hot day. Everyone ignored them – and me.

Michelle Rathborn still had bandages on her face and arms, and she left the talking to her lawyer, Stanley Montrose. Stanley suffers from a severe case of resting scowly face. So naturally, everyone refers to him as "Smiley." He has an office in my building, which means he isn't the kind of shyster you expect to be negotiating multi-million-dollar probate matters. Personal injury and DUIs are more up his alley.

Michelle's siblings had a team of attorneys, two at the table and three in chairs behind whose main job seemed to be handing the Big Two papers that they didn't glance at. Smiley's opening position was that Michelle was only there out of courtesy, that their father's will was very clear that she was to inherit a controlling interest in the Quickie Buy empire, and that she would fight any effort to challenge the will.

The siblings' attorneys pointed out that they could tie up probate for years while challenging the validity of the will. No one would receive any money, and control of Quickie Buy would remain with the executor of the estate. That prospect made Uncle Al turn a paler shade of gray and become even more committed to mediating a solution.

"Michelle, do you really, truly want to run Quickie Buy?"

She touched Smiley's arm, and he spoke. "Her father wanted her to."

Albert Rathborn sighed, as the two sides started arguing with each other again. The conversation wasn't the only thing that was getting heated. The room was becoming uncomfortably hot. Smiley took off his jacket and hung it on the back of his chair. The sibs' lawyers kept their jackets on, but they were starting to sweat.

Uncle Al was the first to reach for a Slurrie. Then Smiley. When Michelle touched his arm again, he got one for her. Then the two sibs' lawyers at the table grabbed one each. They didn't offer to hand any back to their colleagues. There was a short break in the bickering in which the only sound that could be heard was the slurping of icy sugar water through straws.

After a few more rounds of verbal jabs punctuated by Al Rathborn interventions, an agreement was reached. The siblings would not contest the will, and Michelle Rathborn would turn over her shares in Quickie Buy to her siblings, in exchange for a one-time payment. The market value of her shares that morning was about $4.2 million, but the siblings refused to budge on their offer of $3 million. Smiley pointed out that news of a settlement would push the stock higher than its current value, but as a gesture of good will, Michelle was willing to settle for $4 million.

Both sides pretended to dig in, but it was obvious to me that everyone was relieved to have a settlement in sight. Uncle Al came to the rescue again with a compromise offer – Michelle would get $3.5 million, and the Quickie Buy Corporation would donate another $500,000 to the Orman Community Foundation in Michelle's name, earmarked for homeless services.

The siblings and Michelle were happy with that arrangement. It definitely looked good to Smiley, who would reap a six-figure payout for a few hours work. The siblings' lawyers were watching hundreds, maybe thousands, of billable hours fighting the will go up in smoke, but Quickie Buy was a large client so whatever made its owners happy made them happy, too. And everyone was eager to get out of the sweltering conference room.

The lawyers gathered up their papers, and everyone departed with handshakes all around – except for Michelle, of course, who held her bandaged arms at her side and nodded. I hung back and collected up the mostly-empty Slurries.

"Just leave those, Mr. Perdue."

"Oh, I don't mind, Mr. Rathborn. I brought them in, and I like to leave the campsite cleaner than I found it.

Thanks for letting me attend. I like to see cases all the way through."

"Of course! We'll all be glad to put this behind us." Uncle Al seemed quite pleased with the results of the meeting.

I trailed him out of the conference room, holding the tray of Slurries in one hand. In the hallway, I paused for a moment, made sure he wasn't looking, and turned the thermostat back to the "Auto" setting. I may have accidentally put it on "emergency heat" and turned the temperature to 88 on my way in.

"Uh, I need to use the rest room – and there should be a trashcan in there for these."

Uncle Unctuous gave a friendly wave over his shoulder and kept on walking.

In the bathroom, I removed Ziplock bags, a surgical glove, and a pair of scissors from my pocket. The bags already had the names of the various Rathborns on them. I snipped the straw ends with the scissors and put them into the appropriate bags and pocketed them. Then I dumped the rest of the mess into a trash can.

The week before the Founders' Ball went by in a blur of paperwork and reestablished routine. It was obvious that Julia missed Squire's frequent visits to our office, but I enjoyed having just the two of us there, doing busy work and tying up loose ends. They met for lunch on most days, and they would get plenty of time together at the ball. The newly promoted Deputy Chief for

Community Relations apparently was expected to hob nob with Orman's elite at such events, and Julia was her "plus one."

A lot of pieces fell into place, once the police decided to really investigate NLM and Pastor Jan. Special dogs were brought to the site and the body of Sean Ryan was discovered buried in a corner of the property. The fake Ryan in Montana had apparently been tipped off by Pastor Jan and had escaped with his life and freedom, but without the new identity he had paid for. Any records that might have been kept of his actual identity were lost in the fire.

The dogs found another site where the CSI folks were pretty sure one or more bodies had been buried and then moved. The working assumption was that Ryan's body had been buried there first and then moved for some unknown reason. I had a different theory.

Nothing turned up on Darren Stevens, the man whose dental work and tattoos I had acquired during my stay at NLM. Julia had searched every database she could find and had narrowed down the field to just over a thousand individuals of roughly the right age and appearance with variations of that name. I had only heard his first name spoken by Dr. Bayram and never seen it in writing. There are six common ways to spell "Darren." Of course, it also could have been a pseudonym.

There was no trace of Bayram. Squire informed me that the consensus opinion among the various agencies involved in untangling the NLM mess was that he was just a heroin and nitrous oxide fueled figment of my imagination.

They acknowledged that there must have been a dentist involved, but the idea that he was Saddam Hussein's personal dentist was just too implausible for them to accept. Julia had not been able to find any references to a Dr. Bayram in Hussein's orbit, but most of the good source material was in Arabic, so she couldn't dig very deep. I didn't doubt that he had found a way to live to drill another day.

David Levant had turned over the artifacts to the feds, most of them anyway. Gayle Forris' article about the looted antiquities got picked up by the wire services and was read around the world. There were photos of the items in David's office, interviews with him, statements from the FBI and the State Department, and messages of thanks from the Iraqi and Afghan Ministries of culture. None of the photos featured the sword, and it was not mentioned in the article at all.

Ellis Bell was awaiting trial for fraud, embezzlement, and accessory to murder. No charges had been brought on the antiquities, as they couldn't be linked directly to him without acknowledging that I had stolen them from him and left him trussed up like a Thanksgiving turkey at the scene of an arson.

Bell was fishing for a plea deal, dangling the funds stolen from the Levant Foundation as bait. As far as I was concerned, if he returned the foundation's money, lopping off his own hand paid his debt for the fraud and embezzlement. But his part in Gary Carson's murder called for a long stretch in prison. He may not have done the deed, but he knew it was being done for his benefit.

News of the settlement between the Rathborns was made public and Quickie Buy shares rose by 10%, making the deal seem even better to Michelle's siblings. It would take a couple of weeks to complete probate, and then the matter would be closed.

As for Pastor Jan, she had vanished without a trace. While I didn't expect it to lead to her present identity or whereabouts, curiosity demanded that I dig a little deeper into her birth identity as Laura Walker.

Searching on the web, I easily found high school yearbook photos from Framingham High School in Massachusetts and a few mentions of her at Mt. Holyoke College. She was just old enough that social media wasn't around to document her every interest and entanglement.

The internet has made the job of detective a whole lot easier. Information that used to require shoe leather, endless interviews, and borderline illegality is now available to anyone with a decent broadband connection. Youthful indiscretions that were forgotten for people of previous generations achieve digital immortality for children of the 21st century.

Tech mercenaries aren't content with compiling information from the present and the future, though. To properly monetize individuals' information, it's necessary to reach back into the Dark Ages before the reign of the Titan Facebook and of the new gods that would eventually topple it. Free services to help one "reconnect" with past colleagues, classmates, or crushes required only one's social security number, date of birth, school information, or some other personal details.

Since I had all that for Laura Walker, I was able to enroll her in alumni groups, find old class lists, and search student newspapers that had been archived online. There wasn't much of interest from Framingham High School, but Mt. Holyoke offered a few tidbits.

Colleges never like to lose an alumnus who might be good for a donation – even if they had dropped out or been kicked out. Laura Walker's name appeared every year on the alumnae site under the "Has Anyone Heard From…" list of former students who the development department had not been able to find and solicit.

There were half a dozen comments about her in the section for students to share "news" about their classmates, none more recent than ten years ago, and all asking the same question: has anyone heard from her?

I read through the Mount Holyoke News, "proudly produced by Holyoke students since 1917," for every year she was there. The scans weren't searchable, so I had to look at every story on every page. Her name appeared once, giving a quote in a story from her final year there.

A young cafeteria worker had been found dead of a drug overdose in the basement of the Student Union, just a few days before graduation. "Gabriela was such a sweet person – and very smart. It's just so tragic." The story noted that a collection had been taken up by generous students to make sure she had a decent burial, as no next of kin had been identified. There was also mention that the food service department was being investigated over its hiring practices, as Gabriela was an undocumented immigrant.

That was it. The only other place her name appeared was on her year's student list – along with about 2,000 other names. I smacked the computer mouse across the desk out of frustration. I wasn't about to start searching each of about 1,000 names for a connection I knew I wouldn't find.

The screen flickered and scrolled, then the class list for the year ahead of her appeared, the cohort who would have graduated a few days after the cafeteria worker overdosed. The cursor came to a stop toward the end of the alphabet, and a name jumped out at me. Maria Santos.

THE FOUNDERS' BALL

Attendance at the Founders' Ball is obligatory for anyone who is anyone – or who wants people to think they are. It costs $500 per couple, and all the proceeds go to the Orman Community Foundation. The OCF is second only to the Levant Foundation in the size of its endowment and the impact of its annual giving. I had been a guest frequently at similar events – a long time ago, in a galaxy far, far away.

The only thing that had made them tolerable then was that Sarah and I had spent most of the time making up stories based on glimpses of interactions between the guests. We also danced. As an anniversary present to her, I had agreed to attend ballroom dancing lessons. It turns out that even two left feet can be taught to move with a near approximation of rhythm after sufficient repetition.

Maria picked me up outside my office in a white limo. When I got in, she handed me a one-dollar bill. "I know that you are escorting me as a favor, but I also want to be your client. That will allow me to rely on your discretion. These charity balls can get pretty wild. Consider it favor number two completed." I took the dollar.

The Founders' Ball, and every charity event I had ever heard of in Orman, were rather tame affairs. Being a detective on the job rather than an escort seemed a little more dignified, though, so I accepted the money.

When we got to the conference center, the driver leaped out and held the door for her as she exited the vehicle with the grace and poise of a 1940s movie star. I scrambled across the seat and half-fell out onto the sidewalk. No one noticed.

I thanked the driver, whose face was turned away from the car in a gesture I took to be a demonstration of his unimportance compared to his passengers. I wondered if I shouldn't avert my eyes from Maria and the other toffs attending the gala, on the same basis.

The Founders' Ball had a red carpet, complete with local reporters and photographers. As celebrity couples made their way across it, they paused for pictures and mouthed banalities. The mayor and his wife were in the center of it as we arrived. Based on the look on his face, decorum had been breached somewhat by the reporters.

He was probably being asked about the multiple scandals swirling around his pet project, New Life Ministries. It couldn't happen to a more deserving dolt, but I did feel bad for his wife, whose smile was frozen harder than the last bag of ice in a supermarket freezer.

Fifty feet away from the red-carpet entrance was the one for the rabble. No reporters or photographers there, just harried volunteers checking names off lists and handing out name tags and table assignments. Taking Maria's arm, I turned toward the regular entrance. She deftly steered me in the other direction, to the red carpet. I wasn't keen on walking that gauntlet, but I took heart that the way she had directed our movement bode well for the dance floor. I had always danced better when Sarah led.

According to Squire, the term "monkey suit" comes from the fancy dress sported by the monkeys that organ grinders use to solicit donations. Maria was far more dazzling in her emerald gown than any organ grinder, but I may have resembled a simian sidekick that had been forced into an outfit it didn't want to wear. Fortunately, none of the photographs that appeared online or in the newspaper the next day featured more than a glimpse of my elbow or shoulder. Maria Santos, drop dead gorgeous local philanthropist, rightfully took up the entire frame.

The mayor kissed Maria on both cheeks while his wife and I grinned uncomfortably at each other in arm candy solidarity. The mayor gave me a smile that made his wife's earlier one for the photographers seem warm. He couldn't afford to hate the feds, his own police department, or David Levant, but it cost him nothing to loathe me. Maria took my hand and started to move on.

"Hey, I'm still looking for Pastor Jan. Give me a call to talk about it, when you're not too tied up?" I put a little extra emphasis on the last two words, remembering Pastor Jan's reference to His Honor's fondness for bondage. Maria's nails dug into my hand.

She pulled me close and whispered, "You're not here on your own agenda. You are here as a favor to me, my strong, silent companion – emphasis on silent." She punctuated her message by biting my ear lobe, hard enough that I wondered if it might draw blood.

It was both frightening and sexy at the same time. Hell, just about everything about Maria was those things. Any small hope I had nurtured that she and Pastor Jan attending the same college at the same time was a coincidence had withered when I rechecked the name of the LLC that owned the building leased to Pastor Jan for NLM: Marsan – a not very subtle combination of her names.

Maria was wrong about me not being there on my own agenda. I had one, all right, with two items on it. One was a joint venture with Squire, and the other was figuring out just how entangled Maria was with Pastor Jan. The best way to pursue my agenda, though, was probably to attend to hers and play my assigned role of boy toy. Gratuitous needling of the mayor was certainly not going to help.

"I assume you need to work the crowd. Can I get you something to drink?"

"That would be very nice, Adam. There is usually a signature cocktail of some kind. I'll have whatever that is."

I went to the bar and discovered that the signature cocktail was called Cuervo Rancheros. It consisted of a shot of Jose Cuervo Reserve from bottles that had sliced jalapeno peppers steeping in them, tomato puree, lime juice, and a "secret ingredient" added underneath the bar – some sort of custom-made bitters, I guessed.

The drink was served in a tall glass, garnished with a baby onion skewered on a hard spear of rolled and roasted tortilla. The garnish was laid across the top of the glass, not dipped into the drink, presumably because the tortilla would not hold up to prolonged immersion. It was tasty, like a Bloody Mary with the spice dial turned up to 10. By the time I got to Maria with hers, mine was finished.

On my way back for a second Cuervo Rancheros, I was intercepted by Julia. She was stunning in an ankle length shimmering gown that caressed her curves as she moved smoothly through the crowd. In her wake, I could see Squire admiring her date with a "I can't believe I'm here with *her*" look on her face. Squire cut quite a dashing figure herself in her dress police uniform.

Julia took my elbow and walked me to the bar, where the barman produced two Cuervo Rancheros. Her outward elegance and composure provided nearly impenetrable cover, but she has a tell. When Julia is uncomfortable, she smiles just a little more sharply than she does naturally.

I read the deeper than normal lines at the corner of her impeccably lip-sticked mouth as evidence that she was nervous in general and flustered about something in particular. I'm a pretty good detective when I'm not actually on the job.

"What's the matter?

"What? Nothing! Everything's fine." She drained her drink and signaled to the bartender for another.

"C'mon, Julia. It's me. You're upset about something."

"Upset? Not at all. Being at a high-profile social event as part of a same-sex couple with the newly promoted deputy chief of police and recognizing three former clients, so far, among Orman's rich and gracious isn't upsetting. Nah, everything's great. How about you?"

"I'm fine. They didn't recognize you, did they?"

"I don't think so, but what if they do?"

"You haven't had the talk with Squire, yet?"

"Of course, I have. But that doesn't mean she needs my past thrown in her face. Especially here. Now."

"That's not gonna happen. They're just not going to recognize you. Recognition requires context. There's probably a couple of the guys I work out with at the gym here tonight – guys I see twice a week – and we're not going to recognize each other. Unless one of them shows up unshaven and wearing smelly shorts and a t-shirt.

"If you look familiar to someone, he's just going to think that he's seen you at another fancy affair like this one. Besides, I'm guessing that your former clients have a lot more to lose from exposure than you do."

"I don't know." The second drink was also finished, but it took a little longer and she didn't immediately call for another.

"Relax. Enjoy. You're an honored guest accompanying a rising star of the Orman's PD. Don't worry about the past, or the future. Focus on tonight." The lines were gone, and her regular smile was back. "Now, get back to your date. I have boy-toy obligations to fulfill."

Julia put her hand on my arm and squeezed. "Thanks for the pep talk, coach! And don't worry about your boy-toy duties. It's the role you've been practicing for your whole life. Maria is a lucky girl. By the way, Danny says she and you have a surprise planned after the speaking program, but she won't tell me what it is. Spill."

"I've been sworn to secrecy by your beau – or belle, or whatever. Let's just say that the New Life Ministry cases have at least one more twist to them."

"Hah! I told her you wouldn't tell me. She was sure you'd squeal. Like she did!"

"So, you know?"

"Yep. Looking forward to it! Other than the whole thing about you being tortured and drugged for a couple of weeks, this case has been a blast!" She gave a little wave and made her way back to Squire, with a drink in each hand.

Yeah, other than that, I thought to myself sarcastically. But she was right. In the matter of less than a month, the NLM cases had resulted in Julia and Squire finding each other, Squire being promoted to deputy chief, dozens of future victims of Pastor Jan being rescued, and the mayor being publicly embarrassed. Good times.

David Levant approached the bar, looking me up and down. His eyes lingered at my feet. "Nice shoes."

I was wearing a pair of Charles Tyrwhitt Patent Oxfords "from the Ellis Bell collection," as I liked to think of it. "Bell has good taste in shoes. I wonder what goes well with an orange jumpsuit?" Levant laughed.

"Thanks again for the tux. I'll have it cleaned and returned tomorrow."

"Please keep it, Adam. It has been tailored to you now, and one never knows when one will need proper formal attire."

"Thank you. I read about the return of the antiquities. Thanks for keeping my role in their recovery out of the story."

"Thank you for your discretion about any discrepancy you may have noticed in the inventory."

"What will you do with it?"

"Keep it safe. Make sure no one uses it to start the Apocalypse. Nothing special." He gave me a wink, collected a cocktail, and walked away.

"Will you take $50 now to call off our bet?" I turned to see Jimmy Diaz, City Councilor, holding out a fifty-dollar bill.

"No way, Jimmy. Deputy chief is more than halfway there. I'm holding out for the Benjamin. How are you doing?"

He put the fifty into the tip jar on the bar.

"I'm well. Better than the mayor these days, that's for sure." He was joined by an absolutely stunning woman who took his arm. There was an almost visible aura around her. She had the presence of a movie star, a supermodel, or a saint. It was Claire.

I stifled my urge to greet her by saying, "Wow, you sure clean up nice!" and went instead for, "Good evening, Claire. Small world. I didn't know you and Jimmy were acquainted."

"You clean up nice, Adam."

Damn psychic stole my line.

"It *is* a small world, and Orman is an even smaller town. Jimmy and I went to high school together. We've known each other for a long time." She tugged on Jimmy's arm. "I predict that you are going to ask me to dance, Councilor!"

Jimmy winked at me as Claire dragged him away from the bar. "I don't know which of us is in more trouble. Oh, yes, I do. It's you, with the Viuda Negra!"

I scanned the room for Maria and saw her surrounded by men vying for her attention. They were drooling like Pavlov's dogs at the sound of the dinner bell. She gave me a "come hither" look that was part seductive and part commanding. All right, it was pretty much all commanding, but boy toys need a scrap or two of dignity, too, you know.

"Maria, you promised me a dance." I held out my arm. As I led her to the dance floor the looks on the faces of the men who had been surrounding her made me wonder if Pavlov had recorded the reactions of his dogs when the bell rang and no supper was delivered?

"I turned them all down, saying that I never dance at these events. I'm guessing you're not their favorite person right now." Maria is not someone who giggles, but I'm pretty sure I heard a soft one. Giving her the benefit of the doubt, let's call it a chuckle.

We danced several songs in a row, and to my surprise I was totally adequate. Muscle memory kicked in and I managed to not tread on Maria's feet while moving more or less with her, as if I had a passing acquaintance with rhythm. They say that smell is a strong trigger for memory, and Maria was again wearing Le Chevrefeuille, so maybe my body thought I was dancing with Sarah.

I dragged my thoughts away from my lost family and considered Julia's comment from earlier about the NLM case being a blast. She didn't know that the case wasn't really over yet, but she was mostly right. The unnecessary dental work had been traumatic, but it had given me the unusual opportunity to spend some quality time with a war criminal.

I had cheated death a couple of times and helped put away Ellis Bell. I had regained my sense of smell, though given my propensity for hanging out in alleys, bars, and greasy spoons, that is something of a double-edged sword. And, speaking of swords, David Levant had come into possession of an ancient one and been lauded for returning many other antiquities to their rightful owners.

Captain Hook and The Wheelies had put on one of the more entertaining protests in Orman's recent memory. Maria Santos… Claire Voyant…. All in all, it really had been a blast. But there were losses, too. Gary Carson. Sam Watkins. Sean Ryan.

"Michelle Rathborn!" The music had stopped. Maria and I were standing still on the dance floor with our arms still around each other, like a sculpture of dancers.

"Welcome back to the here and now, Adam."

My reverie had been interrupted by the emcee introducing the Quickie Buy heiress, who was cradling between her bandaged arms a $500,000 poster board check made out to the Orman Community Foundation.

"On behalf of my family and the Quickie Buy Corporation," she whispered hoarsely into the microphone, "I am proud to make this donation to OCF to support their work with the homeless community." She thrust the check awkwardly in the direction of the Foundation board chair, who took it from her and stepped up to the microphone.

She made her way off the stage and headed for the side exit stairs, accompanied by her lawyer, Smiley. Squire followed a few paces behind, talking rapidly into her cell phone. Julia was right behind her.

"I'll be right back," I mouthed to Maria and then headed for the door. She held onto my arm and fell in beside me.

"I sense something fun is going on!" she whispered.

When Smiley and his client reached the exit to the street, they were met by half a dozen uniformed police and Woody Wales.

"Jane Doe, you are under arrest. You have the right to remain silent…" While Woody finished the Miranda reading, a cop with handcuffs approached. Realizing that he couldn't really handcuff her given how her arms were bandaged, he placed his hand on the small of her back and led her toward a waiting squad car. She offered no resistance.

"This is an outrage!" Smiley shouted. "I am Ms. Rathborn's attorney and I demand that you stop this nonsense at once." He placed himself between his client and the squad car.

Squire spoke softly. "You may speak with your client at the police station, if you like, Mr. Montrose, once she has been booked. I have to ask that you not interfere with her arrest, though. Step aside, or you'll be accompanying her in handcuffs."

Like private detectives, lawyers are well-practiced at hiding their surprise. It's just as important to their effectiveness that they appear to always know what's coming. What Smiley was less adept at, however, was hiding his lack of surprise. Rather than reel in shock at his client being arrested and addressed as "Jane Doe," he went into damage control mode like someone who had planned for just this turn of events.

He stepped aside, but he didn't stop talking. "Do not say a word unless I am present, Michelle. Decline any request for DNA. Don't accept any food, drink, or cigarettes that could be used to get a sample of your saliva. Do you understand, Michelle?" She nodded.

"Yeah, like a Slurrie. Right, Smiley?" Smiley glared at me, and then my words sunk in and he realized what they meant. He turned and walked away quickly.

In a couple of minutes, the street was empty except for Squire, Julia, Maria, and me.

"That was awesome!" Julia announced.

Maria was in agreement. "Much better than listening to the Foundation Chair make lame jokes about not being able to fold the giant check into his wallet. I do get the sense, though, that I'm not in on the whole story."

I gave her the condensed version, glancing at Squire periodically to make sure I wasn't over-stepping.

"I wish I had kept Smiley's Slurrie straw from the settlement conference. Who knows what databases that creep might be in."

"Running DNA tests on all the Rathborns put the department in enough jeopardy, without running one on a member of the state bar with no reason." It sounded like Squire was trying to convince herself more than anyone else.

"Hey, they all surrendered their straws voluntarily," I pointed out. "No fruit from the poisoned tree. And without it you wouldn't have been able to expose Jane Doe as a fraud and identify Michele's mostly-incinerated remains. Smiley sure didn't seem too surprised by his client's arrest. Do you think he is in on it?"

Squire pursed her lips. "Maybe. More likely, though, he just doesn't care. He figures he'll get paid, either way."

"As long as the Foundation gets their money, I don't care who else gets a piece of the Quickie Buy pie."

"Mmm, pie! What say we blow off this gala thing and head down to Tuck's for some pie?"

"You know I'm always down for pie and coffee at Tuck's. But I am at m'lady's pleasure for the evening."

"I bet you are," Julia said softly with a smirk.

Maria pulled her phone from the stylish bag that didn't look big enough to hold it and directed the limo driver to meet us at the side door.

It probably wasn't the first time that a group in evening dress pulled up outside Tuck's in a limo. But it probably *was* the first time that the members of the group were above prom age.

"Adam failed to introduce us." Squire reached her hand across the table. "I'm Danielle, and this is Julia." Maria put down her coffee cup and shook her hand, while nodding at Julia.

"I kinda assumed that you all knew who each other are, Orman being Orman."

"Knowing who someone is and knowing them are two different things." Maria cast a jaundiced eye in my direction. "Danielle is quite right that you should have introduced us. But there was quite a bit going on when we met at Jane Doe's arrest, so you are forgiven."

"If you are going to spend any time with Adam, you'll have to get used to forgiving him for his manners." With Julia jumping into the conversation, I was starting to feel very outnumbered, but not in an unpleasant way.

That there were three people in the entire world, let alone sitting in Tuck's Diner at this very moment, who cared enough about me to tease me was a revelation that I received more warmly than I would have imagined. I would have to tell Claire about it when we started our sessions.

If she had read my palm a month ago and predicted that I would be sitting next to Maria Santos, feeling the gentle pressure of her thigh against mine, on a double date of sorts with Squire and Julia, my reaction would have been a hearty "WTF!" Yet somehow, it was comfortable and not at all weird.

It couldn't last, of course. Eventually, I would have to confront Maria about her connection to Pastor Jan. But at that moment, I found myself willing to believe that her attending the same college and then leasing her a building 15 years later was just a bizarre coincidence.

The pie arrived and banter was replaced by the sound of forks clacking against ceramic plates and satisfied murmurs as warm, delicious slices of pie were dispatched with extreme prejudice. When the last flake of crust had been cleaned from every plate, Maria offered Squire and

Julia a ride back to the gala where their car was sitting in the valet lot. I gave Squire a dirty look when she let me pay the check without even the pretense of an offer to do so.

The limo was parked across and down the street. The driver was idly polishing the hood, whistling. When we appeared on the sidewalk, he jumped behind the wheel, flicked the lights on, and barreled the limo straight at us before turning parallel to the curb and stopping right where we stood.

Adrenaline pumped in my veins as I was transported back to the night that Gary Carson, standing in for Ellis Bell, had been crushed by a limo and mutilated by its driver.

My companions chatted amiably while taking their seats in the limo. Last to get in, I faked a stumble and cursed aloud. The driver instinctively turned in my direction. I recognized him. Not from the Gary Carson murder – I had never seen that limo driver's face – but from NLM. He was one of Pastor Jan's thugs.

SCORPION AND THE BLACK WIDOW

We dropped Squire and Julia off, and I was tempted to make up some excuse and get out of the limo with them. I was still in shock at recognizing Maria's limo driver as one of Pastor Jan's goons, maybe even the weird whistler who had killed Gary Carson. I tried to think of what to do or say, but nothing came to me. Except Maria.

Before we had left the curb, her hand was running along my thigh as she nibbled on my ear lobe. The ringing of the big head alarm bells receded as the little head trumpets rose to a crescendo. In a last valiant attempt to heed the alarm, I turned toward Maria and opened my mouth to say something about the driver, but her tongue engaged mine in a more compelling conversation. The last coherent thought I had before giving in to the feelings now stirring in every part of my body was: Viuda Negra – the Black Widow.

Somehow, we navigated the exit from the limo and entry into Maria's house while remaining in contact along about 80% of our bodies. If the limo driver smirked – and in retrospect I have to figure he did – I was completely unaware of it. Unaware of anything, really, but the softness of Maria's lips, the quivering tension of her body beneath the silk gown, and the intoxicating scent of *Le Chevrefeuille*.

Half an hour later, we were lying in her bed in a tangle of limbs, partially attached items of clothing, and twisted bed linens.

I cleared my throat. "We need to talk."

"Wow! You just broke the world speed record for speaking the dreaded four words."

"We really needed to talk before this, but something distracted me...."

"Well, I understand some people smoke after sex, some cry, and some fall asleep within seconds. I suppose wanting to talk isn't the worst thing. I do my best talking in the shower." She took my hand and led me to the bathroom. I kicked off the undershorts that were still wrapped around one of my ankles.

Once the water was a good temperature, we stepped under the huge rain shower and let the hot water run down our bodies.

I had run through dozens of scenarios for this conversation and still hadn't come up with a good way to begin, so I just dove in. "I need to know the story about you and Pastor Jan, or should I call her Laura Walker?"

To her credit, she didn't feign surprise or ask, "Whatever do you mean?" She just nodded and considered her response while soaping up.

"What do you want to know?"

"Everything. When did you first meet, what have you done together, or for each other? Do you know where she is now? Were you aware of what she was doing at

New Life Ministries? You know, all the things that you think I want to know."

"We met at college. I wouldn't say we were friends, but we knew each other. Then I didn't see or speak to her for 15 years, until she showed up in Orman and asked to rent space for a homeless shelter. The buildings were empty, so I was happy to oblige."

"Just doing a solid for an old friend?"

"I told you we weren't friends. She asked to rent space, and I had space to rent."

"And you had no idea what she was up to?"

"Not really, at first. She seemed very sincere about the mission of transitioning homeless people from the streets into productive lives. I didn't pay her much attention, to be honest. After you got knocked on the head, though, I suspected she was up to something. Turn around." She rubbed a soapy loofa over my shoulders and back. "Who is Sam?"

"What? Oh, the tattoo. I don't know. Must be the boyfriend or girlfriend of the Stevens guy whose dead body I was being groomed to play."

"I was very worried about you when she took you prisoner. I had one of my people inside her operation. He was keeping an eye on you."

I spun around. "Keeping an eye on me while I was being drugged, undergoing forced dental treatment, and having a stranger's name tattooed on my back?" She lowered her head and gently scrubbed my chest. I realized why I recognized the driver. He was the guard who somehow hadn't seen me when I was escaping from NLM.

"I was not going to let her kill you. But I had to be careful. She had... has... considerable leverage over me." She dropped the loofa and bent over to get it. Her position allowed for her to engage in what I took to be a nonverbal apology for not doing more to help me when I was at New Life.

I put a hand under her chin and raised her back up. "What leverage does she have?"

She soaped up the loofa, handed it to me, and turned around. I scrubbed her back and bottom, the latter drawing pleasant sighs.

She faced me. "You know what they call me, don't you?"

"Viuda Negra." I ran the loofa over her breasts and belly.

"Yes, the Black Widow. A spider who kills her lover after mating. I suppose I got that nickname, because I generally only sleep with someone once. If I were a man, perhaps it would have been 'One and Done' or 'Love 'em and Leave 'em.' But it was useful for me to have a fiercer moniker, given the people I sometimes have to deal with."

"Yeah, the charitable foundation game can be pretty cutthroat." Humor is a coping mechanism for me. And this conversation, under these conditions, required considerable coping.

She gave a weak smile that made the Mona Lisa's look like the Joker's when he has Batman hanging upside down over a cauldron of bubbling acid.

"I bring up this nickname, because if I were to tell you what she has over me, the only reasonable thing for me to do then would be to kill you, to live up to my nickname. I don't want to do that. Please don't insist."

She punctuated her point with a long, gentle kiss – rising on her tip toes to reach my lips. If I were a real gentleman – or a little less terrified – I would have bent down to make it easier. Still, I didn't pull away. She bit my lower lip as she disengaged.

We stood under the hot water, rinsing away the suds as I considered our dilemma. I knew that I wouldn't just let it go. The same logic that dictated she would have to kill me if she told me meant that she would have to kill me if I figured it out. And I know myself well enough to know that I don't stop pulling at a thread until I reach the end.

"I'm guessing it has something to do with the girl who overdosed during your senior year."

She looked sad, and a little scared. "You can't leave it alone, can you?"

I shrugged, shook my head and said, "Scorpion."

She looked confused for a moment, then chuckled. "The story of the frog and the scorpion. Grimly appropriate."

"We're writing our own story here in your shower: the gumshoe and the black widow. I hope we can figure out a better ending."

"Happy endings haven't featured prominently in my life."

"Nor in mine. The school newspaper didn't have much detail about the overdose, but I don't think it was a coincidence that Jan/Laura never came back for her senior year. Did you supply the drugs that killed the girl? Is that Pastor Jan's leverage?"

She shook her head and embraced me, putting her face against my chest. With the steady stream of hot water from the shower, I couldn't really tell but I think she was crying.

"So, if you aren't responsible for the girl's death, what's Jan got?"

It hit me just a beat before she said it. "I didn't *kill* the girl. I *am* the girl."

Pastor Jan's first body swap. The girl who came back from college wasn't Maria Santos but Gabriela, the cafeteria worker. It was Maria who had overdosed.

"Maria and Laura were good friends. I saw them in the cafeteria often. I didn't particularly care for Laura. She was just another stuck-up WASP who treated me like a servant. Maria was sweet, though. She used to joke that we were sisters from different misters.

"We were the same size and did look a bit alike. She gave me her clothes when she was bored with them, but never in front of anybody. I would just find a box of dry-cleaned clothes in my locker. I adored her. I was in the country illegally, trying to assimilate, and Maria was my model. I mimicked her speech, her mannerisms... I wanted to be Maria. Laura teased me about it, called me 'Mini Mare.'"

"So, she over-dosed and you just moved into her life?"

She nodded. I had questions, lots of questions. But the confession seemed to have taken all the energy out of Maria – uh, Gabriela. Her shoulders were slumped and she actually looked smaller, as if the hot water had somehow shrunk her. I guided her out of the shower, toweled us both off, and we settled back in bed. Her head rested against my chest, and I could feel warm tears on my skin.

The problem with pulling at threads is that eventually you end up with a tangled mess that can't be put back together again.

Part of me wanted to stroke her hair and whisper comforting words. Another part of me wanted to grill a suspect who I knew was a good enough actress to *become* another person and pull it off. She had managed to fool people who were far more discerning than a sexually-sated recovering heroin addict with unresolved intimacy issues.

When I'm torn between two directions, I go both ways for as long as possible. I kept on stroking her but channeled my inner Woody Wales.

"You looked like Maria, sounded like her, and even had some of her clothes. But there had to be dozens of people at the school and dozens more back in Orman who would have immediately recognized the switch."

She pulled away and used some pillows to prop herself up in a sitting position. "Really, Scorpion, is that the line of questioning that interests you?" Some of the familiar Maria fierceness had returned to her voice. "The practicalities of pulling off the deception, not how I felt about stealing the life of someone I admired and loved, or throwing away my own identity?"

"Facts before feelings? Yeah, that's kinda how I roll. That can't really be a surprise. But you talk about whatever you want to, as long as it helps me understand what happened and what it means for us today, here and now."

"Facts, then. Of course, there were many people at the college who would have recognized that I wasn't Maria, even if few would have recognized the cafeteria girl Gabriela dressed up like a debutante. But I didn't need to see any of them. Classes were all finished, and I simply requested by phone that my diploma be sent to my home in Orman, as I was returning there on urgent personal business and would be unable to attend graduation.

"That gave us a week to pack up Maria's things and figure out how to handle my return to Orman. Laura knew a lot about Maria's life. Her father had died recently, and she had no siblings or aunts or uncles – no direct relatives at all. The only people back there who had met Maria in person were some local representatives of the companies who handled the trust's finances and the housekeepers. Odds were, the financial people would have bought me as Maria, but to be safe, we fired them and hired different companies.

"That only left the two old retainers who kept the house running in Orman. We offered them early retirement with a pension and paid-off houses in their hometowns in Mexico. My voice impression of Maria was good enough to do that over the phone."

"You keep saying 'we.' Pastor Jan, er, Laura helped you with all this?"

"Laura *did* all of it. I just did what she told me to do. It was like she had thought it all out and was working from a playbook. I remember thinking that it was almost like she had planned it."

"Did you ever suspect that she was responsible for Maria's death?"

"Not then. I would never have gone along if I had. And I never really thought about it until learning what went down at New Life Ministries. But now, yeah. I think it's possible that she gave Maria an overdose on purpose."

"Why?"

"Why do you think? It's not like she helped me move into Maria's life, gave me a kiss, and then disappeared like a fairy godmother. It was for money. She received $100,000 a year for five years. Then she went away. She kept her word; I'll give her that. I assumed she would blackmail me for life, but when she got her half million, she left me alone. Until last year."

"That's a lot of money. I understood that there wasn't a lot of the family money left outside of the trust when your father – uh, *Maria's* father – died."

"No, but there was property that could be sold. And 'scholarships' that could be made to fictitious students. As you have learned, Laura's is an especially creative kind of criminality."

We sat in oddly comfortable silence for a few minutes. I had a lot more questions that needed answering, but the compulsion to go all Woody Wales on her had completely dissipated. I couldn't help wondering about the feelings stuff. Maria/Gabriela wasn't a monster like Laura/Jan. I didn't know how I was going to handle what I knew, and I didn't know how she would handle that I knew it.

What I did know was that I was in bed with a beautiful, mysterious woman who had stirred a passion in me that I hadn't felt in years – and that however things might turn out, I would almost certainly never find myself there again.

For the next six hours or so, we made love, showered, talked, made love again. We made love like it was the first time, the last time, and every time in between. We had tender sex, angry sex, makeup sex, kinky sex – a whole relationship of physical and emotional intimacy in one long night and morning. We even had perfunctory sex. We laughed, cried, purred, growled, and whispered. We shared the secrets of our bodies and souls.

When no questions had been left unanswered, no avenues left unexplored, the sunlight was pouring through the curtains. After one last shower, separately this time, we got dressed and sat across from each other at her kitchen table, drinking coffee. Through the window, I could see the limo parked at the curb, the driver slouching in the front seat.

"Are you going to give that poor fellow a break and send him home?"

"Are you going to give this poor gal a break and not send her to prison?"

"Ethically, I am obligated to maintain client confidentiality unless appropriately ordered to disclose information by a court of law. You wisely made yourself a client last night. The main exception to confidentiality is if I have information about a crime a client intends to commit, or an action that might cause harm to the client or others."

"But if compelled by a court, you would disclose what you know?"

"I would disclose what I had to. No more, no less. It seems unlikely that anyone would ever suspect you, though. By every official record, you *are* Maria Santos. It was brilliant to apply for your notary license when you 'returned' to Orman as Maria and get your fingerprints on the record as Maria's.

"I don't see how even DNA could be used against you. It might prove that you aren't the biological daughter of Maria's father and mother, if relatives of theirs could be found who agreed to be tested. But no one could prove that they didn't raise you as their daughter."

"Would it violate your ethics to disclose nothing of what you know but encourage your friend Squire to investigate?"

"Not my professional ethics. But I also have personal integrity that comes into play."

"And that would prevent you from alerting Squire?"

"As things stand, yes. That could always change, though, to be honest. If you posed a threat to others that could be eliminated by exposing you, I would have to consider that option."

"But, for today, my secret is safe?"

"For today."

She picked up a cell phone and I could see the limo driver sit up straight and put his phone to his ear. "I won't be needing you anymore... for today."

There are three main cemeteries in Orman: St. Paul's, Forest Lawn, and Gethsemane. St. Paul's is the oldest, and it's where the founding families and Orman's wealthier citizens find their eternal rest. Its tombs, crypts, monuments, and rows of head stones are spread haphazardly across rolling hills and meadows. The oldest graves are from the mid-nineteenth century.

Forest Lawn was built in the early 1960s. In order to make perpetual care more affordable, headstones are installed horizontally, parallel to the ground, so that mowers can cross over them. It's laid out in a perfect grid, with a columbarium – a wall for cremated remains – along one side. Both the cemetery and the columbarium were originally built with special sections for Jews and Blacks, though those designations had been removed in the 1970s.

Gethsemane is about as old as St. Paul's and has been taking all comers since its founding, without regard to race, creed, or national origin. One section is owned by the City of Orman and serves as the public cemetery, the euphemistic name for what was once known as the "paupers' field."

Another is leased by the Veterans Administration, and the rest is a hodge-podge of single graves and family plots. Some parts are overgrown, with fallen headstones and rusted fencing. Others are kept up by families of the deceased and look as nice as the best sections in St.

Paul's. Gethsemane Cemetery is probably the most integrated neighborhood in Orman.

Gary Carson's funeral was held graveside in the public cemetery. There were about a dozen people there, including several members of the Salvation Army shelter staff and some of his co-workers from Fallows' Grocery. Major Tom gave the eulogy, and Gary's sister talked movingly about how her big brother had always taken care of her when they were kids, and her regret at not having been able to take care of him in his final years.

She threw a rose in on top of his casket, and the mourners all passed by the open grave and tossed clods of dirt on top. When my turn came, instead of dirt, I dropped a five-dollar bill in. Major Tom gave me a strange look. "He shouldn't arrive at the pearly gates with an empty kettle," I mumbled.

Sean Ryan and Sam Watkins had a joint burial service in the veterans' section at Gethsemane. A few family members of each man attended, along with a couple dozen comrades-in-arms from their time in the service, and most of the current population of the shelter at the Veterans' Assistance Center.

The VAC's Honor Guard was there, and a pale and fragile-looking Trent Argent played taps on a bugle. Ellie from the Wheelies was a member of the Honor Guard, turning and "marching" her chair through the rough earth with her comrades as they presented the colors and fired three volleys over the graves. Before the men's caskets were lowered into the ground, the flags draped over them were removed by white-gloved members of the Guard, folded into taut triangles, and presented to the families.

When most everyone else had left, a middle-aged man in Marine dress blues remained at Sam Watkin's grave, his eyes cast downward.

"I'm sorry for your loss."

He looked up. "Did you know Sam?"

"Not really. We met quite recently."

He looked at me more closely. "You're the private eye. The one who was wanted for his murder." I nodded. "They haven't arrested anyone else for it, have they?"

I shook my head. "He deserved better."

"He did. He never forgave himself for breaking under torture. That's what the rat tattoos were about. He thought of himself as a rat. No one else did, though."

"He was having the tattoos removed. He was trying to turn his life around."

I'm not sure he believed me, and I'm not sure it was really true. But the Marine nodded, whispered "*Semper Fi,*" saluted, and walked away.

Michelle Rathborn's funeral was held in St. Paul's Church, and her remains were laid to rest in the family plot. The funeral was private, but there must have been a hundred or more people at the cemetery for the burial: family, friends, reporters, and gawkers. Also, a number of the same folks from the VAC who had been at Sean's and Sam's service.

I nodded to Gayle Forris, who – to her credit – looked uncomfortable to be there in her professional capacity. I scanned the crowd, not sure what I was hoping to see. Maybe Pastor Jan fuming in rage at losing whatever her cut was of the $3.5 million that the fake Michelle was going to receive?

"Adam." I turned to see Horace Alpert, the success story from Pastor Jan's speech outside City Hall.

"Can I have a minute of your time?"

"Sure. Did you know Michelle?"

"I'm sorry, no. I didn't know her or any of the others. I had no idea what was going on. I couldn't believe it when I saw the stories on TV. New Life Ministries helped me turn my life around at the same time it was destroying other people's. It's left me feeling a bit off. But that's not why I'm here."

I waited.

"I need your help. One of my workers has gone missing, and I think he's in trouble."

Printed in the USA
CPSIA information can be obtained
at www.ICGtesting.com
CBHW030441021024
15219CB00027B/277

9 798991 335416